TANZI'S LUCK

C.I. DENNIS

For Soren

TUESDAY

DR. JAFFE POINTED TO her computer screen. I put on my reading glasses and leaned across the clutter of paperwork on her desk to see. "Here's where the bullet stopped, in Brodmann area 4," she said. "We had to leave some small fragments, but it's healed better than I thought it would."

The surgeon was fast-forwarding through a series of images that displayed cross sections of my brain as if it had been run through a deli slicer. Noelle Jaffe had removed a nine-millimeter slug from it two and a half years ago, and I had almost fully recovered. There are occupational hazards that go with being a private investigator, although stopping bullets with your head isn't usually one of them.

"You really think it's healed?"

"Yes, Vince," she said. "Either that or it's just a bunch of rocks in there."

"My ex-wife would agree with that diagnosis," I said.

"How's the limp?"

"It's under control. I walk the beach every day, and that helps."

"Don't talk to me about the beach," she said. "We're supposed to have a frost tonight, and we don't appreciate you Floridians rubbing it in."

"You didn't see anything else? Anything bad?"

"Why? Are you worried about something?"

I didn't want to get into the whole business of the whiteouts, because they had only recently started happening, and I was hoping that they would just fade away. If I brought them up, the doctor would probably tell me to quit driving, and there was no way that I could manage that. I had too much work, and I needed to care for Royal, my two-year-old son. Besides, I could tell when the episodes were coming on, so I would just pull over to side of the road, recline the seat, and pretend I was napping. That was how I had handled it for the month before my trip to Vermont, and so far, so good.

"Nothing worth mentioning," I said.

"Excellent," the doctor said. She smiled as we stood up and I reached for my jacket. "How long are you here for?"

"I'm going to my mother's for a couple days, and then back to Vero. I have my boy to chase around."

"Royal is the reason you're doing so well," Dr. Jaffe said. "See you in six months."

It was a long trip from Vero Beach, Florida, to Burlington, Vermont, just to see my surgeon, but I liked her. And more to the point I trusted her, since she had saved my brain, which is my second-favorite organ. The doctor was right about my motivation. Spending time with my little boy had been a big factor in my recovery from a near-fatal injury, and from my latest train wreck of a marriage.

It took a moment to remember what my rental car looked like—it was tiny, anonymous, and the cheapest one they'd offered at the airport. I located it at the back of the hospital lot and then steered through the University of Vermont campus. As I got onto the Interstate I knew that I'd timed my trip perfectly. It was the first week of October; the foliage colors were at their peak. The surrounding hills of the Green Mountains reflected the late afternoon light and were anything but green—they'd been temporarily repainted in tie-dye hues of red, orange, and yellow, and might have made a suitable backdrop for a Dead concert.

I would arrive at my mother's by the dinner hour and would bunk in my old room, enjoy her cooking, and possibly do some leaf-peeping over the next couple of days with the rest of the fall tourists, many of whom were also from my adopted state of Florida. I missed Royal, but my ex was covering for me, and I would only be gone for a little while.

It seemed like a reasonable plan.

*

My wardrobe has gone downhill since the divorce, but I keep an eye on my waistline, I have all my hair, I brush my teeth, I hold the door open for ladies, and I even put the toilet seat down, unprompted. My mother, my sister, a gaggle of early girlfriends, my first wife Glory, and my second and now ex-wife Barbara have, over time, helped me to evolve from a knuckle-dragger to someone who can make it through a meal without a good portion of it ending up on his shirt.

That is, unless we're talking about my mother's lasagna.

I was finishing off a second helping of four layers of homemade pasta sandwiched between a ragù made from veal, pork and pancetta, and a creamy béchamel sauce, plus a heavy hand on the garlic press, when my mother got up from the table to answer the door. Donna Tomaselli stood at the threshold, dressed in one of the black outfits she always wore even though her husband had been gone for thirty years. Mrs. Tomaselli loved to eat, and she had a knack for showing up right as the food came out of the oven. My mother fixed her a plate without bothering to ask if she wanted one. I poured her a glass of Montepulciano after receiving a strenuous embrace into her ample bosom that might have suffocated a shorter man.

"So, how you doing, Mrs. T?" I was quickly slipping back into the Barre-speak of my youth.

"Awful, Vinny," she said. She took a big drink from the wine glass and wiped her lips on a napkin. "If it wasn't for your mother I'd be in the mental ward. She's the only one keeping me sane."

"What's the matter?"

"Carmela," she said. I prepared myself for the latest installment of the long-running Carmela Tomaselli soap opera that had been going on ever since Mrs. T's daughter and I had been classmates in high school. At the last count, Carmela had ditched husband number four and was hanging out with a young mechanic from the Saab garage in Montpelier who must have had a penchant for fixing up the classics—Carmela had been a stunner in her day, but bad marriages, chain-smoking, and frequenting the downtown bars had taken their toll.

"What's she up to now?"

"It's not her, it's her daughter, Grace. My granddaughter. Everybody says she's fine, but I think they're wrong, and Carmela keeps telling me she's all right, but she never gave a tinker's damn about her own daughter, forgive my language, and now I'm stuck with the goddamned dog." She paused to cross herself after the profanity. "He already bit your mother."

"What?" I put down the fork that was about to about to descend into a third portion of the lasagna. It didn't really count as another helping; I was just making sure that the edges were evened off in the pan. "You'd better start at the beginning."

"He's a good dog," my mother said. "He didn't mean to bite me. He's scared, because Grace is gone."

"Who is this dog?"

"She calls him Chan," Mrs. Tomaselli said. "After the actor. He's a brute, and he barks at everybody."

"He's terrified, Donna," my mother said.

"You could sue, Francine, and we'll go on a cruise with the money. Carmela has insurance. It's left over from one of the husbands."

"He nipped me, that's all," my mother said. "He's a nervous wreck."

"So am I," Mrs. Tomaselli said. "Grace left college two weeks ago. She goes to Johnson State. She sent her mother a letter on the computer, one of those, you know—"

"An email," I said.

"Right. She said she was going hiking on the Long Trail, and to come get her dog."

"So why isn't the dog at Carmela's?"

"He was, for a couple days, but he barked all the time and her landlord made her get rid of him. So I got stuck with him. But I'm worried, Vinny."

"About what?"

"Grace doesn't go hiking. She doesn't even own a pair of sneakers. She's a town girl."

"Maybe she's with a guy?"

"And they take off hiking in the middle of the semester? Not my Grace. She's a good granddaughter, and she's been trying hard as a student, not like her mother. Do you remember her? She's very beautiful."

"It's been a few years."

"I have a picture," Mrs. Tomaselli said. She opened her purse, took out a wallet, and thumbed through a sheaf of photographs in plastic slipcovers. "This is her. My Gracie."

It was a headshot taken by a professional. The photographer's lens had blurred the edges for a glamorous effect, which was unnecessary, because the granddaughter was beautiful, all right. The picture reminded me of black-and-white photos that I'd seen of Donna Tomaselli back in the day when any man in Barre would have given up a testicle for a date with her. Grace's hair shined like a freshly-buffed shoe, and her dark eyes and sensuous lips radiated both innocence and sexuality.

"What's her last name?" I said.

"Hebert," Mrs. T said. "That was Carmela's husband number two."

"And she's been hiking for two weeks?"

"That's what Carmela says."

"Have you talked to anyone at the school? Or the police?"

"No," she said. "Will you go see Carmela? You know that she and I don't get along."

"Of course I will," I said. "But I have to be back in Florida the day after tomorrow."

"Oh, I love my Vinny," Mrs. Tomaselli said. "Now that you're single again you'd better watch out. I can still make whoopee, you know."

"Donna, for god's sake," my mother said.

"Duly noted, Mrs. T," I said. She was trying to lighten the mood, but I could see the worry in her expression.

I would stop in on her daughter in the morning, and would make a few calls to the college and to some police friends from my days on the Barre force. With any luck I would clear this up in a couple of hours and get on with my leaf-peeping, although it didn't feel like it would be that simple. Trouble has a smell, and in this case it was as strong as the garlic that was wafting up from the remains of my meal.

WEDNESDAY

CARMELA TOMASELLI WORKED AS A nursing assistant at Woodridge Rehab, which is a part of the Central Vermont Hospital complex that sits on a hill overlooking the Winooski River Valley. I parked in the lot, entered the nursing home, and was greeted by the odor that they all have: Humanity vs. Lysol. A receptionist in floral-print scrubs was on the phone. She signaled me to wait while she finished her call.

"I'm here to see Carmela Tomaselli," I said. "Vince Tanzi. She knows I'm coming."

"I'll page her," she said. A couple of minutes later Carmela came around the corner, fishing out a pack of cigarettes from her purse as she approached.

"Outside," she said, waving the back of her hand at me as if I was a mosquito. "I need a smoke."

"Nice to see you, Carmela," I said, although what I was thinking was more like: holy crap, you're the same age as me? Do I look that bad?

"Mom said you want to know about Grace," she said. Carmela led the way out into the parking lot and lit up a Virginia Slim. She still had the body of a pole dancer, but her face was puffy and florid and was framed by a tangle of bottle-blonde tresses that reached to her shoulders. You could see the black roots underneath, which was the color that her hair had been when we were kids.

"She said you told her that Grace went on a hike. How long has she been gone?"

"Am I supposed to keep track of these things?" She took a deep drag, exhaling it into the light breeze. "She's old enough to take care of herself. I was on my own at her age."

"You're not worried about her?"

"My mother is the worrier. Grace is an adult. She can run off, get married, I honestly don't give a damn, Vinny. I got her through high

6

school, and believe me it was a struggle. She's on a scholarship, and if she wants to throw it all away, it's her problem."

"Do you really think she went hiking? Your mother isn't so sure."

"Look, I know this sounds harsh, but she has to make her own mistakes. I did. Senior year, when I ran off with Fast Eddie? You remember?"

I remembered. Carmela Tomaselli and Fast Eddie Boudreault had been the talk of our high school for weeks. They'd taken his father's Trans Am and driven all the way to Orlando, where she had gotten a tan, a Mickey Mouse hat, and an abortion.

"What makes you think that she's making a mistake?"

"The email she sent me was bullshit. You know what her major is? Theater and Drama. Give me a break, Vinny. If you're trying to help my mother, just get her some wine and tell her to relax. I let her believe the hiking thing, but my guess is that Grace is off with some guy."

"Do you know who she might be with?"

"No idea. She's such a child, really. I can hardly believe she's mine, she's so goddamn naïve sometimes. She has no idea what I go through on a daily basis. The crap that I put up with just to get by."

I wondered what it must have been like to grow up with this woman. The booze, the cigarettes, the revolving door of boyfriends and husbands, and the hard-as-nails attitude. "I'm going to stop in at the college," I said. "I'll let you know if I find her."

"Don't bother," she said. She dropped her cigarette on the pavement. "You're just wasting everybody's time, including mine."

I walked across the lot to my car. The sun was stronger now, and the morning had only become more spectacular, but I hardly noticed. I was thinking about the old days, and about the former high school hottie who was now a bitter, self-pitying shrew. People like to tell you that life has dealt them a bad hand even when they've chosen most of the cards themselves.

*

Much of my work as a private investigator has to do with finding those who don't want to be found. But some do want to be found, and they leave a trail a mile wide. Especially the girls, who may be royally pissed off at Mom and Dad over some incident but are terrified at the thought of being on their own. In this situation I employ what I call the Clueless Runaway Action Protocol, or, CRAP:

Step One. Log onto their phone, their laptop, and their social media accounts. It's all in there somewhere, carefully laid out in tortured prose. Or worse, in poetry.

Step Two. Cherchez le boyfriend. If she's not hiding in his bedroom, try the basement or the garage. I once found a runaway in a Porta-Potty out behind her boyfriend's house. Some guys sure know how to show a girl a good time.

Step Three. Lean on their friends. Kids don't keep secrets very well. Not that adults are any better.

A Johnson State campus safety officer named Duffy let me into her room, and we methodically tossed the place. He knew how to go about it: you have to be thorough, but there is no need to leave a mess. Grace Hebert's phone and laptop weren't there. So much for Step One.

The first thing I noticed was that there was no sign of a dog staying in the room—no bowl, no food, no hair from shedding. Her closet held an assortment of clothes, all on hangers and neatly arranged by color. A bureau contained socks, underwear, carefully folded jeans, tights, and jerseys. A drawer in her writing desk held pens, pencils, notepads, an older iPod, and a small purse with some change. No scribbled notes, no diaries, no photos of boys on the wall—it was the most OCD college dorm room that I'd ever seen.

In fact, it looked staged.

"She has a dog here, right?

"They're not allowed on campus," Duffy said as we closed up. He stood about two inches taller than me, and I fill up a doorway. I pegged the blond, walrus-mustached man at something past the usual retirement age but in excellent physical shape. He had the unflappability of someone who had been doing this work for a while. "These kids will take off without notice sometimes. I can call it in to the Lamoille County Sheriff, but you said she wrote her mother a note?"

"An email. She said she was going to hike the Long Trail. This was two weeks ago. The mother was supposed to come get the dog."

"And you're sure she's not hiking?"

"No, I'm not sure."

"You just don't like it, right?" he said. "I'm not a hack, Mr. Tanzi. I was NYPD for nineteen years before I took this job."

"You didn't strike me as a campus cop."

"Give me your number and I'll ask around, OK? These kids are like my grandchildren."

"Thanks," I said. "Do you know where the trailhead is? For the Long Trail?"

"It's a couple miles east on Route 15. It's marked, and there's a parking lot. You're not going to hike it, are you?"

"I haven't really thought about it."

"You need serious gear if you do. If you go north it's fifty miles to the Canadian border, and you have to summit Belvidere Mountain, and then Jay. It's a bitch, and—hey, no offense, but you'd never make it with that limp."

"How about southbound?"

"Forty miles to Camel's Hump. My wife and I did it last summer, and it's the hardest stretch of the whole trail. You summit Whiteface, Madonna, Spruce, Mansfield, and Bolton, and by the time you're finished you don't ever want to set foot in the woods again."

"Do you think that this girl could handle it?"

"Plenty of them do, if they're prepared. Young legs, you know. But if she's solo, all she has to do is break an ankle and she's done. That could be why she's been gone so long. Let me call this in, Mr. Tanzi. I'll take care of it."

"I'm going to give it another day," I said. "I leave for Florida tomorrow. I'll let you know, either way."

He shrugged, and I hoped that I was making the right decision. If Grace Hebert was up on the high peaks with a broken leg, then I was dead wrong. But from the looks of her squeaky-clean dorm room, I couldn't imagine her on the side of a mountain, or even outdoors, unless it was beneath the umbrella of a sidewalk café. Grace was definitely a "town girl", as her grandmother had described her, and a bunch of cops and rescuers looking for her in the deep woods would be a waste of resources.

It was time for Step Two, and maybe Step Three: I needed to locate a boyfriend or a best friend and see what I could sweat out of them. In the nicest possible way, of course.

*

The Dibden Arts Center was a short walk across a leaf-strewn lawn that was the center of the Johnson State campus and was dotted with kids leaning against their backpacks, talking, reading, playing Frisbee, and enjoying the day. The 1970's-era brick building was framed to the south by Sterling Mountain, which was also known as Whiteface, because for a good six months of the year it was draped in snow. People from Vermont enjoy a selective amnesia that kicks in around May after the impossibly long winter, and by the balmy days of midsummer you find yourself thinking—it snows here? Nah, that can't be. It's just green and gorgeous like this all the time. Who needs snow tires? And then, come November, it snows, and snows, and snows, until April rolls around, and the woodpile is down to a few sticks, and you're thinking will it ever get nice again? And you repeat the same cycle, year after year, unless you bail to somewhere warm like I did thirty years ago. Basically, Vermonters are crazy. But it's a good crazy.

When I entered the building I expected to find the usual purple-dyed, black-clad art majors, but I was pleasantly surprised by a young man in torn khaki shorts who looked like a surfer, and a freckle-faced, pigtailed woman in gray sweats. They were the only people in the entry hall, and I got right to the point.

"Hi there, I'm looking for Grace Hebert. Can you help me out?"

"She took off, I think," Surf Dude said. "Are you her dad?"

"I'm a private investigator," I said. "I'm working for her grand-mother."

"Seriously?" the girl said.

"Yes," I said. "She's been gone for two weeks, and her family is worried. You know her?"

"You mean the princess?" The girl turned up her nose. "Every-body knows her. This is a small campus. We all know way too much about everybody."

"What do you mean by *princess*?"

"Well, she's ridiculously good looking, for starters," the girl said. "And she's, you know. An ice queen. She's a totally amazing actress—she was the prostitute in the Brecht play we did last year, and it was, like, scary."

"So, are you friends with her?"

"She doesn't hang with the students," the guy said. "Just with the profs."

"The professors?"

"Yeah," the girl said. "Like I said—we know too much about the people here."

"Does she have a boyfriend?"

They both looked embarrassed. The girl spoke first. "Shouldn't we be asking for your ID or something?"

"Duffy said it was OK for me to ask people questions," I said. "He's helping me look for Grace."

"Duffy's cool," the boy said. They looked at each other, and I said nothing.

"You should talk to Mr. Lussen," the girl finally said. "His office is upstairs. He's her advisor."

"Among other things," the boy said, and the look on his face finished his sentence for him.

Oh really? *Cherchez le boyfriend?*

"Thanks, you guys," I said. "This is a big help. Just one more question. Is it possible that she'd be hiking? Like, somewhere on the Long Trail?"

"Grace wore heels to everything," the girl said. "She was nice, but she didn't fit in. I'm not surprised that she's gone."

The young woman probably hadn't meant to use the past tense like that, but if I had smelled trouble before, right now it was like I had just run over a skunk.

*

I located Donald Lussen's office, but the light was out and his door was locked. A janitor told me that most of the staff was at lunch, so I hoofed it across the campus to my car and checked out the student parking lots. Grace Hebert's faded-purple Ford Aspire sat in the lower section, just off of the road that led in and out of the college. Her car was parked at the far end of the lot and was covered in leaves. I went back to one of the dorms and borrowed a coat hanger, and a couple of minutes later the door popped open. Keyless entry, so to speak.

The back seat was folded down and a tattered foam mat took up most of the space. A metal bowl was wedged under the dash behind a thirty-pound bag of Taste of the Wild dog food. Maybe this was Chan's kennel, and she kept him here while she studied? Did that mean that he also slept here overnight? That seemed like a bad arrangement, seeing how the cold weather was just around the corner.

The Ford Motor Company must have named this tiny, cramped model the Aspire because it wasn't a real car, it only aspired to be one. I twisted myself into a position that a yogi would have admired and got inside. Next to the dog food was a small black overnight bag that I unzipped: two pairs of panties, a rolled-up nightshirt, lipstick and other cosmetics, a three-pack of condoms, a toothbrush, a hairbrush, assorted feminine products, and seventeen crisp hundred-dollar bills zipped into a side pocket. What was this, a hooker's emergency kit?

Maybe Grace Hebert had played the part of a prostitute so deftly because she already knew the ropes. Or, was this simply an overnight bag for a woman who also liked to keep some serious cash around, just in case? There was more money in the zippered pocket than the car was worth, and Grace was taking a risk leaving it around, but that could be why the dog slept here: according to Mrs. Tomaselli, he was a brute.

There was nothing out of the ordinary in the glove box: the service manual, the registration, and a bill from the Montpelier garage where her mother's boyfriend worked. I combed the area under the seats, looking for any additional items. Sometimes the smallest thing can provide a clue, but all that I could find was a bottle cap, a couple of paper clips, a few bits of the dog kibble, and some wadded up tissues. In other words, nothing.

I popped open the tailgate of the hatchback and lifted up the dog bed and the carpeted floor panel underneath to reveal the tire compartment. The space held three items: a temporary spare, a jack, and something heavy that had been wrapped in a hand towel, which I carefully unfolded.

Inside the towel was a .44 magnum Ruger Super Redhawk, freshly oiled, fully loaded, and with the safety off. What the hell? A gun that size would create so much recoil that Grace Hebert would sprain her wrist if she used it. And no experienced gun owner would ever leave a weapon loaded and ready to fire—during my years as a deputy sheriff I'd seen the consequences of that all too often. I engaged the safety and put the gun in my car. If Grace reappeared, she could collect it at her grandmother's along with her dog.

If the dorm room had revealed nothing, the car had told me too much. Your typical college student didn't pack heat like that, not to mention wads of hundreds. I decided to go back to the drama building to see if Professor Lussen had finished his lunch. Maybe her student advisor could explain what was going on, or maybe not. Either way, I doubted that I was going to be on the flight home tomorrow.

*

If I were a good-looking, twenty-one-year-old female drama major with a loaded revolver, a cash hoard, a dog, and a dark secret of some kind, and not a fifty-three-year-old ex-cop with a bullet hole in his head, I would have curled up on the rug at Donald Lussen's Birkenstock-clad feet and purred like a kitty cat. He had the kind of male beauty that would make even the most sensible woman want to strip down to her Fruit of the Looms and start twerking uncontrollably. The professor's hair was prematurely gray, which only enhanced the appeal of his tanned face, chiseled features, close-cropped beard, and pale blue eyes. He wore one of those perma-smiles that instantly put you at ease, although sometimes people like that will keep smiling regardless of what you say, and it's unnerving. I told him who I was, why I was here, and that I was deeply concerned for Grace Hebert's safety, and he smiled back helplessly like he couldn't turn the damn thing off.

"Tell me your name again?"

"Vince Tanzi. She told her family she was hiking the Long Trail, but that was two weeks ago. Is she taking classes with you?"

"She's not in the fall production. We're doing *Macbeth*, and I wanted her for Hecate, but she wouldn't do it. I haven't seen her—I thought she was out sick."

"But you're personal friends?"

The smile finally began to fade. "I'm her faculty advisor. We meet a couple times a semester."

"Here? Or off campus?"

"What do you mean by that?" the professor said. I had him off balance. I was playing the dual role of good-cop-bad-cop, and it was time to reel him back in.

"I'm sorry," I said. "I didn't mean it to come out that way. There's some scuttlebutt on campus about you and her, probably because you're both very attractive, and people like to make assumptions that they shouldn't."

"That's right," Lussen said. "I know where the lines are drawn."

"What can you tell me about her dog?"

He hesitated. "She has a dog?"

My bullshit alert suddenly went off. Answer a question with a question, lose one credibility point. "Why would she own a gun? And keep a lot of cash handy?"

"No idea," the professor said. "Guns aren't allowed on campus. Not even for the campus cops. All they can do is write tickets."

"Are you married? You live in town?"

"Yes, I'm married, and—listen, this is quite enough. No more questions. You're not with the police, right?"

"No."

"I'll speak to the police if they want me to. I'd be happy to help, but I don't like what you're insinuating. So please go."

I paused for a moment before speaking. "Look, Donald. You can talk to the police, and by the way I'm calling them next, or you can tell me what you know, right now. And if you level with me, we'll keep your wife out of this, all right? All I want to do is find the girl."

Lussen sat back in his office chair, which squeaked as he reclined. An old Regulator railroad clock ticked away the seconds on the brick wall behind him while I waited.

"No," he said. "No deal."

"Here's my card," I said. He waved it away, so I left it on his desk.

"Take a hike, Mr. Tanzi," he said, and the smile reappeared.

*

Donald Lussen may have not meant it literally, but the idea of being in the woods for a little while to sort things out sounded like a good idea. Afterward, I would call on Lieutenant John Pallmeister, a friend from my Barre days who was now in charge of the Middlesex barracks of the Vermont State Police. The barracks was on the way home, and even if this turned out to be nothing, it wouldn't hurt to get his opinion. Grace Hebert was old enough to make her own decisions, as her mother had said, and maybe this was nothing more than some kind of intrigue with a philandering professor, and it was none of my damn business. I could almost have bought into that—except for the gun and the money. They didn't fit, and the dog didn't either.

Maybe the dorm room *was* a stage set, and Grace and her dog spent their nights elsewhere. Did the professor have a secret love nest? If the state cops took this one on, they had the tools to find that out in a day or two. Acting on my own, and without access to her phone records and all those other things, it might take me weeks. It made sense to go see Pallmeister whatever the outcome, but for now I was going to steal an hour of the beautiful autumn afternoon and see if my legs and my balance were up to taking a brief hike in the Green Mountains.

The trailhead parking area was two miles outside of Johnson, across the road from an old cemetery that was surrounded by a picket fence. There was only one other car in the lot: a rusty green Subaru like my mother's, with an empty kayak rack on the top. I parked my rental car and tightened up the laces on my sneakers. I was dressed in chinos and a white golf shirt, and I had nothing at all in the way of hiking gear except for a plastic bottle of water, but my plan was to go no further than a mile each way—I just wanted to get a taste of the outdoors and try some terrain other than the level Florida beach.

White blaze markers pointed me down a path across a field to the wood's edge, where the trail began a modest ascent over a small hill. I was up one side and down the other without a problem, and the soft breeze and rustling orange-and-gold foliage was lulling me into a quiet contentment that I hadn't experienced for a long time. Maybe if Grace Hebert really was out on an extended trek, it was a good thing.

The trail led to the side of the Lamoille River, where a suspension bridge had been built specifically for the hikers. It wobbled under my gait, and I was soon on the other side, where I crossed a paved road and reentered the forest. This time the trail was much steeper. A sign pointing to Prospect Rock provided me with a goal, and after a half an hour of sweating and grunting I was rewarded with sweeping a view over the river valley and the farms, church spires and settlements below. I sat on a wide rock outcropping, well away from the edge because I don't do heights—the third rung of a ladder is the limit before my palms begin to sweat.

I opened the bottle of water and drained it, as I already knew the way back and I wasn't worried about getting dehydrated. I was pleased with myself for being able to handle the modest climb and was thinking that when Royal was a few years older and we were visiting his grandmother, I should take him into the woods. Close to nature. I filled my lungs with the cool mountain air and was glad that I had taken a break from looking for Grace Hebert. This was heaven, and I was about to lie back on the sun-warmed rock when I fell face forward to the edge and passed out cold.

*

The first of the whiteouts had come in August after I had dropped Royal at his mother's and was driving back to my house. He and I had walked the beach together that afternoon, part of the time with him in the backpack but most of the time I held his little hands and let him stumble in and out of the shallow water at the edge of the surf. I'd had a bit too much sun that day, and five minutes after I left Barbara's driveway I started getting light-headed. Everything was too bright, as if the bulb wattage had been increased. I pulled over into the parking lot of the Indian River Mall and checked out my eyes in the rearview mirror: they were dilated, and the brightness became a glaring white flash that made my head throb. The episode was over in less than a minute, but it was good that I had pulled over, because if I'd still been driving I could have killed somebody. It had happened four more times in the month before my Vermont trip, and each time I'd had plenty of warning and had been able to get off the road.

There had been no warning this time.

I had keeled over forward and was now trying to get up, but the back of my neck was throbbing, and I could feel blood drying on my face. I realized that I had been lying only inches from the edge and that directly in front of me was a hundred yard drop to the treetops and boulders below. I'd had no advance notice, no light-headed feeling, no brightening of the light. This had been a blackout, not a whiteout, and I wondered why the back of my neck hurt so much when it was my face that was bleeding.

A young hiker in dreadlocks came rushing to my assistance and helped me stand. He recoiled at the sight of my bloody face, and after we backed away from the edge of the rock he sat me down and dabbed at my forehead with a towel soaked in water from his canteen.

"You cut the skin at the top of your forehead," he said. "I think the bleeding has stopped. How long have you been here?"

"Don't know," I croaked. My neck was really beginning to throb now, and I wondered if I could make it back down the trail. "Did you see anybody?"

"Just you," the kid said. He was dressed in shorts and a T-shirt, with leather hiking boots and tall wool socks. His backpack rested near him on the rock. From the look of it he was a through-hiker, not a day-tripper.

"You going north or south?" I asked. The wet towel felt good on my forehead, and I was slowly getting my wits back.

"North, but right now I'm taking you back to your car. Is that your Subaru in the lot I passed? Or the other one?"

"Mine's the red one," I said. "Did you see anybody else?"

"Just the Hummer," he said. "The guy was leaving when I came through."

"A Hummer?"

"White, with blacked-out windows. Florida plates. It's illegal to black out the windows on a Vermont car. Plus, nobody around here would drive one of those things."

"Did you get a look at the guy?"

"Not really. I just saw the car and said, you know, what's *that* doing here? Those people don't hike."

"I think I can handle getting back. You go on ahead."

"But—"

"I'm OK, really. Thanks. You go."

He shrugged, picked up his pack, and started north. I stood up and began walking in the opposite direction. I had no problem at all with my balance, or staying on the trail, and I was back to the parking lot in no time, because I was pissed. That was no whiteout.

Someone in a Hummer had followed me all the way into the woods, sneaked up on me, and coldcocked me, and I was going to find out who it was, because that hadn't been a random attack. It was a message, and I had a message for them:

I can hit back.

*

John Pallmeister wasn't at the Middlesex State Police barracks when I stopped in, which was fine, because what I really wanted to do was go to my mother's house, open a beer, recline in my deceased father's Barcalounger and wait for this headache to go away. I would call the lieutenant in the morning, and in the meantime I put in a call to my friend Bobby Bove at the Indian River Sheriff's office, where I had worked for twenty-five years before getting the boot. I asked Bobby to run a DMV check on the white Hummer. He said there were a total of one hundred and thirteen in that color registered in Florida, and he would email me the info.

As I pulled into the driveway of my mother's house I saw two women approaching down the leafy street that I grew up on. One of them was holding a leash and was being pulled toward me by a small horse or a very large dog—it was hard to tell from a distance—but as they drew closer I recognized my mother and Mrs. Tomaselli, who was getting her arm dislocated by some kind of monster. The dog stood as tall as her waist and had to weigh a hundred pounds or more. He didn't look happy to see me. In fact, he began barking as they drew closer to the car, and the sound was making my head want to burst open like a dropped cantaloupe.

"I'm sorry, Vinny," Mrs. T yelled over the commotion. "He hates men. He tried to eat the UPS man."

"Nice doggie," I said, tentatively reaching out a hand toward the dog's muzzle, which probably wasn't the smartest move, but the dog immediately stopped barking and recoiled. He gave me an incredulous look, like: *Nice doggie? Did you really say that?*

"What is this thing?" I asked the women.

"It's an Akita," my mother said. "They're Japanese. That's why Grace calls him Chan. After the movie star."

"Jackie Chan is Chinese, not Japanese," I said. "What are you feeding him?" The dog was sniffing at my trouser legs, and he allowed me to pet him on the back of his neck, which I could reach without bending over.

"I've already gone through a whole bag of Purina," Mrs. Tomaselli said. "I need to go to the store."

"He eats a different brand," I said. "I saw it in Grace's car. I should have brought it."

"Did you find her?"

"No, but I have some leads. I'm going to talk to the police in the morning." The dog continued to sniff at my pant legs, and then he suddenly yanked the leash free from Mrs. Tomaselli's hand. He leaped though the open window of my rental car, leaving scratches on the red paint, and climbed into the back seat where I had put Grace Hebert's overnight bag and her revolver. The dog stuck his nose into the bag and sniffed for a moment as I opened the door and attempted to grab the leash, but I couldn't reach it. He raised his muzzle and let out a low, mournful howl that was the sorriest noise I had ever heard coming from an animal. After a while he stopped and his brown eyes focused on me, as if I was directly responsible for his misery:

Find her. It was as clear as if he had said it out loud.

"I intend to," I said.

"Vinny? What was that?" my mother asked.

"Let's go inside," I said. "I need a beer. And then Chan and I are going to go buy some dog food. He likes the expensive stuff."

*

The modern detective needs to be on top of technology, because computers, search engines, databases, tracking programs, listening bugs, remote cameras, and license plate readers have made solving most cases as easy as pushing a button. Meanwhile, those same devices have also stripped away every shred of privacy, and it's unnerving to know that somewhere, someone knows that you Googled one of your high school girlfriends just to see if she was still alive, or married, or still hot, or that you wear a size thirteen loafer, or that you have pretty much survived on Hot Pockets and ramen noodles since your wife took off.

It's a challenge to square these concerns with my profession, seeing how invading privacy is the whole point of the job. So I do what any Fortune 500 CEO would do: I outsource it. Roberto Arguelles, my teenage friend and tech guru, has been guiding me through the technological woods since he was thirteen. I figured I had about six months of his attention left, since he was a senior at St. Edwards School in Vero Beach and would be off to college soon. I would miss him.

I had forwarded Bobby Bove's email with the various Hummer registration details to Roberto and was resting in the Barcalounger with Chan by my side. I was lazily stroking the fur of the dog's back, who lifted his head and looked at me as if to say *don't get used to this*.

"Right," I said out loud, and my mother glanced up. She was in her chair across from me with the local paper, and she returned to her reading when she realized that I wasn't talking to her.

Roberto sent me back an email with an analysis of the one hundred and thirteen white Hummers with Florida plates. Seventy-two were located in Dade County. Fifty-nine of those were registered to names that had Spanish roots, but somehow that didn't click. Roberto had come to the same conclusion, and his research had led him to a car that was domiciled in Pensacola, the westernmost city on the Florida Panhandle before you get to Alabama. I'd been there once for the Crawfish Festival, but it was a part of the state that I was not that familiar with, even though some people say that Pensacola has the best oysters in the South, and my internal GPS pretty much directs me from one raw bar to the next.

The white Hummer was registered to the New Commitment and Love Society of Jesus Christ, which Roberto had already cross-referenced on the search engines, and he had included several links in his email. The first one showed maps of the Society's recent real estate acquisitions, one of which happened to be in Vermont. In fact, the organization had closed the previous year on a piece of land along the Lamoille River that had formerly been known as the West Eden Bible Camp: a collection of unheated bunkhouses, a mess hall, and a central meeting house that had been a religious retreat since the mid-nineteenth century. Camp meetings used to be common in Vermont, where the participants prayed, baptized each other, sang hymns, and socialized for a few weeks each summer at rustic locations. The attendance had waned over the years, and some of the nicer properties were now private homes. West Eden, according to the Society's website, was to be maintained as a special retreat for "select leaders" of the New Commitment and Love Society, presumably because religion was such a grind and the top brass deserved a few perks.

Roberto had also included a link to the "About Us" section of the Society's webpage. Prominent among the executive staff, friends, and benefactors was a photograph of a handsome, seventy-something man in a goatee whose name I recognized: Clement Goody, the founder of Goody's Peanuts and one of the wealthiest men in southern Georgia. Goody had become ordained as a Baptist minister, and he had a Sunday morning radio show with a devout listenership that numbered in the thousands. It was said that he had cashed in his peanut fortune and had given it all to God, but from the looks of the website he was the control person for whatever the Society was doing, and they owned a lot of high-end real estate. There were holy places in London, D.C., New Orleans, midtown Manhattan, and a few thousand no-doubt sacred acres in Colorado, near Vail. Praise Jesus and pass the warranty deed.

I zoomed in on the map to see exactly where the Vermont property was. The location was along a stretch of the river near Johnson, about two miles west of the village, directly adjacent to the Long Trail. Right next to where I had parked, and taken a hike, and been whacked in the neck by someone who may have been driving a white Hummer.

I sent a text to Roberto: *Bullseye*.

I'll put it on your bill, he replied.

I was eager to return home and see my son, and Roberto, and get back to my life. But whether or not I would be able to enlist John Pallmeister's help in finding Grace Hebert, I would be heading north in the morning, and if Mr. Clement Goody was in residence at his newly acquired prayer camp, he had better start praying.

THURSDAY

CHAN WAS ON MY BED when I woke up. He covered a third of the mattress with his front and back legs stretched out like a steeplechase horse going over a jump. The dog had effectively pinned me under the bedclothes. I jostled him to get him to move, but instead I got a look:

No way.

"Move, you big lunk," I said.

I'm not a morning person.

"You're not a person," I said. He rolled over, let out a huge sigh, and fell back to sleep while I extricated myself from the covers and stumbled into the kitchen.

My mother is a product of the Betty Crocker generation, gastronomically speaking, but in her later years she has become addicted to the Food Network, and a few minutes after I poured myself a generous mug of black coffee she put a plate down on the table in front of me.

Mama mia. Eggs Benedict with Parma ham, a side of hash browns, and a Hollandaise sauce so lush and rich that it ought to be a controlled substance. If the world's governments ever served food like this to their arms negotiators, there would be no more war, just mutually assured arteriosclerosis.

Chan and I were on the road by eight. The dog spread out on the back seat of my rental car while I sat at the wheel listening to an old Talking Heads song on a Montpelier radio station. Chan dozed and I drove the little vehicle north through the fog-draped morning, wondering what my next move would be.

When faced with a choice between making a discreet inquiry and barging through somebody's door, I tend toward the latter, or at least I had in the days before my brain injury. I wasn't on such firm ground now. I had been thinking that I would hang out in Johnson for the morning—check out the places where the townspeople congregated, like the coffee shops, or the post office, and ask a few questions, but the back of my head was still tender, and my inclination was to drive balls-first into the West Eden Bible Camp and raise some hell. My health concerns were trumped by the fact that someone had assaulted me, and I'd already had to reschedule my return to Florida, which didn't make me happy, so whatever I could do to expedite the process would be a plus. My strategy was to find Grace Hebert, give her back her gun and her money, and thump the bastard who had thumped me up on Prospect Rock. It seemed like a reasonable plan.

You keep saying that.

The dog was right. I needed to stop trying to control things and go with this. Investigations take time. The trajectory of events is unpredictable, and you can't rush them—like hurrying a Hollandaise sauce—or they will turn into a curdled mess.

The entrance to the bible camp was at the bottom of a gravel road that led up a hill. I stopped when I reached a grassy meadow dotted with small buildings, mostly simple structures with white clapboard siding and with no sign of chimneys or insulation—this was a summer-only place. A large barn stood in the center with a dark green crucifix mounted above the central door. A basketball court at the far end of the meadow was flanked by tall white pines that loomed over the recreation area. I noticed another road that led up the hill but was closed off by an iron gate. An electrician's van was parked at the foot of the extension road. I pulled my car next to the van. A young man in coveralls and a Red Sox cap leaned into the open back door of the vehicle, and he jumped when he heard me approach.

"Jeezum, mister, don't do that. Ya made me screw up this solder connection." He smiled, revealing a set of perfect teeth that belonged on a dental hygienist.

"Sorry," I said. "Nobody else around here?"

"Just me," he said. "You looking for Mr. Goody?"

"Yes."

"They took off an hour ago. Didn't say when they'd be back."

"You work for them?"

"Nah, I'm independent, but I have to say he's a good customer. I been rigging this place up since he bought it. Name's Eric."

"Vince Tanzi," I said. "What are you working on?"

"This here's a Fence Hawk," the young man said. "Electric fence, all the way around the main house. Meaning the one up there, up on the hill." He pointed up the road that led out of sight beyond the gate.

"That's where Mr. Goody lives?"

"Yeah," Eric said. "It's a real nice place, and he's spent a bundle. Got a home theater and everything. I wired the shit out of it."

"So the fence is to keep animals in?"

"Nope. This fence is to keep people out. You know what a prepper is?"

"You mean a survivalist?"

"Yup. He's got a whole frickin' arsenal up there, and a couple years' worth of food, too. Real nice guy, but kind of a whack job. I put in a generator and a big fuel tank, but if the shit hits the fan these preppers won't last much longer than the rest of us. Wasting his money if you ask me. But don't say nothin', because I need the work. Sorry, I talk too much. At least that's what my wife says." He flashed the perfect teeth again.

"When you said that they left, who else was in the car?"

"Just Miss Lila. You know what a MILF is?" I got another blinding grin.

"She's his wife?"

"Don't know about that," he said. "People in town say she's his girlfriend. But he's got more than one. A gal I know cleans for them, and they have these sex parties. No secrets around this town, no sir."

"Sex parties?"

"I heard he was a rich preacher," he said. "But you ought to see the women. Jeezum crow, I should a gone ta church more often." This time he laughed, and he had to hold onto his teeth, which I realized were dentures.

My phone rang in my pocket and I got it out to take a look. VT STATE POLICE TROOP A showed on the display, and I knew who it was: John Pallmeister, calling me back.

"Where are you?" he said, not bothering with small talk.

"Johnson," I said. "I might need to get you involved in something. I'm looking for a missing girl, and I think I'm getting close."

"Stay right there," Lieutenant Pallmeister said. "I'm on my way to the college. I'll meet you at the Campus Security office."

"What's up?"

"You know someone named Donald Lussen?"

"I met with him yesterday afternoon. He's the advisor for the girl I'm trying to find."

"He's dead," Pallmeister said. "A jogger found him on the Water Tower Trail this morning, next to the campus, with a hunting arrow through his skull. Bow season started on Saturday, but the Lamoille sheriff doesn't think it was an accident."

"Why not?"

"Because there was another arrow in his chest."

"Uh-oh."

"He had your business card in his pocket. We're going to need a statement. I'll be there in half an hour."

Donald Lussen was dead? I shuddered involuntarily. Somehow he had seemed too perfect to die, but death doesn't care how good-looking you are.

*

Duffy Kovich had been a New York City cop, and he had no doubt seen some truly bad things over the course of his career. That didn't stop his hand from trembling enough to spill a good portion of the coffee I'd brought him onto his desk. The ambulance had left, the State Police forensics guys had packed up, John Pallmeister and a stocky, cropped-blonde sergeant named Janice had taken Duffy's and my statements, and it was down to the two of us in the cramped office where the older man worked dealing with lock-outs, noise complaints, students' cars that wouldn't start, lost laptops, and kids who had partied too hard and were passed out on the library steps. Finding the dead body of a theater professor with one arrow through his eye socket and a second one that had punctured his lungs was not supposed to be part of the job.

The last time I'd been through something like that I had gone home, picked up Royal from his crib, and walked him around on the cool floor tiles of my darkened house, even though he was still asleep. When you've been slapped in the face by some gruesome event, you have to find a way to reaffirm that life isn't completely depraved. I wondered who Duffy turned to.

The big ex-cop had been in the room when I'd spoken to Pallmeister and his partner, so he'd heard what I had told them about my morning trip to the West Eden Bible Camp. I asked him what he knew about Clement Goody. "He's on the campus now and then," he said. "He gave money to the theater program last spring. He underwrote the play that your girl was in."

"Grace?"

"Yes. I didn't go. Not my thing. But Goody's OK."

"How well do you know him?"

"Not well, I just hear what I hear."

"About the sex parties?"

"Who told you that?"

"Local scuttlebutt," I said. "But I'm supposed to leave it alone. Pallmeister asked me to lay low while his team looks around."

"You're going to do that?"

"I don't know," I said. "I'm not the lay low type. And I still haven't found Grace Hebert."

*

I had to steer through a throng of reporters, camera operators, satellite relay trucks from the Burlington TV stations, scared students, freaked-out staff, and the usual ghouls who had seen the report on the news to get to the parking lot. I didn't go directly to the West Eden Bible Camp. Instead, I drove around the village for a while, because I needed to mentally reboot. Finding a loaded gun and a bunch of money, and then getting hit on the head out in the middle of the wilderness—that was motivation enough to stay in Vermont to figure out what was going on. But with this new element, I was even more fearful for Grace Hebert's safety. Someone very close to her had been murdered.

Donna Tomaselli's worries were becoming mine. Her grand-daughter had been friends with Professor Lussen, and the two kids who I had met yesterday had intimated that the student-advisor relationship went well beyond that. The Vermont State Police's crime scene search team was now combing through the professor's office, and they would be logging every email, text, and cellphone call that Lussen had made. If there had been any unusual extracurricular contact with his young student, it would be revealed. Pallmeister promised that he would keep me in the loop, but I wasn't convinced that I could be that patient. Police investigations are slow by nature because they have rules and protocols to follow and also because they have the press watching every move. I'm not so encumbered, and I wasn't thrilled about sitting by the phone like a teenage virgin, hoping that the lieutenant would call. I didn't think that time was on our side, and it wasn't because I needed to get home. It was because this was October. October is arguably the most spectacular month of the year in Vermont. It is also the start of hunting season, and I needed to resolve this before Grace Hebert became the prey.

We were in the parking lot of the Johnson Woolen Mill factory store. I had been pondering whether to go inside and buy anything for my Florida friends, but I didn't think that a red and black checked bomber hat with pull-down earflaps would be an essential fashion accessory anywhere south of Johnson, Vermont. Chan growled from the back seat just as a white Hummer sped past us, and I caught a brief glimpse of the tags: they were the "Choose Life" version of vanity plates that the state of Florida offered. That had to be Clement Goody. I gunned the rental car's tiny engine and wobbled out of the lot. We followed the big white car through the village and a couple of miles east to Hog Back Road. I knew exactly where we were headed because I'd gone this same way earlier in the morning: the West Eden Bible Camp.

I pushed the little sedan as hard as I could until we were a couple of car lengths behind the SUV; I knew that the driver would notice me now if he hadn't already. We swerved together into the camp's driveway, and I had to drive through the Hummer's dust from the gravel road's loose surface. The SUV pulled up to the gate at the bottom of the drive that led to Goody's house, and I waited, expecting the gate to open and let the Hummer enter. I would try to scoot in behind before it closed. None of this could be called subtle, but neither was taking a whack on the head in the middle of the woods. Somebody had to answer for that.

The gate stayed shut, and the driver's door opened. I was expecting a grey-haired man with a ponytail, but instead I got a smile from a blonde woman in black yoga tights and a yellow fleece jacket. Chan sat up in the back and let out a nervous whine.

"Are you lost?" She was walking toward my open window, and she got better looking with every step: medium height, with the shoulders-back, tits-out posture of a beauty contestant. My defenses went up: females who are that attractive bring out the testosterone-cursed cretin in me, and I didn't need that right now. I have built something of a wall around my love life since the divorce.

"I'm looking for Mr. Goody," I said, smiling back. "That's your car?"

"No, it's Clement's. He's not here. You're a policeman?"

"Private investigator," I said. "Were the police here already?"

"He went to Morrisville to meet with them. You heard about Donald Lussen?"

"You knew Lussen?"

"I worked with him," she said. The smile was gone. "I'm Karen Charbonneau. I'm the chair of his department. We're all in shock."

Uh-oh. Attractive, and smart too. "And you know Clement Goody."

26

"I live here," she said. "He's away a lot. Cindy and I take care of the house."

The passenger door of the Hummer opened and another woman got out, dressed in a jean jacket and brown Carhartt dungarees. She wore no makeup that I could tell, but it was obvious that the passenger was the driver's sister—in fact, they appeared to be identical twins: one Miss Vermont and one dressed-down Miss Podunk.

"Come on, Karen!" the other one yelled.

"What do you want with Clement?" Karen asked through my open window.

"I'm looking for a student named Grace Hebert. She's the grand-daughter of a friend."

The woman considered this information for a moment. "Pull your car over there and you can ride with us," she said. "Clement doesn't like the dog."

I parked the car under a tree, opened the windows a few inches, and patted Chan on the head. "Back in a while."

The animal glowered at me. *Tell him I don't like him either.*

*

The Charbonneau twins ushered me into the foyer of what had once been a cozy brick Cape-style house, typical of the ones that dotted the Vermont landscape, and that had either enjoyed—or suffered—a recent addition the size of an airplane hangar. I took a seat in a soft leather chair that reclined so far back I was almost horizontal. Karen Charbonneau had left me with a cold can of ginger ale and a pile of magazines, and then disappeared. They hadn't said when my host might show up, but I had a feeling that I'd made the right move. All I had to do was wait. Clement Goody would be here eventually, and I would grill him, and would find out who had assaulted me, and find out where Grace Hebert was. I might even kick some butt in the process.

There was only one problem.

Ever since I'd gotten in the back seat of the Hummer and had taken the ride up the hill to Goody's place, I had been fighting off a whiteout. The light at the hilltop had become harsh and opaque, and I had barely been able to take in my surroundings when I'd arrived. This episode felt like I was surfing the outer curl of a glassy, soon-to-be-suffocating wave. It was different, and it was also sobering, because it dawned on me that one of these things might kill me. It could be some kind of ministroke, and it might get a lot worse unless I leveled with my neurosurgeon. I had already cheated death once, and just like death doesn't discriminate, it doesn't like to be fooled.

I flipped through the magazines, hoping that by distracting myself the unbalanced sensation would pass. At the bottom of the pile was a heavy one, printed on the kind of thick stock that was reserved for high-end real estate or art auctions. But this publication had nothing to do with real estate, or the art world. It was porn.

The photographic content was carefully crafted, and no expense had been spared on the production. This wasn't a skin mag that you might see at the local barbershop. This was the top-shelf stuff, although as perfectly lit, staged, and composed as the pictures were, they were also completely depraved. I turned some of the pages thinking: *do people actually do that?* The answer is yes. There's a thin line between the erotic and the unthinkable, but my position with these things is to take the veteran cop's approach: let them have their fun as long as nobody gets hurt.

I thumbed through the magazine, hoping that my mother wasn't going to burst through the door flanked by a group of angry nuns. I no longer go to Mass, but growing up Catholic, one's sense of guilt is as indelible as a birthmark. On the twenty-third page I stopped browsing, and it wasn't because it was getting boring. It was because the model— a young woman with dark hair and full lips, shown in a variety of poses and accompanied by men whose equipment would have shamed a sex- shop dildo—was Grace Hebert.

The photographers had edited out the moles, the skin blotches, and the red marks, but they hadn't been able to do anything about her eyes. It was a look that I'd seen many times before: Grace had the vacant stare of a junkie, and I realized that even if I did find her, she might still be lost.

*

"Mr. Tanzi?" Clement Goody was standing above my reclined chair. He had tapped me on the shoulder and roused me. The light from the foyer's window was fading. I'd suffered a whiteout, and I had no idea how long I'd been here.

"What time is it?"

"We got back a while ago, and then went out on our bikes. You feeling all right?"

"I'm fine," I said, although I wasn't so sure about that. I'd come here to grill the guy and had passed out in his lobby.

"Welcome to my house. This is Lila Morton." He gestured to a middle-aged woman who had taken a chair across a glass coffee table from where I was seated. Both of them wore friendly smiles and looked as if they were thrilled that I had decided to drop in.

I pushed a button to make the chair sit up. Goody stood about six feet even and had a neatly pointed goatee that set off his blue eyes. He was dressed in black tights and a multi-colored bicycling shirt that clung to his fit physique. Lila Morton wore an identical outfit and wasn't quite as pretty as the Charbonneau twins, but the Breast Fairy had definitely stopped at her house. I turned my attention back to Goody before I got caught staring.

"I have some questions," I said. "Your caretakers let me in. I'm looking for Grace Hebert."

"No cause to rush things," Clement Goody said. He had a strong, Southern-tinged voice that would easily carry over a large congregation. "Lila and I need to shower, and then we'll have drinks. We worked up a sweat." He wore the same frozen smile that I'd seen on Donald Lussen. It might have been an effort to put me at ease, but it was having the opposite effect.

"Just a couple of quick questions," I said. "It won't take more than a minute."

"After we clean up," the preacher said. "If we're going to discuss Grace it will take more than a minute. Come on, Lila."

He took her elbow, and she turned to me and gave me a sly wink. "Join us?"

I smiled just enough to be polite. It was a joke, right? I would have believed that, but she waited a little too long for my answer before disappearing down the hall.

*

I decided to look around. I gave myself a tour of the first floor, starting with the original section. It had a dining room, a parlor, and several other small rooms that looked unused but were tastefully furnished with oriental rugs and antiques. The newer wing consisted of the foyer, multiple bathrooms, side rooms, and closets that I would have examined more closely if I'd had more time. The newer section was dominated by what builders call a Great Room. This one measured about sixty by thirty feet and contained a living area, a kitchen with barstools along a long counter, and a grand piano along one wall. At the far end was a stone fireplace with a fire already set. I stood next to it, trying to shed a chill that had come over me.

It must have been a whiteout. If it was, it was a different kind from the ones before, because although I remembered getting light-headed at the top of the hill, I'd been escorted by the Charbonneau twins to the chair in the foyer, I'd drunk from the ginger ale can, and I'd checked out the high-end porn that Clement Goody left out for visitors. I remembered nothing after that, but according to Goody, I'd been out cold.

I killed half an hour in front of the fire worrying about my situation. I'd come up here ready to punch out someone's lights, and instead I had passed out. Maybe I couldn't pull this off anymore, and my return to the investigating business was a bad idea. Someone else would have to find Grace Hebert. I would slink back to Florida, take care of Royal, and try to live on my pension from the Sheriff's department. Dr. Jaffe would have my driver's license taken away, and I would be washed up for good. How would I transport Royal anywhere? Hell, I'd have to hitchhike to the Market Basket for groceries. I had worked myself into a multi-episode miniseries of misery when Lila Morton finally emerged into the Great Room and gave me a radiant smile.

Whoa, I almost said aloud.

She wore a black dress that reached to her knees and revealed just enough cleavage to promise a vast world of fun. Her gray-blonde hair was pulled back with a clip, exposing her neck, with gold hoops on her ears and a matching necklace. I pegged her at mid-forties, but with a body that had escaped gravity. Was there some sort of rule against normal-looking women living here?

"Clement's making phone calls," she said. "Gin and tonic? We make our own."

"You make your own gin?"

"No, we make the tonic. The store-bought kind is full of corn syrup," she said. She walked over to the kitchen area and took out several bottles from the bar. "This is much better for you. Cane sugar and real quinine. It's a lot of work to make it, but Clement insists."

"He's a gin drinker?"

"He's a teetotaler," she said. "But he likes his guests to be happy." She handed me a hand-blown goblet of the gently bubbling beverage, topped with a wedge of lime. I took a sip—whoa, again. Maybe this would be the cure for the whiteouts.

"Do you know where Grace Hebert is?"

Lila Morton finished mixing her own drink. She came over to the barstool where I was sitting, and put her hand on my arm. "We'll get to that later," she said. "Let's talk about you."

"About me?" Hold on. I had a few questions that I wanted answered, and then I would be on my way.

"Yes, you," she said. "You haven't been very lucky in love, have you? I'm curious why not."

"Ms. Morton—"

"Lila."

"You know nothing about me," I said.

"Your first died, and your second wife left you. What was that old song? If it wasn't for bad luck?"

"I wouldn't have no luck at all," I said. "How do you know about my marriages?"

"Clement had Cindy research you. She likes to have the background on people. And she's not too good with men. She's straight, but sometimes I think she'd rather beat them up than take them to bed."

"So it was Cindy who assaulted me? Yesterday, on Prospect Rock?"

"What are you talking about?"

"Someone parked your car—the Hummer—at the trailhead, and snuck up on me. They hit me in the back of the neck, and I passed out. Another hiker saw the car. Middle of the afternoon."

"We were in Burlington," Lila said. "Clement likes to shop at Costco. Karen was at the college, and the rest of us weren't back until after dark."

"In the Hummer?"

"No, we had Cindy's van," she said. "The Hummer was here. Nobody had access to it. The only one here was—"

"Was who?"

"I—can't say. You'll have to wait for Clement."

*

The three women were making dinner while we waited for the master of the house to get off the phone. Cindy and Karen had also put on dresses, and I was feeling more and more like a homeless person who had stumbled through the back door of an exclusive disco. The women were almost too pretty, like a doll collection. I was nursing my drink, and I passed the time talking with Karen, who dodged any inquiries about Grace or Donald Lussen. When I brought up his death she shuddered, but she seemed determined to keep up the small talk. She was apparently under orders to not discuss anything important. I tried various approaches, but she would say: *you'll have to ask Clement.* He had her well trained, and I wondered how that had happened, because she didn't seem the type to be taking orders from anyone.

"How much longer is he going to be?" I asked Karen. "I need to feed my dog."

"He's still on the phone," she said. "I'll feed him for you. Please stay."

I got up from my chair. "Be right back."

"Please," Karen said. "Don't leave the house. Clement won't like it."

"That's a problem?"

None of the three women spoke. What exactly was the deal here?

"I'll be right back," I said.

Chan was not pleased to see me after my long absence. I poured him a bowl of kibble, and he took a few bites and then looked up. He sniffed at my pant leg.

She's there.

"You know this somehow?"

Yes. Dogs know.

I realized that I was standing out in the starry Vermont night talking out loud to a dog, which was batshit. I wasn't under the illusion that this was a two-way conversation—I was simply using the animal to work things out in my own mind. I'm no crazier than the next person, although sometimes you have to wonder about the value of that endorsement.

"I have a dinner invitation with Pastor Goody and his girlfriends," I said as Chan finished off his meal, "and then I'm going to get some answers."

Make good choices, Vince.

No, the dog didn't say that—I did. My life has included some questionable choices, and there was no room for that now.

*

It took Clement Goody another half hour to show up in the Great Room where the rest of us waited. By that time I had finished off a bowl of peanuts, half of a summer sausage, a wheel of Brie, and everything else in sight that was edible. I was about to start gnawing on a chair leg when Goody finally appeared, beaming a huge, glassy grin like he'd just taken off the nitrous oxide mask. I took one look at his outfit and thought: *uh-oh*.

He wore an open black leather vest on the top half, and that was it—no shirt, just his surprisingly muscled bare arms and tufts of grey hair on his chest. His pants were canary-yellow leather, tight at the crotch, Jim Morrison-style, and on his feet were black suede boots that folded over at the top, Santa Claus-style. It was one of the more bizarre outfits that I'd seen on a man, and I've been to South Beach. I might have cleared out right then, questions or not, but Cindy Charbonneau was serving osso buco, a meal for which I would gladly crawl across broken glass, or even dress up in a biker vest and canary-yellow nut-huggers.

We served ourselves and took seats at a long wooden table on the other side of the kitchen area. Lila had lit at least a dozen candles and placed them around the room, and Goody took a chair at the head of the table and played with a remote control until he had tuned the stereo to a smooth jazz station. All very nice. The Sultan of West Eden, enjoying a meal with his female consorts and me. Too bad I had to spoil the mood with a reality check.

"Grace Hebert," I said. "I know she's here."

"Yes, and she can't join us for the meal, unfortunately," Goody said, wiping his lips after a sip of his sparkling water. "How do you know this? Donald told you?"

"Donald Lussen? No."

"He was the only person outside of this group who knew where Grace was," Goody said. "We're careful about these things. I know you're an investigator. Please tell me how you found out."

"Her dog," I said.

Goody looked displeased. The three women said nothing. "This is for her security, Vince. I don't want people knowing where she is. If somebody told you, we'll have to move her."

"Why?"

"She's at risk," Goody said. "I told you that this would take some explaining."

"You mean because she's a junkie?"

He took a few moments to collect himself before he spoke, which is a characteristic of the wealthy and powerful, and also of some of the more calculating criminal-types that I'd met over the years. They choose their words carefully.

"Cindy told me that you'd been shot in the head, but it obviously hasn't affected your abilities."

"The porn mag, in your foyer," I said. "Page twenty-three. Find a pretty girl, fuck her up on heroin or crack, and get some pictures. Is that a sideline of yours?"

The color rushed to Clement Goody's face. It was almost worth the hours that I'd had to wait before grilling him. "The magazine was a gift from Grace," he said. "The photographs were taken in London, the summer before last, when she was studying there, and yes, she had a drug problem. The NCLS found her, and I took her on personally. We saved her."

"NCLS?"

"The New Commitment and Love Society of Jesus Christ. We are the Lord's servants, helping young women in need."

"Everyone at this table was a junkie, as you call us," Cindy Charbonneau said. If Goody had appeared displeased before, Cindy stared across the table like she was about to hurl a plate of food at me. "The Love Society is the only reason that I'm not dead, and the same is true for my sister. So don't fucking jump to conclusions, OK?"

"You can tell her grandmother that she's safe, Vince," Goody said. "I'm sure you want to get home to Florida."

"Why does she have a gun in her car? And a wad of cash?"

"That came from me. Protection."

"Protection from what?"

"Who told you she was here?"

"Her dog," I said. "He smelled her scent on my trousers."

"Is that the truth?" Goody asked. "I need to know. Someone else didn't tell you?"

"Yes, it's the truth," I said.

He looked relieved. "She's had death threats," he said. "She won't tell us from whom, but she's terrified. We took her in two weeks ago, and she can stay here as long as she needs to. She used to come over from the college with Karen a couple times a week, so she's comfortable here. She participated in the shows."

"Shows?"

He took a sip of his water. "Do you know what the cure for heroin addiction is, Vince? You're a former policeman. You've seen addiction."

Seen it and done it, I thought. I'd had a fling with oxycodone several years back. Modern pharmacology had made it easy to ruin your life. "I know a little about it, yes. There are different treatments. Different approaches."

"Love," Clement Goody said. He leaned forward, his face reflecting the candlelight. "Nothing else works. Not permanently. You have to *commit* yourself to the unconditional love of Jesus Christ, both giving it and receiving it."

"Religion works for some people."

"That's not what I'm talking about." His voice had now risen to the volume of a preacher addressing his flock. "You commit with your whole self. Your soul and your flesh. You give your body up unto the Lord, just like his Son did for us. You take communion of one another. Love, sex, forgiveness, and the strength to go on without the drugs. All wrapped up in one package. That's what we do here. Believe me, I've known a lot of addicts too, and this is the only thing that works every time."

"Praise Jesus!" Lila said, and I suddenly felt like I was in one of those European films where everyone is bonkers except for the narrator. Did he just say *sex*? Was I really getting a mini-sermon from a bare-chested seventy-year-old in a Rumpelstiltskin outfit?

"Forgive me, Vince," Goody said. "Here I am, talking religion at the supper table. I just wanted to explain that Grace is in our care. She'll be safe now. I trust you about the dog. You can tell her grandmother that she's all right, but keep her whereabouts confidential."

"Did you tell John Pallmeister about the death threats?"

"Who?"

"The State Police investigator you spoke with today."

"No, I didn't. And please don't."

"Why not? They can trace these things and find the person."

"I don't trust the police."

"Clement, you and I are going to make a deal. I'll keep that information to myself, but I want to see Grace Hebert right now, and then I'll leave."

"Not yet," Lila said. "Thursday is our dance night."

"No," Karen said. "Donald is dead. We can't do this."

Clement Goody raised his palms into the air. "We will demonstrate our love for Donald Lussen," he said. "Donald was one of us, and this evening we will celebrate his life."

"Clement—" Karen began.

The older man interrupted her. "Y'all finish your meal," he said. "It's show time."

*

I was the sole occupant of a twelve-seat theater that Clement Goody had built underneath the addition to his house. The seats were softly padded armchairs with side tables to hold refreshments: mine was a snifter of Armagnac that Goody had served me, despite my protests, before he and the girls had disappeared backstage. Soft music played through speakers in the ceiling while I waited for the heavy, plush curtain to open. The mini-theater was dark except for the faint glow that came from a line of gold-painted scallop shells along the walls.

The lights went out, the music came up, and the curtains parted.

Goody was the first act, clad in the leather get-up. He held up two translucent globes, illuminated from within by colored LEDs and attached to his wrists by a length of rope. He began to whirl them around in circles in the near-darkness of the theater, and the effect was amazing. He had chosen a thumping, bass-heavy electronic piece as the soundtrack, which added to the intensity of the performance. Goody could make the globes spin over his head and under his legs, crisscross each other, and change colors while he pranced over the floor. I had followed him into the home theater in no mood for entertainment, but this was impressive, and it explained the bizarre leather outfit: Goody was a showman, and these were his gig clothes.

He concluded his act with a standing backflip while still spinning the globes. I couldn't help but clap my hands when he landed it. The piece ended and the theater went dark again; the only sound was my solitary applause. The house lights turned on, and Goody came out from backstage and took the armchair beside me.

"Impressive," I said. "What are those?"

"They're called Pod Poi. I use the flaming kind when we're out-doors. Cubes dipped in kerosene." He took a sip of his water, and the lights went down again as more pulsating electronic music came on the sound system.

This time the stage was bare except for thin spears of blue light from above. I heard a hissing noise as a puff of artificial fog drifted across the floor of the performance area. One by one, four women entered from backstage, each dressed in a shimmering silver bodysuit and wrapped in long scarves that floated behind. They began to dance, using the scarves to trail circles and patterns around each other. The women wore black masks, but I could recognize Cindy, Karen, and Lila from their shapes. The fourth girl was a brunette, with an ease of movement that made the room feel elegant. It was Grace, and the young woman lived up to her name: she was the most effortless dancer that I had ever seen.

Goody leaned over. "I deliver on my promises," he said.

"She's amazing."

"Do you want her?"

"Pardon me?"

He grinned. "Do you want to make love to her?"

"No," I said. And now I got it. I had been invited to a sex party, just like Clement Goody's housecleaner had described to everyone in Johnson.

"She's yours for the asking," he said, and he leaned back into his chair. "You can choose any of them, Vince. They need your love. You're helping them stay clean. It's God's will."

God's will? That would be a one-eighty from what the nuns had drummed into me in my childhood years. God didn't have anything to do with girlie shows that I knew of, and I didn't want to be part of anyone's drug-rehab-sex-fantasy world, nor was I a likely candidate anyway. I was a middle-aged, semi-disabled P.I. with a penchant for screwing up my personal life, and this freak show suddenly had a flashing neon sign above the stage that was saying: *Get The Hell Out Of Here.*

"I have to go," I said.

"The door is locked," Goody said. The light from the stage illuminated his face, which looked tired. The grin was gone. "You can leave when we're finished. Please don't be rude."

My cop brain kicked in: OK, I'm locked in here, what are the options? Do I strong-arm him? Put him in a headlock until he opens the door? Would there be another door backstage? Or am I being paranoid, and the guy is just a garden-variety pervert, and when the show is over I'll just head down the driveway and go home like a good boy?

The music swelled in intensity. One by one the dancers disappeared backstage and then reappeared with the scarves but minus the bodysuits or any other clothing. Their movements became more erotic, and their hands caressed each other as they executed dance steps that you would not see on Lawrence Welk. Each of the women approached us and gave us a personal display, which motivated Goody to get up from his chair and gyrate while I stayed where I was and watched. It might have been stimulating, but I felt like a lab rat. I don't like being locked in. Clement began to shed his own clothing, and I took that as my cue.

I walked to the back of the room and tried the door. It wasn't locked. Goody had lied, although he had kept his promise to show me that Grace Hebert was in his house. I looked back toward the stage where the five of them were dancing to the pounding music, and I realized that I had completed my assignment. I had found Grace, and I would report back to Mrs. Tomaselli, although I had no idea what I would tell her.

*

The Hummer barreled down the driveway so fast that I had to leap into the tall grass to get out of the way. Had I pissed off Clement Goody so much that he was trying to run me over?

I'd made it halfway down the hill to get back to my rental car and my dog, whose bladder would by now be the size of a weather balloon. It took another five minutes of walking after the Hummer had buzzed me, but when I reached the car and opened the door to let Chan out, he was gone. No dog, no bag of kibble, no water bowl. Holy crap. I checked behind the seat for the .44 magnum revolver. Also gone. At least I had transferred the money to my wallet.

For the second time tonight I considered my options. There weren't any, other than to drive up to the house, interrupt whatever merriment might be going on, and kick some ass until I found out what had just happened, and why. Or, I could call it a night, flop into some local motel, and kick some ass for breakfast. Either way, I was in a foul mood, and Goody had to be the cause of it. I was ready to take one of his little swinging rope lights and wrap it around his neck.

I started the car and prepared to drive back to the house, but as soon as I turned the headlights on I knew what had happened, because a message had been scrawled on the windshield in red lipstick:

I don't want to be found.

Grace Hebert had been driving the Hummer. She'd stopped at my car before I got down the driveway, and grabbed the gun and the dog. I had spooked her, and she had flown. Why?

Meanwhile, I had figured something else out: Grace was the one who had hit me on the head at Prospect Rock. She had been at Goody's while the rest of the crew was away, and she had access to the Hummer. Lussen must have tipped her off, and my rental car with New York plates would have been easy to spot.

Grace could have pushed me over the cliff on that spectacular autumn afternoon, but she didn't, because she wasn't a killer. She just wanted to get me off of her trail. She was a frightened young woman, and Clement Goody with all his money, his reassurances, and his religion couldn't make the fear go away.

I had lost her again, and I was twice as worried as I had been before.

FRIDAY

I CONSIDERED MYSELF RELEASED FROM my promise to keep Grace's whereabouts confidential, seeing how she was gone. I had spent the night in my car at the bottom of the driveway in case she came back, but she hadn't, and if she was getting death threats the police needed to know. Lieutenant John Pallmeister answered his phone at six in the morning sounding wide awake.

"Where are you?" I asked him.

"At my desk. Where are you?"

"At the bottom of Clement Goody's driveway, freezing. I camped out in my car."

"Why?"

"Because Grace Hebert was in the house, but she took off. She has her dog and a .44 magnum with her."

"What's going on, Vince?"

"She's been getting death threats," I said. "Goody was hiding her at his place. He's a wingnut, by the way. A rich one."

"They're the worst kind," Pallmeister said. "He didn't give up much about Lussen. He said they were acquainted because he supported the theater program at the college."

"He has another professor living at his place. You might want to go up there again and squeeze them harder."

"Yes, I might."

"Do me a favor? Have your people look for the Hummer. I'll email you the plate number. And I'd really like to see Grace Hebert's phone records and location data."

"I can get that," the lieutenant said. "You want to stop by my office?"

"No, I'm going to hang out here and freeze for a while longer in case she comes back."

"I'll call you if we find out anything. And cheer up. It's supposed to get into the forties today."

"Oh, great," I said. "I'll put on my shorts."

Stakeouts remind me of detention back in parochial school. There was nothing to do to keep me busy. I'd taken a break from my former knitting hobby, figuring that the wool was better off on the sheep. I didn't have a book to read, I'd slept fitfully, wrapped in a blanket that I'd put down for Chan, and I needed a shower, a shave, a quart of hot coffee, and a couple dozen donuts if I was going to continue here. Maybe I could call the nearest bakery and arrange for an airdrop.

Four hours later, still no sign of Grace. I took off the blanket and started the car. I would return to my mother's house, clean up, and regroup. Damn. If I had stayed the night at Clement Goody's house I might now be in postcoital bliss under the sheets with one of the Charbonneau twins, peeling grapes to pop into each other's mouth. But I was glad that I'd declined, and it wasn't because I was being a prude. Sex complicates things. The biggest lie in the world is *no strings attached*, because intimacy is always a commitment. And that isn't the Catholic in me talking; it's from lessons learned the hard way.

I changed my plan when I saw Karen Charbonneau come careening through the open gate in her Jaguar. It was an older model but was still a nice ride for a college professor. She didn't notice me, tucked back under the shade tree. She drove like she was late for something, and I guessed that it was work. Unshaven or not, I decided that I would get a coffee somewhere, drive over to the college, and drop in on her. She and I had enjoyed a good conversation before dinner, and during the so-called dancing part of the evening she had looked uncomfortable. I also knew that she'd once had a drug problem, and I wondered if that had been on her résumé at the college. Not that I was going to blackmail her, but there would be some implicit pressure just by showing up at her workplace. When someone's life is at risk, I'm not above being a jerk.

*

Karen Charbonneau's administrative assistant had been crying. She'd made no attempt to hide her emotions, and neither had the steady trickle of students who had come to the faculty offices to talk with anybody they could find in an attempt to process the tragedy of the day before. Donald Lussen's murder had left shock waves that were still reverberating through the college. The campus was still under siege: reporters and camera operators were wandering the grounds, and I'd had to pass through a phalanx of state cops and Lamoille

County deputies to get in. My first stop was Duffy Kovich's office, but he wasn't there. I'd wanted to get him up to speed and put him on the lookout for Grace.

Instead, I was now in the foyer of the drama department, waiting my turn to see the department head. Three students were in front of me, and the woman at the desk had told us that everyone was allotted ten minutes, so I had half an hour to kill. I spent it by nodding off in my chair until I was awakened by Karen Charbonneau's gentle nudge on my shoulder.

"You must be chronically short on sleep," she said. "You did this yesterday. Come into my office."

"Sorry," I said. I followed her into a space that was larger than Donald Lussen's quarters and was furnished in a jumble of well-worn office gear that might have come from the Goodwill store. Stuff was scattered everywhere, and I had to move a stack of papers to sit down. Professor Charbonneau may have kept scrupulous care of her face and body, but her office looked like a teenager's bedroom.

"You snore," she said as she sat down at her desk.

"That's why I left," I said. "If I'd stayed, nobody would have gotten any sleep."

"Clement said that he offered you—he—"

"He said that I could take any one of you to bed."

"But you left."

"I'm old school. Sorry."

"No need to be," she said. "Out of curiosity, who would you have chosen?"

Now that's a damned-if-you-do, damned-if-you-don't question, and I wasn't going to touch it. Besides, she was suddenly blushing, and I hadn't expected that reaction from a woman who was certainly no ingénue. "I'll take the fifth on that," I said.

"Lila would sleep with anyone Clement says, but she confessed that you weren't really her type."

"Gosh, I'm devastated," I said. "So, what are Fridays? Bingo night?"

"Clement works on Friday and Saturday evenings," she said. "He prepares his radio sermon for Sunday morning. We have a gathering on Sunday, after dark."

"What do you mean by a gathering?"

"It's usually just Clement and us. He has lots of—energy. But if he finds someone he likes, he may invite them along. Like you."

"I'm sorry if I was a letdown," I said.

"I was fine with whatever you decided," she said, lowering her eyes. "I like you, Vince. You give me hope for Grace."

"That's why I'm here."

"What do you want to know?"

"Who would want to threaten her?"

"I don't know."

"Did Donald Lussen go to the parties at Clement's?"

"Yes. He was deeply in love with Grace. It got out of hand."

"How so?"

"His work went to hell. He would have lost his job, eventually. And his wife."

"What's she like?"

"She didn't kill him, if that's what you're wondering. She was in Connecticut yesterday."

"Did you really have a smack habit?"

"Yes."

"You don't fit the profile—at least not the one that I used to know in Florida."

"Cindy had a boyfriend at the hospital. He got her some pain pills. She broke an ankle, and she got strung out on them. It's too easy."

"I've been there," I said. "Go on."

"My sister and I are very close. She couldn't get the pills after a while. Nobody could—the whole supply thing got tightened up, and people started doing heroin instead. It was cheap, and it's everywhere, even out here in the sticks. I tried it too, and I can't explain why, but Cindy and I have been like that our whole lives. That was two years ago, and I know I would be dead if I hadn't met Clement. It really does work, you know. I was never a religious person, Vince, but he's right. People live for love, and sex is a big part of it."

"What happened after I left?"

"Clement wanted Grace, and she refused. They had a shouting match. She told him to fuck off, and she ran out the door with his car keys. Cindy was going to go after her, but Clement said no, Grace would come home. But I think he's wrong."

"Why?"

"Because she's using again," Karen Charbonneau said. "She was trying to hide it from us, but I can tell. Addicts know. I didn't have the heart to tell Clement."

"One step forward, two steps back," I said.

"Please find her, Vince. She needs to go through a regular detox program. This one worked for me, but not for her."

"Where would she go?"

"Ask her mother."

"Her mother wants nothing to do with her," I said. "She's a hard case. I know her from high school."

"I've met her," Karen said. "She knows more than you think."

My phone rang and I moved to turn it off, but it was John Pall-meister. "Excuse me," I said, and I put it to my ear.

"Grace Hebert's cellphone is in Barre," he said. "She hasn't made an outgoing call in weeks, but she's received a bunch of texts."

"From who?"

"The recently-departed Donald Lussen."

"That fits," I said. "Where is it, exactly?"

"It's inside Carmela Tomaselli's apartment," he said. "We're waiting on a warrant. I'll see you there."

*

There are no secrets in Barre. It boasts a population of nine thousand people, large by Vermont standards, but it is a big small town, and if the State Police are parked in your driveway, no one will have to wait for the next day's paper to find out why. The town's grapevine is faster than the Internet and is equally unreliable when it comes to the facts, but facts don't matter to gossips.

Carmela Tomaselli had been the subject of gossip since puberty, and the cops had been to her house before. It was a miracle that her four marriages had ended in divorce and not death, because she was a wild animal if you crossed her. By the time I arrived on the scene she was cussing out Lieutenant Pallmeister and Janice, his female sergeant associate, and you could have heard her yelling from my mother's house, which was four blocks away up the hill.

The State Police had summoned her from the nursing home to let them in and locate Grace's missing cellphone. I'd worked with John Pallmeister for one year during my very brief stint as a rookie cop on the Barre force, and he was one of those guys who never, ever confronted people, much less yelled back. It was like he didn't have a temper to lose—he would just wait people out until they were exhausted, and then he'd get the job done, whatever the task was. I always wished I had his kind of cool, but I'm too Italian for that.

Carmela saw me approaching. She kept up the volume for a few more moments, but I could tell that she was coming to the end of her rant. The neighbors who had gathered in the street parted to let another car in the driveway: a mostly-yellow Saab 900 convertible with a torn roof and one flat-black fender panel that was primed for repainting. A wiry, thirtyish man got out of the car. I figured that this was Carmela's current flame. His hands were stained with the kind of grease that never fully washes off, with tattoos running up and down both arms. It was not a warm day, but he was dressed in a sleeveless T-shirt and red basketball shorts. I caught a glimpse of his face: handsome, in a bad-boy sort of way, with thick, waxy hair and deep-set, dark eyes. Cleaned up, he might have been a model, except for the arms—there were needle marks among the tattoos. Apparently he had the same monkey on his back that Grace did.

He strutted toward the cops with what I call the Asshole Swagger: shoulders back, arms hanging loose—hey man, be cool. People like that bring out my natural urge to just handcuff them and throw them in the back of the car, and ninety percent of the time it would save a lot of trouble.

"Chill out, everybody," the young guy said to the group. "I know where it is. I'll go up and get it for you. Wait here."

"You have Grace's phone?" Carmela said to him. Her voice was hoarse from the confrontation with the cops.

"She dropped it off," he said. "Didn't want it no more."

"What? Listen, Matty—"

"Later, babe," I heard him say, and he went inside the house. I approached Pallmeister.

"Are you going inside?"

"No need, if he gives us the phone," he said. The lieutenant was my age, but aside from the close-cropped gray hair under his hat, he could have passed for forty. That said, he didn't look like he'd had any more sleep than I had. "You got anything new?"

I steered him away from Carmela, out of earshot. "Yes," I said. "Grace has a drug habit. On and off, but it's currently on."

"You wouldn't believe how bad that is around here," the lieutenant said. "We make a heroin bust every couple of days."

"She was detoxing at Goody's, but it didn't last. Did you see the tracks on that punk?"

"Yes, and I'm tempted to toss the whole house, but the warrant is specific to the cellphone," Pallmeister said. "You know about warrants."

Yes, I knew about warrants. I'd performed a search without one and had been caught, and a killer had gotten off. It was the reason that I'd lost my job as a deputy sheriff after twenty-five years on the Indian

River County force. Pallmeister knew that, and he couldn't help bringing it up. "Are you going to question these two?" I asked him.

"Not unless we find something on the cell."

"I might stay around for some chit-chat," I said. "Carmela and Matty. He'd be husband number five."

"Five times a charm," Pallmeister said, just as the young man was coming out of the house with the phone in his hand.

"Here you go," he said, giving it to the lieutenant and displaying a smirk that was just begging to be wiped off by someone's fist. "Now fuck off, man. Leave us alone."

Pallmeister ignored him and got back into the cruiser where Janice was on the phone. I approached Matty and Carmela who were in a heated discussion. "Got a moment?"

"Who are you?" the kid said.

"I'm a private investigator. Carmela and I know each other. Let's go inside and talk."

"Vince, not now," Carmela began. She was puffing on the second cigarette that she had lit in the five minutes since I'd arrived.

"Hey, you can fuck off, too," Matty said. He gave me the same contemptuous sneer that he had given the cops, with an implied invitation: *Go ahead and start something.*

As tempted as I was to rearrange his dental work, I channeled John Pallmeister's reserve and turned to Carmela. "I saw her last night."

"Where?"

"She was staying with a friend for a while. But she's moved on. I'm still working on it."

"You know where Grace is?" Matty said. "Who are you again?"

"Grace's grandmother is concerned about her," I said. "I'm making sure that she's all right."

"Shit, man," he said, and the tough-guy posturing evaporated. "I didn't know that. I'm worried about her too, even though Carmela says I shouldn't. But I sure would like to find her."

"Let's go inside," I said.

"Can't," he said. "I have to get back to my shop."

"Carmela?"

"Don't bother, Vinny," she said. "You already know what I think about this. You're wasting your time."

"You know that she's doing heroin? And that somebody has been threatening her?"

Carmela said nothing, but I caught a fierce look that was exchanged between her and her boyfriend, and I recognized it, because I had seen it often enough over the course of my two marriages:

You and I are going to have a little talk.

*

I decided that the most productive thing that I could do until I heard back from John Pallmeister about the cellphone would be to go to my mom's house and wait. Grace Hebert's secrets would soon be revealed. Your cell is your most unreliable, blabbermouth, tell-all friend. It has no ethics, no sense of loyalty to you, and it feels no remorse for laying out every sordid, humiliating detail of your personal life for the world to see. Your movements, the calls you made, the late-night drunk texts, and, of course, every single selfie that you took, clothed or not: all of that will live on forever like a prehistoric bug embedded in amber.

I stopped at the Quality Market and loaded up on cold cuts and sliced cheese. The delicatessens in Florida simply don't get the same products that you can find here, and I was jonesing for capicola, mortadella, some good Genoa salami, and a pound or two of provolone to take home and roll up in little tubes, sit back in my father's chair, and nosh on while my mother and I talked. I didn't know how much I would tell her about Grace, although she would have seen Donald Lussen's death on the news, and she would have made the connection to Johnson State. I was thinking that I might lay it all out and get her opinion. My mom has always been a shy person, but she has a good feel for things. Maybe she could shed some light.

John Pallmeister phoned me as I was driving back from the market. I pulled over to the side of the street to take the call. "This isn't going to help you," he said.

"Meaning?"

"It's a five-year-old Motorola. It can text and make calls, but that's it."

"A college girl who doesn't own a smartphone?"

"I know. It must be her choice. Some people are that way."

"So what do you have?"

"It was at Johnson State until September 18th. That was two Saturdays ago. Then it went to the Comfort Inn, by the Barre exit, and then up to Shelburne, somewhere out on the point. We couldn't triangulate it exactly. And then it went back to Barre the same afternoon and stayed there. At her mother's apartment."

"Anything else?"

"Seventy-one texts from Donald Lussen's phone, sent between the 19th and two days ago. No outgoing texts."

"So he was trying to reach her?"

"You could say that."

"Are you looking at the other texts? And the location data?"

"Yes, but nothing stands out. I can email it to you if you want to look. Off the record."

I told him that yes, I wanted to see the data, and I figured that Roberto Arguelles might burn some virtual shoe leather for me and possibly provide us with a few more clues. A dumbphone? Damn. For a college girl, an up-to-date phone wasn't just an accessory; it was a vital organ. It didn't fit, but maybe I didn't yet know as much about Grace Hebert as I should.

Tonight I would do my homework. I would spend some time with Donna Tomaselli, because Carmela was stonewalling me, and because grandmothers often knew more about their granddaughters than mothers did. Roberto could work on the phone forensics. Grace had been clever enough to not display her personal life on a smartphone, and that would make it harder for me to find her, but it also gave me an odd kind of respect for her. She was an outlier, and if someone were truly threatening to kill her, that might increase her chances of survival.

*

Mrs. Tomaselli didn't have much to tell me about Grace that I didn't already know, and she was more relieved than concerned when I told her I had found her granddaughter—briefly—in Clement Goody's questionable care. She had the grandma blinders on, meaning that Grace could do no wrong, and at the same time Carmela could do no right. Mrs. T had shown up precisely at suppertime. The meal was one of my mother's old standbys: sausage and peppers, and I had helped out by cooking the meat on the grill over real charcoal. The crisp fall night had turned rainy, and I'd had to use an umbrella to get the food inside without getting soaked.

I didn't want to bring up the heroin issue over the dinner table, as it would unnecessarily worry the older women. That didn't mean that I wasn't turning things over in my head while trying to keep semi-involved in the conversation. I parsed the afternoon's events while I ate. The good news was that Grace's phone had been found, but that was the private investigator's conundrum: one answer begets a hundred new questions.

Matty—last name unknown—had a bad attitude and a smack habit. He also happened to be in possession of Grace's cell, which had taken a ride from the college to a chain hotel at the Barre exit, then up to Shelburne Point, an old-money enclave on Lake Champlain, and then all the way back to Carmela's apartment in Barre where the State Police had been able to locate it thanks to the carrier records. Someone needed to fill in the blanks on that one, and I figured that it would be Matty. If the State Police were too busy to ask him, I'd happily take care of it for them, and if he gave me any attitude he would regret it.

But he had seemed genuinely worried when I'd said that Grace was still missing. Carmela didn't give a damn, but he did. Matty and Grace were both strung out on heroin. Maybe he held some responsibility for that, and he was feeling bad about it. Or maybe Matty wasn't such a tough guy, and he actually cared about his girlfriend's daughter. He looked closer to Grace's age than Carmela's. Hell, maybe they were lovers, and the Comfort Inn stop had been a shack-up. The mind of a P.I. is a fertile place, although you have to keep in mind that fertilizer is generally made from cow shit, including a hefty dose of bullshit. Don't get ahead of yourself, Vince.

Mom had made cannoli for dessert. Mrs. T and I pushed back our chairs, protesting that we were already full to the bursting point, but a space magically opened in my digestive system and I was able to accommodate two of the sweet, rolled-up cholesterol grenades. OK, three.

John Pallmeister emailed me the location records and call logs for Grace's phone, which I in turn sent to Roberto in Florida. I was back in my father's chair, regretting the cannoli decision, when Roberto sent a text: *Kind of a dead end on the phone thing.*

What makes you think that?

Long lapses in activity, he wrote. *She might use a messaging program on her laptop. It's slightly more secure.*

Any late night calls? I sent to my young friend. When you're looking at someone's phone records, the three AM ones were where you started. That was when a person might call somebody they weren't supposed to.

I traced one to her college, he wrote. *Five AM, back in May. It went to the theater department, according to the directory.*

Grace had called the theater department at five in the morning? Of course—Donald Lussen, and I bet he was an early riser. The State Police had no doubt examined the same records that we were looking at, but they might not have made the connection.

Interesting, I wrote back. *The dead guy was her drama teacher. They had a thing going.*

Aha.

Thanks. You need anything from up here? I'll be back as soon as I wrap this up.

Nope. I'm buried in an essay for my college applications.

What are you writing about?

You, he sent.

Seriously?

Yes. About the experience of being mentored.

That ought to kill off any chance of getting into college, I sent back. The little bugger was writing about me? I was touched, and I wished that I was back in Vero, where I would be now if the whole Grace Hebert thing hadn't happened. But it had, and I was already filling in my calendar for tomorrow.

I would call John Pallmeister to compare notes. I would also drop in on Matty at the Saab shop, and we'd chat. And I might go back up to Johnson, to see what else I could find out about the relationship between the faculty advisor and his attractive, addicted student. His death and her disappearance seemed to be intertwined, and I didn't think that I was getting ahead of myself this time, cow shit or not.

SATURDAY

THE RELENTLESS BARKING WOKE ME. I grabbed a rain jacket from the front hall closet and went outside to my mother's driveway. The racket was coming from inside my rental car, which I hadn't bothered to lock. I recognized the bark.

Chan.

I let him out of the car and he quieted down, but he didn't look at all pleased to see me. There was no lipstick message on the windshield this time. Instead, I found a note on the front seat. I took the note and the dog inside to look for my reading glasses.

The message was written in careful, feminine longhand on the back of an envelope. *Please take care of him. I can't take him where I'm going. If you have to give him away, find a good home.*

Damn. Grace Hebert had swooped down like an owl in the dead of night and dropped off her gigantic dog, entrusting him to me. She couldn't take him to wherever she was going? I filled Chan's water bowl from the fridge while I tried to figure out what to do next. Call the Barre police and put out an alert for the Hummer? Not at 3:30 AM, the time that was displayed on the microwave's digital clock. This wasn't a big city—there would be no more than one or two cars on duty, and Grace undoubtedly knew the back roads.

So, my quarry had come to me, but I'd missed the opportunity. By now she could be anywhere. I had only been asleep for a few hours; I needed more rest if I was going to be good for anything at daybreak. I glanced at Chan, who had finished slurping from the water bowl and was looking anxious. I led him outside into the drizzle for a late-night pee.

"We're going back to bed," I said. "I'll take you to Matty's shop after breakfast. You can bite him if he doesn't cooperate."

Chan perked up. *Now you're talking.*

*

Three hours of fitful sleep later the dog and I were on the way to the Saab repair shop on the Barre-Montpelier Road. The Swedish company had stopped making the cars several years ago, but Vermont was still full of them—they performed well in the snow and lasted forever, assuming that you knew a good mechanic. The local joke was that SAAB stood for Something Almost Always Broken.

Matty's shop was on a side road behind a fast-food restaurant. The parking lot was littered with cars in various stages of decomposition: a few looked fixable, but the rest were slowly rusting carcasses that would be plundered for parts. The lights were on inside a solitary metal-sided building, and the only other person nearby was a man who dropped off a car, got into a waiting van, and drove off. I left Chan in my rental sedan and let myself into the premises.

The area that served as a waiting room was empty, presumably because it was so filthy that no patron would consider taking a seat on one of the grease-stained couches. A Fox News commentator spewed outrage from a vintage television that was chained to the wall. I spotted an unkempt cluster of business cards on the counter: *Matthew Harmony, SAAB Service & Sales.* Adjacent to the waiting room was a double garage. Matty stood at the corner of the far bay, dressed in a grimy blue coverall with a welder's mask tilted up from his forehead. He held an acetylene torch in one hand and a flint igniter in the other.

"Fuck do you want?" he said as I approached.

"A couple of questions, that's all."

"Already told you to fuck off." He flicked the igniter twice and the torch lit. I bent down to the base of the tank and turned off the gas supply. He began to protest, but I took out my wallet, removed one of Grace Hebert's crisp hundred-dollar bills, and held it up in his face.

"A hundred bucks says you can't go without saying the f-word for five minutes."

The mechanic blinked at me like I was crazy. Maybe I was, but if it would get rid of the attitude, it would be well spent. "What are you, an English teacher?"

"You said you'd like to find her," I said. "Why?"

"I—wanted to give her the phone," he said. "What do the cops want with it?"

"It's a part of a murder investigation," I said. "It may hold evidence. A professor was murdered."

"She knew the guy?"

"He was her faculty advisor. And her lover. That's what the kids on campus say."

"Grace?" He looked surprised. "No way. She woulda told me."

"You two were close?"

"Me and her? Not really. I mean, Carmela and me—"

"But you did drugs together? You supplied her? Or the other way around?"

"Man, that's bullshit. I'm clean for like two months now."

"But she's using again."

"No she ain't."

"I saw her, and she's using."

"Saw her where?"

"Not important," I said. "She's gone again. I've got the dog."

"That fuckin' dog," he said. I withdrew the hundred-dollar bill. "Aw, fuck. I knew I couldn't do it."

"Double or nothing," I said, holding two of the bills now. "But no more bullshit. What were you doing on Shelburne Point?"

"Shelburne Point? What are you talking about?"

Like Donald Lussen, he had answered a question with a question. Stalling. I held the bills up again and waited.

"I—got a customer there," Matty finally said. "It was a pick up. I drop off my car and drive theirs back to the shop."

That was possible, but it had taken him too long to answer. Something was wrong, and I decided to do a Chan. Bite him in the ass and see what happens.

"You were screwing her, weren't you?" I said. "Both of them. The mother and the daughter." I waited for a reaction.

Matthew Harmony's reaction was to walk over to a tool chest and remove a chrome-plated combination wrench that was two feet long. He pointed it at me like a sword.

"Get out of my shop," he said. "And you can take your fuckin' money with you."

*

Chan and I were passing the shore of Lake Elmore where it follows the highway. We were taking the slightly longer but more scenic route to Johnson, and I caught his eyes in the rearview mirror: *Why are you still driving?*

"Too much going on," I said. "I can't afford not to."

Tell that to the people you kill when you nod off at the wheel, he said. He was right, of course. Once I'm on a case I am just as strung out on it as Grace Hebert was on heroin. Addictive behavior is a Tanzi family tradition. It drowned my father in booze, crippled my brother Junie with drugs, and kept my sister Carla in a permanent marijuana fog. And I was just as guilty. One more hit, one last drink, and one more day at the wheel, seizures or no seizures, because hey, this was really, really important, and that trumped everything else. Until it all came crashing down.

I should have called Dr. Jaffe and booked an appointment, but I couldn't do it. It would have felt like calling the morgue and saying save me a spot. I had been through so much over the last few years with my head injury that I had been conditioned to fight for survival, and then recovery, and then a semblance of a normal life, and giving up even the slightest bit of ground meant failure. The pride that had helped me heal was strong medicine, but it was now clearly getting in the way of common sense. I knew that, but I kept on driving.

Matty had told me a lot by saying a little. When I'd needled him about Donald Lussen's amorous connection to Grace, a signal flare had gone off. And when I'd trotted out my suspicion that he and Grace were lovers, he hadn't denied it. Instead, he'd threatened me. People think that they can safeguard every dark secret within themselves, and if you allow them to, they will. That's why I have trained myself to be obnoxious when necessary, even though it goes against my nature. It produces results. Matthew Harmony hadn't actually mouthed the words, but I was convinced that he and Grace were lovers. Or maybe they had been, until Donald Lussen came along...

Aha.

A motive, Chan said from the back.

"Possibly."

Donald Lussen sent seventy-one text messages to Grace's phone over the course of the two weeks that Grace had been missing. Did Matty read them, flip out, and kill Lussen? Why was Lussen texting her if he already knew that she was hiding out at Clement Goody's house?

"See what I mean about the one-answer-begets-a-hundred-questions thing?" I said to Chan, but he was asleep again. With or without the dog's confirmation I had just placed Matthew Harmony on the suspect list. He was the only one on it, so he was at the top. I would call John Pallmeister when I got to somewhere with a cell signal and would float this by him. Matty seemed more like a punk than a killer, but every text from Lussen might have felt like another pin in the voodoo doll. It fit, for lack of anything better.

This didn't solve my own problem, though, which was to find Grace. My visit to Johnson would include a few house calls: I had Donald Lussen's home address, and I was going to drop in on his widow. That one would be a bit delicate, and I would need to tread carefully.

I also wanted to revisit the West Eden Bible Camp. This time I would take a good look inside the closets, provided that no one else was there. The house would be locked, but I had a set of lock-picking tools at my mother's, left over from my somewhat-misspent youth, and I knew how to use them. Even if Goody had installed decent hardware on the doors of his house, it was nothing that I couldn't handle. I didn't know what I would find inside, if anything, but you don't want to sit still in my profession. You have to keep circulating, asking people obnoxious questions, and lifting up rocks to see what unpleasant things might lie beneath. You get your hands dirty sometimes, but I hardly noticed, just like Matty might not have noticed that his shop was filthy and he was caked in grease.

I love my job, and I was ready to get my hands dirty. I wasn't about to shuffle off to the sidelines because I had experienced a couple of fainting spells. Grace Hebert needed me.

*

The Lussen residence was two miles up Clay Hill Road, beyond the college. It looked like it had once been a working farm back when you could eke out a living on a few dozen acres as long as you grew all of your own food and heated your home from the woodlot. The property consisted of a white clapboard house about the size of Clement Goody's cape before the addition, a main barn stained in the classic faded-red, and several other outbuildings. Everything was in perfect shape, and the grounds were dotted with ornamental trees and perennials. A half-dozen Belted Charolais stood in a pasture looking like bovine Oreos with their black heads and hindquarters separated by a white band around their middles. They weren't milkers—more likely the place was a hobby farm, and the cows were four-legged tax deductions. I smelled manure, and money. Keeping livestock around for fun wasn't cheap, and I wondered if Donald Lussen was a Trustafarian: a city boy who had gotten the farming bug, but who lived on the dividend checks that arrived monthly from the wealth managers in Boston.

Chan was still asleep, so I left him in the car and approached the house. I stood on the freshly-painted front porch and rang the bell. A thin, prematurely gray woman of about forty opened the door. She had the high forehead and clear, piercing eyes of someone who you might see at a book discussion group or working in a library. She looked exhausted, which was no surprise as her husband had been brutally murdered a little more than forty-eight hours ago.

"Mrs. Lussen?"

"I won't speak to the press," she said. "I'm entitled to some privacy. People have been here all morning, and I need some peace."

"I'm not a reporter," I said. "I'm sorry about what happened. This is about something else."

"Then state your business."

"I'm looking for Grace Hebert. She was a student of your husband's. She's been missing, and I was hoping to see if you might help."

"How would I help? I don't know any of Donald's students." The slender woman stood at the threshold like it was electrified and if I came any closer I would get a nasty shock.

"He knew her well. They were close." I hadn't meant to drop a bomb so soon, but this was going to be a very short visit if I didn't.

"You can come in," she said. I followed her into what the old farmers called a parlor: a small room to the side of the entryway where the family would gather and sing along with a piano or a mandolin. "Sit," she said, pointing to a Victorian-era couch. She took a seat as far across the room as she could. "Who are you?"

"My name is Vince Tanzi. I'm helping Grace's grandmother. Grace has been missing for weeks, and I spoke with Donald three days ago, but he said he didn't have any ideas about where she might be."

"So why do you think I would?"

"He wasn't telling me the truth," I said. "She was at Clement Goody's place on Hog Back Road. She's been hiding out there. Someone was threatening her life."

"Donald wouldn't lie."

"He did. Goody said he knew where she was. You know Clement Goody?"

"Who are you exactly, Mr. Tanzi?"

"I used to be a cop. Do you know Clement?"

"I've met him at gatherings," she said. "He underwrote one of Donald's productions. So if you already know that she's there, how can she be missing?"

"She took off again. I saw her at the house, but she's gone."

"Then you have a problem, don't you?"

"It's more complicated than that," I said. I was summoning the will to drop another bomb.

"Meaning?"

"Did your husband socialize with Goody? Go to his house?"

"They were friends," she said. "Associates more than friends. Donald helped Clement with his sermons, and Clement was talking about producing one of my husband's plays. Donald was a playwright as well as a professor."

"Really?"

"Yes, and quite brilliant, too. He should be famous, but he never had the confidence."

I noticed a desk covered in papers at one side of the room, under an antique window. The mottled, imperfect glass panes let in a wobbly sunlight. "Is this where he wrote?"

"No, this is where I pay the bills," she said. "Donald wrote in his sugar shack, as he called it. He would go there when the college wasn't in session and write nonstop. It was an obsession."

"Where is this shack?"

"Belvidere Mountain, in Lowell," she said. "It belonged to the asbestos quarry. Donald bought it for twenty thousand dollars with fifty acres of land. No heat, except for a fireplace. You couldn't drag me there. I don't know how this relates to your missing student."

I decided to hold Bomb 2.0 in check. The woman's husband had just died, and if she didn't know about his dirty laundry, there was no reason to trot it out. She was telling me a lot, and my mental wheels were turning. I wondered if the State Police had already visited Donald Lussen's getaway cabin. If they hadn't, I would.

I was about to ask another question when the front door opened. I glanced out the front window and saw a black Lincoln Town Car in the driveway with the engine running and a tall man in a chauffeur's uniform standing outside it. A much larger man entered the parlor—I might have described him as obese, except that he carried the weight like muscle. He was about the same age as Clement Goody but twice his size. He wore a button-down blue dress shirt under a black fleece vest, with gray flannel trousers and casual shoes. His pink face was framed by neatly combed white hair. The man gave me an assessing glance and then ignored me. "Car's waiting, Trish," he said to Donald Lussen's widow.

"I'm already packed," she said. "You'll have to excuse me, Mr. Tanzi. I'm going to my father's house until things quiet down."

"No problem," I said. "Thanks for your help on this."

"Help with what?" The huge man asked her, not me.

"I'm looking for a missing student," I said, and he gave me a disapproving glare. I knew that face, but I couldn't place it. Everyone knows everyone in Vermont, but I'd been in Florida for thirty years. "Do I know you?"

"Angus Driscoll," he said. "And no, you don't know me. I remember everyone I've met."

This was true. Angus Driscoll was a Burlington stockbroker who was also the political kingmaker for the state of Vermont. He was the ultimate networker, fundraiser, and back room wheeler-dealer, and it was said that he never forgot a face. You didn't become governor, senator, or dogcatcher without his blessing.

So—it wasn't Donald Lussen who had the money, it was his wife: Trish Lussen, née Driscoll. Mrs. Lussen had excused herself to fetch her bag, and I moved toward the door. I waited for her, because I had one more question. It had been prompted by Angus Driscoll's introduction, because there was something else that I knew about the Driscoll family: they lived in an exclusive, Kennedy-like compound on Lake Champlain at the far end of Shelburne Point.

"Do you know Matthew Harmony?" I asked her as the three of us went down the front steps to the driveway.

"Why don't you leave her alone, fella?" Driscoll said.

"Matthew fixes my car," Trish said. "Donald knew him."

Angus Driscoll gave me a look like if I said one more thing he would sit on me, which would be like one of the Belted Charolais stepping on a frog.

We got into our cars, and Chan began to growl. "What?" I asked him.

The driver.

I looked more carefully at the car next to me. Angus Driscoll had gotten into the back seat with his daughter. The man sitting at the wheel was looking back at me, and it had been a long time since we'd seen each other, but this time the connection was as fresh as if it had been yesterday.

Driscoll's limo driver was a mug from Barre named Fish Falzarano. They called him that because his eyes were so widely separated he looked like a grouper, and his small mouth and puffy cheeks made it worse. The last time I'd seen him he was a seventeen-year-old street punk and I was a rookie on the Barre force. Fish and two other kids had broken into a corner store and were loading cases of Budweiser into a car that they had hotwired an hour before. I'd had the dubious honor of presiding over Falzarano's first juvenile arrest, and others had followed. What was he doing working for a legit guy like Driscoll? He must have recognized me too, because he gave me the finger before backing the Lincoln out into the road.

I stayed in my car and watched them leave. I could have let myself back in the house with my tool bag, but I had already intruded enough into Trish Lussen's life. Besides, I wanted to revisit Clement Goody's place, and I try to limit myself to one felony breaking-and-entering per day. For now I would head back into town, walk Chan for a while, find a coffee shop, and connect the dots by phone with John Pallmeister. I would tell him about Falzarano, and Driscoll, and the fact that Matty was the Lussens' mechanic of choice. Matthew Harmony seemed to be more than casually involved in all of this, and Pallmeister had the resources to help me find out how, and why.

*

"Her phone was at the Comfort Inn for no more than five minutes, according to the carrier log," John Pallmeister said. The cell reception was weak, making the policeman's voice reverberate like he was speaking through a metal culvert. "So it wasn't a quick shack-up."

"Even I'm not that quick."

"There goes your theory, Vince."

"It still feels like they had a thing going," I said. I took a sip of the coffee and sat back on a plush sofa in the front room of a nineteenth-century house that had been converted into an eatery called the Lovin' Cup. The waitress had given me a menu, but I had already carbo-loaded at my mother's before the visit to Matty's garage.

"How do you know that it was Harmony who drove the phone to Shelburne?" Pallmeister asked. "It could have been the girl you're looking for, and then she drives it back to her mother's house."

"Yes, but Trish Lussen confirmed that he works on her car. I asked him, and he came up with the same thing."

"Trish Lussen was in Connecticut that Saturday," Pallmeister said. "She's been going down to her sister's. The sister has cancer. We've covered this, Vince. You're rehashing things that we've already looked into, and frankly, you're stretching."

"Matthew Harmony is involved. I wouldn't waste your time if I didn't think he was."

"So we question him, and maybe get another warrant to go through his house? Because you think he killed Lussen out of jealousy?"

"How did Lussen die? I mean, I know he got shot with a bow, but what are the forensics guys saying?"

"The killer used a compound bow. You could drop a bear with it. The arrows were carbon fiber—the expensive kind, and there weren't any prints. The medical examiner says the shooter was a man, or a very strong woman. The first arrow was the lung shot, taken from a distance. He finished him off at close range with the headshot. The arrow went right through the skull and pinned his head to the ground."

My coffee suddenly tasted like battery acid. "Christ."

"You want to sign up for a badge, I'll take you on," the lieutenant said. "But you're kind of becoming a distraction here, if you don't mind my saying so. You should have left Trish Lussen to us. We've been through the place."

"I just want to find the girl."

"I know," Pallmeister said. His voice was going in and out because of the weak connection. "You stay on that, and we'll cover the homicide."

"One favor," I said.

"What is it?"

"Find out if Matt Harmony ever had a bow-hunting permit."

"Fair enough," John Pallmeister said. "And then I want you to drop this."

"Did your people go to Belvidere Mountain? To Lussen's cabin?"

"What cabin?"

"You don't know?"

"Not until now."

I took a long sip of the coffee and put the cup down. The acid taste had gone away. "Maybe I should be a distraction more often."

*

Sometimes this P.I. thing is a breeze. A child could do it. Karen Charbonneau's white Jag passed me going the other way on Hog Back Road, and there were at least two people inside, so the odds were better than even that nobody would be at Clement Goody's house when I arrived. The gate at the bottom of the driveway was wide open, so I didn't have to worry about electrocuting myself. I drove right up to the dooryard, parked, rang the bell, and waited. If someone answered, I would use my old standby: sorry, I think I left my cellphone somewhere. But no one came to the door, and I went back to the car to fetch my bag of tools from the trunk.

After ten seconds of working the tumblers I realized that the door had been left unlocked. I opened it and looked into the foyer where I'd had my whiteout-nap. Nobody. Either these people were very unconcerned about their home security, or I'd missed something. Vermonters generally don't lock their houses, but Goody wasn't a Vermonter, and his house was full of valuable things. Eric the electrician had told me that Goody was a prepper, and those types aren't slack on protective measures. I sauntered through the wide-open door, wondering if it was about to slam shut on my fingers.

The answer to that worry was simple: be quick. One by one, I opened the doors to the first-floor rooms and checked everything out, including the closets. I went through the bathroom cabinets looking for pills. I pawed through a recycling bucket and read Goody's mail, which was mostly junk. He probably had a shredder for the important things. I found what looked like a master bedroom and opened every drawer and closet. The room was clearly Goody's because the clothes were men's attire and all his size. Most of it was what you might expect a seventy-year-old man to wear, but there were also several performance outfits in a rainbow of primary colors.

The second floor held bedrooms, bathrooms, and a sitting room over the addition. This section was where Cindy and Karen stayed, again judging from the clothes in two of the bedrooms. I hadn't discovered Lila's quarters yet, but I opened a door above the original area of the house and—wow. The entire space had been turned into one room, which resembled a honeymoon suite in a high-end Vegas hotel: a huge circular bed in the center, with fluffy, garish furnishings surrounding it. On the wall next to me was a panel of electrical switches, which I tried out, one by one. One switch made the bed rotate clockwise like a gigantic lazy Susan. Others controlled lights that swiveled, changed color, and might have made you seasick if you'd had one too many Armagnacs before bedtime. The closets along the walls held not only Lila's clothes but also a number of costumes: chambermaid, nurse, soldier, schoolteacher, and a selection devoted to leather straps, spikes, and gear that would have made a Hell's Angel feel underdressed.

Lila's bedroom was also wired for video and sound. I found a closet full of camera equipment, microphones, and boom stands.

Perhaps this was where Clement Goody recorded his Sunday morning sermons?

Nah. If any worshipping was done in this room, it was at the temple of Eros. This was the center of Clement Goody's kinky universe. It made me wonder if the preacher was serious about his religion or if it was simply a conduit to self-glorification and easy cash from his followers. The slick, telegenic types never struck me as people you would seek out for spiritual guidance. Give me the priest of my childhood who showed up every Sunday to lead his ever-dwindling congregation in a drafty church under a leaky roof. His homilies may have put us to sleep, but he was always there to lend an ear when someone was in a bad way. The true saints among us are the listeners, not the talkers.

I made my way downstairs, and then down a further set of stairs to the basement where I had been entertained on Thursday night. The theater space was dark. A passageway led in the other direction, and I checked the doors one by one as I advanced down the hall.

The first room held an oil burner, a water heater, and an electrical panel. Nothing out of the ordinary. The next two rooms contained canned food, five-gallon jugs of water, and other supplies. If Clement Goody was a prepper, he and his friends could survive for a while, but I agreed with Eric the electrician: what was the point?

Next down the hall was a windowless office with a wall of books. Goody was a fiction buff with tastes that tended toward the erotic. Barbara owned a few of those things and I had tried to get through them, but if I want to be aroused I'm better off with food magazines.

The next room was locked. I appreciate locks for two reasons: one, it usually means that there's something worthwhile inside, and two, I can pick most of them, given enough time and the right tools. I still had my bag with me, and I got to work.

I hadn't even inserted the pick when I heard an electrical hum and a loud click. Goddamn. Somebody had opened it remotely, or, from the inside. I jumped back, but I didn't have a place to conceal myself quickly enough. If they were coming out, I'd be caught flat-footed.

No one came out. I gave it fifteen seconds and turned the handle to open the door.

No wonder it had been securely locked. Inside was a cache of weapons, and I've seen lots of them, but this one was different because it was so neatly organized. Ammunition in drawers, arranged by caliber. A highly illegal box of homemade pipe bombs, tucked under a shelf. Armaments displayed on the walls, segregated by type:

hunting, target, and personal weaponry. It was more than a collector's gun closet, although except for the pipe bombs it didn't reach the level of paranoia that I'd seen on display in other basements.

I carefully closed the door to the room. I wondered what had triggered the lock to open, but I couldn't figure it out. Perhaps it was on a timer? A motion detector? You would think that it would lock, and not unlock the door if a sensor had picked up my movement. It didn't make sense, but I was still glad to get into the room so easily.

One more door remained at the end of the hall. If the basement were true to the house's footprint, the room beyond it would be a big one.

The double door swung open before I reached it. Inside was a gym with an array of exercise machines, a basketball half-court, parallel bars, a pommel horse, rings suspended from the ceiling, and a balance beam. The sole occupant was a woman dressed in black tights, a sport bra, and sneakers, pulling hard on a rowing machine. Cindy Charbonneau was working out while watching the screen of a tablet computer on a stand in front of her. She stopped and turned to me.

"Took you long enough," she said. "You're a nosy one."

"I—left my cellphone here," I said. I almost didn't bother attempting to use my alibi because I realized why my B&E had been such a picnic: I'd been played from the start.

"Oh yeah," she said. "Your phone. That would be the phone that I've been tracking since Thursday? If you're looking for it, it's in your pocket."

"You saw me?"

"Come here." She was clearly enjoying this. Not only had she beat me at my own game, she'd roped me in like a calf, and I was about to get my ass branded. "Check it out. I'll put it on fast-forward. It's funnier that way."

I took the computer from her and watched while she got up from the rowing machine and grabbed a towel. The screen was replaying video taken from the numerous security cameras that Clement Goody had installed on his premises, cameras that I had missed. The software was sophisticated enough to keep the lenses trained on me in every room that I had passed through. I hadn't noticed a single one of them.

"Whoa, kinky," Cindy said as the video showed me rummaging through Lila Morton's underwear drawer. She stood next to me, laughing and toweling off sweat. I viewed myself wandering around like a street punk robbing a Seven Eleven.

"You control all that from the tablet?"

"Yup," she said. "And don't feel bad. The cameras are embedded into the sheetrock. That's how the CIA does it. Clement's like, seventy, but he appreciates technology."

"And you're his tech guru."

"Yes," she said. "Like your friend Roberto."

Cindy Charbonneau knew about Roberto? She was a far better researcher than I'd thought, and it was an uncomfortable feeling to suddenly be on the other side of an investigation.

"He's a kid," I said. "Leave him alone."

"I'm not going after you, Vince," she said. "I just want to know what you're up to, and if it poses any kind of threat to Clement, because I won't let that happen. His work is very important to a lot of people."

I was looking at a bright, resourceful woman. Cindy may have been the less-refined sister, but she had the same intelligent, deep-green eyes as her twin, minus the mascara. "I'm here to find Grace," I said. "That's all."

She and I did a visual Mexican standoff that lasted long enough for each of us to understand that the other was serious. "If you find her, what will you do?"

"Get her out of here," I said. "I'd put her into a real rehab program."

"Clement can't control himself around that girl," she said. "Maybe we're on the same side."

"Maybe we are."

"I—might help you." Her look had softened slightly, for the first time since I had seen her at Clement Goody's front gate.

"I would really appreciate it if you did."

"Just so you know," she said, "I won't go to bed with you unless Clement tells me to. You're not my type."

"That shouldn't be an issue."

"Go upstairs and wait in the foyer," she said. "And don't fall asleep."

*

Cindy had changed into a black T-shirt and gray sweatpants. Her hair was wet from taking a shower, and she combed it out as we sat across from each other on the leather furniture in the foyer and talked. She had surprised me by wanting to talk shop, and had quizzed me on the various devices and techniques that I had used over the years. The investigating business fascinates some people, although most novices quickly get bored with it, because it's slow. Solving a case takes time. You don't just waltz into someone's house and romp through all their stuff—that only happens in the movies, or, when you were being had. Fortunately, Chan was still in the car and had witnessed none of this, because I could only imagine his reaction. I was certain that I'd be hearing about it later.

Ms. Charbonneau confessed that she had taken my phone while I'd been asleep on Thursday, and had installed a tracking app. I have used the exact same one, several times. So Cindy knew about my trip to talk with her sister at the college, the drive to Carmela's house, the morning visit to Matty's shop, and my stopover at Trish Lussen's. I could have been annoyed, but I was only getting a dose of my own medicine.

Cindy hadn't seen Grace Hebert since the young woman had bolted down the driveway in the Hummer. She asked me why the police hadn't yet located such an obvious vehicle. Good question. I asked her about Don Lussen, and she confirmed that he was smitten with Grace, and that Clement Goody had intentionally kept them separated for the last two weeks, partly because Lussen was making an ass of himself, but also because that was when the death threats had started.

"How did they arrive?" I asked her. "Emails?"

She grimaced as she pulled the brush through a tangle of hair. "Regular mail, sent to her college P.O. box. Just a single sheet of computer paper with a printed message."

"What did it say?"

"Quotes from the Bible, that kind of stuff."

"Do you still have the letter?"

"Clement tossed it in the fireplace. He told Grace she had to stay with us."

"Were there other threats?"

"I guess so, but Clement wouldn't discuss it."

"Nobody told the police?"

"He doesn't like to attract attention," she said. "Some people don't understand what we do here."

Like me, for example, but that didn't matter at the moment. "So—where would Grace run to, if she's not here, or at her mother's, or at the college?"

"Grace is beautiful, and men will do anything for her. She's probably far away by now. London, or somewhere like that. Sorry, Vince. My guess is that you've lost her."

If Grace had left the country, John Pallmeister could find out through customs. I was already making up another mental list of favors to ask him. Meanwhile, I peppered Cindy Charbonneau with more questions.

"Karen told me that Trish Lussen might have known that Donald was fooling around."

"It wasn't just fooling around," she said. She looked exasperated, and I sensed that her willingness to answer my questions was coming to an end. "Donald was a big part of everything."

"I understand," I said. Sort of. "Do you think that his wife could have—"

"No. She's like, Ms. Politically Correct, you know? Owns the perfect farm, drives an old Saab, makes her own bread, volunteers at the elementary school, all that shit. No wonder Donald was bored."

"Understood," I said, but once again, I didn't quite. Both Charbonneau sisters had now told me that Donald Lussen's wife might have known about his extracurricular love life, and that wasn't good. I added Trish Driscoll Lussen to my list—in pencil, and well below Matty Harmony's name, but it would be a mistake to not include her. Each of them could have acted from the same motivation: jealousy. Jealous people could do things that no one dreamed them capable of, like launching two arrows from a high-powered bow into the body of a cheating husband.

*

Chan reacted, all right. I let him out of the car for a whiz, and I even tried to bribe him with some hamburger that I'd purloined from the Goody house fridge after Cindy had gone into the bathroom with a hair dryer, but it was no use. He wouldn't touch the meat, and he was looking at me like I was the most pathetic thing he had ever seen.

Is there such thing as a rescue program for humans?

"Look," I said, "I'm making progress. I just need a little luck."

If you need a little luck, then you've already lost. He was right, of course.

We were at the bottom of the driveway where I had parked next to one of the bible camp buildings. The clapboard structures didn't seem like innocuous places of worship anymore; they looked foreboding. Maybe Grace was hiding in one of them?

No—Cindy Charbonneau was right: Grace Hebert was long gone. My skills were no longer needed here, unless I was willing to get out my passport and chase her around the globe. How was I going to explain all of this to Mrs. Tomaselli?

My phone buzzed. I didn't recognize the caller, but I answered anyway, partly to get away from Chan's glare.

"Tanzi?"

"Yes?"

"Duffy Kovich. The Hummer is in the tennis court lot, here on campus. The girl's car is gone. I have no idea how long it's been there."

"Did you look inside the car?"

"Yeah," he said. "Nothing I could see that was out of the ordinary."

My phone rang while I was on the call, and I checked the screen: John Pallmeister. "Call you back," I said to Duffy, and we clicked off.

"I have a number of favors to ask you," I said to the lieutenant.

"They'll have to wait," he said.

"My runaway might have left the country. I need you to check with customs."

"I can't do that."

"Meaning?"

"You stepped on some toes, Vince. You're shut off. I'm not supposed to be talking to you anymore."

"What? Look, John, I have a lot of information for you. You can sit on your duff in your office all you want, but I've found some things out. Like, for instance, you should be looking harder at Trish Lussen. Talk about a motive."

"I can't," he said.

"Explain?"

"I can't do that either, Vince. You crossed a line."

"What? You have a homicide case here, and a missing person, and you know that they're connected. And you're refusing my help?"

"It's not my decision."

"Meaning that somebody above you told you to shut me down?"

"I can't go into it. You're on your own. I wish it wasn't that way, but it is."

John Pallmeister and I had started our law enforcement careers the same year, as rookie Barre patrolmen. I'd moved to Florida shortly afterward, and he had transferred to the State Police and had risen through the ranks. He was a far more accomplished cop than I had ever been. But when you get to be a lieutenant, the politics start to become a factor, and someone had waved him off. Pallmeister had a career to think about, and our friendship was too thin for that. I drew a preliminary conclusion about where this was coming from.

"I get it, John," I said. "Somebody is in Angus Driscoll's pocket, right?"

"I can't comment." Meaning that I was right. Driscoll didn't like me snooping around his daughter, and he'd made a phone call.

"You remember Fish Falzarano?" I said. "He's his driver. I saw them both at Trish Lussen's house this morning."

"Fish earned a Distinguished Service Cross in Afghanistan," Pallmeister said. "He was career Army. He straightened out, not long after you and I busted him as a juvenile, and he's been out of the service for a few years now. He does security for the Driscoll family."

"You seem to know a lot about the Driscolls."

John Pallmeister waited for a while until he spoke. "Lay low, Vince. Please. I'm not in anybody's pocket. With any luck we'll find your girl."

"Then you've already lost."

"Beg pardon?"

"My dog," I said. "He comes up with these things."

*

The farther I get pushed back from my objective, the more it comes into focus. Adversity breeds clarity. Maybe I should get that tattooed on my ass.

Angus Driscoll had called somebody, and I no longer had access to what the State Police knew, because I was considered a pest. Or had I come too close to something that he wanted to keep hidden? Did he know about his son-in-law's secret life? If so, why was that a big deal? These days, people gave about as much thought to having affairs as they did to deciding what to have for breakfast. The Internet had offered up a wild new cornucopia of temptation in every possible flavor, and monogamy was as passé as parachute pants. No, a guy like Driscoll would be far too pragmatic to concern himself with something like his daughter's marital problems. Donald Lussen and Trish Driscoll could get a divorce, their assets would be divvied up, and life would go on. Lussen's infatuation with Grace was a distraction, not a motive for murder.

My investigating had bothered Angus Driscoll in some other way, which I didn't yet understand. It may or may not have had something to do with Grace. I would chase it down eventually, but I tend to work off of a list, and Driscoll was way down the list from the two things at the top. Number one was to find out if Grace had left the country. And number two was to check out the Belvidere Mountain sugar shack where Lussen wrote his plays. I was halfway there, and I had just enough of a signal to make a phone call while I drove. That is illegal in Vermont these days, but I didn't care because I was already in hot water with the cops.

Robert Patton answered on the first ring. "Tanzi? Don't tell me. You want to tell me how warm it is in Florida and how much you're getting laid."

"I'm up here."

"In Vermont?"

"I'm in Johnson, headed for Belvidere Mountain."

"That's my back yard," he said. Patton was the head of the Border Patrol, and he knew every square mile of the territory near Canada. We had met a few years before, and I had become friends with the gruff, bulldog-faced law officer who might have even intimidated the huge animal snoring in the back seat.

"I need a favor," I said.

"Say the word."

"A young woman named Grace Hebert. She's a student at Johnson State. She may have left the country. I want to know if you can find her on the exit records."

"When?"

"Sometime between Friday morning and now."

"Does this have anything to do with the professor who got killed?"

"They were lovers," I said. "He had a cabin up in Belvidere."

"Really? Isn't John Pallmeister handling that? I saw him on a TV conference."

"He's not cooperating," I said. "Apparently I stepped on someone's toes."

"Whose toes?"

"Angus Driscoll's. The victim was his son-in-law."

"Those are big toes," Patton said.

"Yeah."

"You seem unconcerned."

"I'm not running for office," I said. "I'm just trying to find the girl. She's Donna Tomaselli's granddaughter."

"Mrs. T?" Patton said. They had both done shifts at my bedside after I had been shot, and Mrs. Tomaselli was one of those people who if you spent five minutes with her, you loved her.

"That's right," I said.

"I'll check it out," he said. "How's your health?"

"Fine."

"Don't bullshit me, Vince. You sound tired."

"I've been better," I said. And that was the truth, because ever since I'd left Clement Goody's house I'd felt tired and on edge. I would make a fast trip to the Lussen cabin, and then get back to Barre for some rest. It would be dark soon, and I was eager to be home, knock off eight or ten leftover cannolis, and climb into bed.

Robert Patton and I hung up right as the signal went dead, with Belvidere Mountain just coming into sight. I had made myself a crude map from the land records that I had pulled off of the town's website: up the Old Mine Road several miles and then a left turn on what used to be a logging road. The former asbestos mine bordered the property, and when I'd looked it up, I had found out why Lussen had been able to purchase his getaway shack for so little money: the hundred-year-old mine had closed in 1993 after asbestos fibers had been confirmed as a carcinogen. The now-bankrupt company had left a two-mile-long scar at the base of the mountain that resembled a moonscape. It was not what people thought of when they pictured rural life in Vermont. More like a toxic wasteland, although the huge piles of tailings and the polluted streams were already being reclaimed by nature, albeit slowly. The Green Mountains were formed several hundred million years ago, and it would take another hundred million for the scar to heal.

Chan had transferred himself to the front seat and was helping me navigate. His ears were perked up, making him look anxious. We found the logging road and followed it for less than a quarter mile before we came to a chain that was secured with a padlock. Unfortunately, it was a combination lock, and you can't pick those unless you're clairvoyant. I would either need to return with a hacksaw, or hoof it up the hill to Lussen's cabin. I had no idea how far that would be, or if I could make it there and back in the fading light.

I parked the rental car and put on a fleece jacket. It was going to be a cold night—not uncommon for the month of October in Vermont. A brief hike in the cool air might do me some good. At least I hoped so, because I was starting to feel as nervous as Chan. I didn't need any more bad things to happen—I needed a break in the case. The whole thing was about as clear as the clouds that were now coming in from the northwest, enveloping the top of Belvidere Mountain and obscuring the already weak sun.

Maybe Chan was right when he'd said *dogs know*. And maybe the same held true for private investigators who had taken a nine-millimeter slug to the head, because both of us sensed trouble. We stepped over the chain and started up the hill past tall hemlocks that cast dark shadows on the forest floor. Bursts of wind scattered leaves and pine needles across our path. The air felt cold and dense in my lungs, and I had to shorten my gait as the road steepened. Chan stayed close beside me, not venturing ahead. Somewhere along the line, someone had trained him. Either that, or he was afraid.

We followed the logging road up the hill until we came to a clearing. A small wooden cabin sat in the middle, flanked by a rustic outhouse. The door to the cabin was wide open, banging in the wind. And as I got closer I noticed a car obscured by a stand of trees. It was a yellow Saab convertible with a torn roof and a blacked-out fender, and for the first time since I had arrived in Vermont I wished that I'd brought a gun.

*

I don't like blood. It's not that it makes me squeamish, or light-headed, or want to run out of the house and puke on the lawn, although there have been some close calls. I just don't like it. It's messy, it's impossible to clean up, and it leaves an unpleasant smell, like dirty pots in the sink. Blood should be kept inside the body, not outside. Not sprayed across the floor of Donald Lussen's writing cabin in a grotesque Rorschach blot that had only one possible interpretation: violent death.

Matthew Harmony still wore his mechanic's coveralls, which were strangely free of the sticky red liquid now drying on the floor behind his supine body. The top of his head was missing, and the barrel of a gun was jammed into his mouth. Grace Hebert's gun. Actually, Clement Goody's gun, which had been lent to Grace, found by me, and then reclaimed by Grace.

From ten feet away you would say suicide. The young man had lain down on the floor, put the barrel of his girlfriend's borrowed .44-magnum revolver into his mouth and had checked out in the messiest possible way. Heartbroken ex-lover. Junkie. Lost soul.

But good police work isn't done from ten feet away. I had managed to get enough of a cell signal to dial 911, and the blue lights had quickly accumulated in the cabin's yard during the hour since Chan and I had discovered the body. The small clearing looked like an alien ship had landed: rooftop speakers blasting police communications, outdoor floodlights being set up, Orleans County deputies, local EMTs, and even a beat-up, rusting fire truck from a nearby village. It was all I could do to preserve the scene for the State Police forensics team, because everybody wanted a look at the body, and in my time as a deputy one of the things that I had learned was how easy it was for well-meaning public servants to screw up a crime scene. I'd had to reprimand several of them, and by the time John Pallmeister and his crew arrived my voice was hoarse from barking orders. I had taken charge, partly because I had a proprietary interest in this and partly because I had to wonder, in the farthest recesses of my mind, whether I held some responsibility, seeing how the first thing that I had done today was to break Matthew Harmony's stones. I would leave that one to the cops, but it was going to take some explaining as to why I kept having conversations with people who had subsequently turned up dead.

Another hour later I had been demoted from my self-appointed managerial duties to sitting in the back seat of Pallmeister's cruiser with Janice the sergeant watching over me. The lieutenant and I had spoken for less than five minutes, after which he'd gestured to his car and said: *wait inside*. He'd no doubt had his fill of me, seeing how I had thrust him into two investigations in as many days. Chan lay on the back seat of the cruiser next to me, and we decided to go with the flow. Let them do their job. Not make it any harder than it was, because investigating a crime scene—or a suicide—was a bitch. You had to examine everything, log it all, keep the evidence untouched, and in some cases, deal with relatives, reporters, and curious assholes. I watched the team do their work, and I realized that I didn't miss any of that. You can pick your messes when you're a private investigator, but when you're a cop you have to be part superhero and part garbage man, and if you did the slightest thing wrong you would be taken to task in the local papers. No thanks.

Chan was catching up on his sleep, but my fatigue had disappeared the moment I'd found the body. My mind was working overtime trying to figure out how Grace might have played into this. Matty had somehow ended up with her gun. He'd freaked out when I had accused him of being her lover. He had also denied any knowledge of the relationship between Grace and Donald Lussen, but here he was, dead, in Lussen's cabin. I had some thinking to do, because as perplexing as the two deaths might be, I was still faced with the same problem: Grace Hebert wasn't here.

SUNDAY

"YOUR PRINTS WEREN'T ON the gun," Pallmeister said. I was in my mother's kitchen with a cup of coffee and Chan curled up at my feet. The dog and I had made it back to the house at four AM, and it was now almost noon. I had stayed up way past my bedtime in Pallmeister's Middlesex office playing what-if, but it was all guesswork until the forensic reports came in. The good news was that the lieutenant had dropped any reluctance to share information with me. I didn't press him about who had put the clamps on in the first place, because I already knew.

"It must have been wiped," I said. "Mine should be on it, and Grace's. And possibly Clement Goody's, since it's his gun."

"But that isn't the big news."

"What's the big news?"

"We found a compound bow in the Saab shop. It has an attached quiver that holds four arrows, but only two were left."

"Carbon fiber?"

"Yes, and they match the ones that hit Lussen. No prints at all on the bow or the remaining arrows, but they had traces of a solvent, like you might use in an automotive shop. It looks like Matthew Harmony killed Lussen and then himself. The coroner said he'd been drinking, and there was an empty bottle of vodka in the cabin."

"Wouldn't that be convenient," I said.

"You don't buy it?"

"No."

"Why not?"

"Did you ever find out if Matty had a bow permit?"

"He didn't," Pallmeister said. "But some of these guys don't bother."

"Did he even hunt?"

"We'll be asking his family, and Carmela Tomaselli."

"Did anyone go see her yet?"

74

"Janice is with her right now."

"I'm going to talk to her too," I said. "I don't think I've been getting the straight story." Karen Charbonneau had told me in her office that Carmela knew some things, and I hadn't followed up, but I would now. Carmela might be in more of a talking frame of mind now that her boyfriend was dead. Events like that usually make the guilty more secretive, and the innocent more forthcoming. I couldn't imagine that Carmela was anything but innocent, and if she had a brain in her head she would cooperate fully, for the sake of her daughter.

"So why don't you like this?" Pallmeister said. "Everything fits, so far."

"Because it's too easy," I said. "You know better, John. Real life doesn't work that way."

*

Chan and I were walking through my mother's neighborhood. He was still on edge, which was understandable after the events of the previous evening, as he had gone into the house with me and seen the mess. I had quickly escorted him outside, not wanting to introduce anything into the crime scene that would confuse the investigators, like dog hair or paw prints that didn't belong there.

I heard myself thinking: *crime scene*. Not suicide. Faking a suicide was no simple task, but it could be done. If that's what had happened, there might be blood traces elsewhere on the property, because if you somehow get a gun into someone's mouth and pull the trigger, you're going to get some on you. Matty's hands had shown traces of gun-shot residue according to the cops, but that was relatively simple to stage: you just had to make the dead person take a posthumous shot out of an open door or a window. The team could look for signs of another vehicle, but after the circus that had ensued, any tire tracks and tread patterns would be long gone. The Vermont State Police's crime scene team was as good as they come, but there is only so much that you can get from the actual location.

My money was on the old-fashioned detective work: interviewing friends and family, checking the computer and phone records, and burning gasoline and shoe leather by making the rounds to all of Matty's haunts and hangouts until you finally turned something up. There weren't a lot of shooting deaths in Vermont, and Pallmeister had the resources, unlike a big city like Philly or Baltimore where somebody took a bullet every few hours and the detectives had open caseloads that would fill up a whole file cabinet.

Of course they could just say it was a suicide, tag Matty as Donald Lussen's killer, and call it a day. Why the hell not. The Pats were hosting the Jets, so let's crack open a beer, make some popcorn, and watch a bunch of three-hundred-pound men give each other concussions.

I wasn't sure why I wasn't buying into the murder-suicide. Like John Pallmeister had said, everything fit. But I didn't get how Matty found his way to Lussen's cabin, opened the combination lock, closed it behind him, and then did himself in without bothering to shut the door. Too many loose ends for my bullet-damaged brain.

"Help me out here," I said to Chan. I decided that we would to go back to my mother's house. I had him on a lead, but instead of following me, he sat on the sidewalk, not budging. "What?" I stopped, and he looked up at me.

Cold.

I turned in the direction of Carmela Tomaselli's apartment. It was less than a block away. *Getting warmer,* he said.

*

Donna Tomaselli intercepted me in the driveway of Carmela's house. She had just come out the front door, dressed in an all-black outfit except for a huge grey shawl that looked like something I might have made in my knitting days when I didn't know how to stop. Baby blankets had become throws, throws had expanded into afghans, and afghans had ended up as bed covers for a California king. My physical therapist had encouraged the hobby to develop my dexterity, but I didn't really have the knack for it, and everything came out super-sized.

"She's as drunk as a poet on payday," Mrs. T said. "I wouldn't bother going in."

"You spoke with her?"

"I dropped off a casserole," she said. "She's about five minutes away from passing out."

"What happened to the lady cop?"

"She left right after I came. She didn't learn anything from Carmela. Oh, Vinny, I'm so worried. This isn't good for Grace, is it?"

"I don't know yet."

"That makes me even more worried," she said.

"Do you think that Matty—"

"Was the suicide type? You never know, do you?"

"No."

"I didn't like him much. Not a shred of manners. But he loved Carmela, and he was nice to Grace. He was the one who went to the college to pick up the dog."

"I'm going inside," I said. "I won't be long. I can walk you home afterward."

"No, I'll just run along, don't you worry, Vinny. Maybe she'll level with you now."

"What do you mean?"

"My daughter knows more about things than she says. She's been that way since she was a little girl. Ask her about Grace. I'll bet she knows where she is."

*

"You want a bite of this?" Carmela asked me. Mrs. T was right—her daughter was already slurring her words at 12:30 in the afternoon. "American Chop Suey. Tastes like candle wax. My mom never could cook for shit."

"No thanks," I said. I had shown myself to a chair at a kitchen table that was littered with unwashed breakfast dishes, bills, a scattering of mini-vodka nips, an open bottle of Bailey's Irish Cream, and a coffee mug that smelled more like liquor than caffeine.

"Drink?" she asked. "I'm way ahead of you."

"I'm sorry about Matty," I said.

"Only the good die young, right Vin?" she said. "Us old fucks, we live forever. 'Cept maybe you, since you got yourself shot."

"Carmela, do you know where Grace is? It's important."

"Why? Why is Grace so goddamn important?" She was standing across the kitchen from me, wearing white jeans with a loose purple top. She shifted from foot to foot, like an elm swaying in the wind. "Why can't you find her? You're the big detective."

"I did," I said. "She was at the house of a man named Clement Goody. He's one of those TV preachers. He's rich, and he has a place up in Johnson."

"Never heard of him."

"Grace spent two weeks at his house. Somebody was threatening her life."

"So?"

I eyed the Bailey's bottle and decided that I could use a small drink. Chan was curled up outside on the front step, it was a Sunday, and I hadn't had five minutes to relax since I'd touched down at the airport.

"Pour me a sip of that," I said.

Carmela picked up the bottle, got a fresh mug from an overhead cabinet, and filled it to the top with the booze. "You want some coffee in it?"

"Too late."

She put the cup down in front of me and sat down. "So you found her, but you don't know where she is?"

"She took off again. She may have left the country."

Her expression changed like she'd been slapped. "Fucking weasel."

"What?"

"He took his passport with him," she said. She refilled her own mug, spilling some because her hand was shaking. She drank half of it. "Yesterday morning. Him and I were supposed to go up to Williston to shop. But Matty said no, he had to go check out a car that he wanted to buy. He said he'd be gone all day, back late, and then I saw him get his passport out of the drawer. I didn't ask why. Oh shit, Vinny, I'm such a goddamned fool—"

She broke down, looking all of her years and then some. I tried to put an arm around her, but she shrugged it off. She sobbed into a paper napkin while I stared into my mug, filled with the sweet, creamy drink that I no longer wanted.

"So they were lovers?"

Carmela's eyes were glazed over, but they still had some fire. "Bitch."

"Why would Matty kill himself?"

Carmela stood up from the table. She raised her hand in the air with one finger extended like she was about to make an important point. Instead, she collapsed on the floor. I gathered her up and carried her to the nearest bedroom. She was lighter than I thought she might be.

"Didn't," she said, slurring the word as we proceeded down the hall. "Cops got it wrong."

"Did he bow hunt?"

"Fucking cops," she said. I lay her down on a blue polyester duvet that covered the mattress of a cast iron bed. "Asked me the same thing. You're all the same."

"Did he hunt?"

"Matty took the spiders outside," she said. Her head lolled back on a pillow, and she gave me a drunken grin. "Wouldn't even squash a daddy longlegs."

I was going to ask her more questions, but she grabbed my neck as I tried to release her, and she wouldn't let go.

"Vince," she said, momentarily regaining her focus. Our eyes were inches apart, close enough for the scent of the liquor to be overpowering. "I loved him, you know? I loved Matty, and he loved me back. All of this is my fault. Me. I did this."

"How?"

"Because I sold her," she said, and she passed out cold.

*

Sold her? What the hell did that mean? This was the 21st century, and you didn't sell women, especially not a feisty drama major who packed a .44 magnum. Carmela must have confused things in her alcoholic stupor. I would have considered staying around until she sobered up, but I doubted that she would explain anything further unless she got drunk again, and once was enough for today.

Carmela's boozy breath and foul mouth made me want to go back to my mother's and take another shower. The four blocks between our houses wasn't enough distance for me to process what I had heard, so I continued walking Chan through the streets of my old neighborhood. I showed him some of the highlights, like Marie Rocchio's second-floor walk-up, where she and I would frolic on Saturday afternoons while her parents worked and her brothers were away at hockey games. I had turned sixteen that winter and played hockey too, but I'd lost interest in team sports after Marie had introduced me to the joys of one-on-one competition. She even let me win sometimes.

The house across the street from hers belonged to Gary Petrullo, a mean-tempered, overweight kid who had reached puberty before the rest of us and could beat up anyone in our grade. He'd bloodied my nose out behind the school, and the nuns had disciplined us both—me because I wouldn't rat him out, fearing certain death if I did, and Gary, because in parochial school the kids like him were presumed guilty not innocent. I'd ultimately had my revenge when I had busted him twice for DUI during my year as a Barre cop. He sat on the stoop of his house, fatter than ever, dressed in a yellow-and-black striped rugby shirt that made him look like a morbidly obese honeybee.

"Yo, Vinny," he said, surprising me, as we hadn't spoken in three decades. "Ya seen her?"

"Seen who?" I wasn't about to be drawn into a conversation with Petrullo. Carmela was a social drinker compared to him.

"The girl," he said. "Carmela's girl. Word is you're lookin' for her."

"That's right."

"I seen her," he said. "And hey, I'd fuck her."

"That's helpful to know, Gary."

"You would too, right?"

"I stick with my own age group."

"You got about as much chance as me, Vin," he said. "She's a limousine girl. Probably doesn't go for us big and tall guys anyway."

"What do you mean by limousine girl?"

"They pick her up at her mother's," Petrullo said. "Late at night, when nobody's outside except me. I can't sleep no more. I walk around until I get tired."

"Guilty conscience?"

"*Vaffanculo*, Tanzi," he said, spreading his palms. When you cuss somebody out in Italian American slang you have to use your hands or it doesn't count.

"Who picks her up?"

"A limo, like I said. So Vinny, what's with the limp? You walk like a cripple. And you know what? I could still whip your ass."

"Maybe you could," I said, "but you'll still be ugly."

Gary Petrullo laughed. Here we were, hurling schoolyard insults at each other, and the absurdity of it must have struck him. "Not as ugly as Fish," he said. "That guy's fuckin' ugly. What do the kids call it now? *Fugly*."

"Fish Falzarano?"

"He drives the limousine, you dumb shit," Petrullo said. "Are you listening to me?"

Yes, I was listening. And I had been thinking about taking a swing at my former playground nemesis, but not anymore, because he had just handed me a big fat gift: according to the neighborhood insomniac, Grace Hebert had been getting late-night rides in a limo driven by Fish Falzarano. Grace, who had been "sold" by her mother. I was never that good at geometry, but I can draw a triangle: Sex, Money, and Trouble.

My plans for the afternoon began to fall into place. I would return to my mother's and call the airline, and Barbara, because I was getting the feeling that this was going somewhere. After that I would make an appearance at the Driscoll residence out on Shelburne Point. Perhaps somebody there could explain why a twenty-one-year-old woman was being squired around in the wee hours by Angus Driscoll's chauffeur.

*

"Stay as long you need," Barbara said. "You're doing the right thing. It's your nature."

"You're being passive aggressive," I said. "It's your nature."

The phone went quiet, and I wondered if the call had been dropped, or if I'd been hung up on. The five-second silence was more than enough time for me to realize what a lousy thing that was to say.

"Barbara? Are you still there?"

"I'm still here," she said.

"I didn't mean that."

"Yes you did," she said. "I know you're still angry."

Damn. How had I so easily slipped into the post-break-up blame game? Didn't being divorced mean that you no longer had to dissect everything under a microscope?

Chan looked up from his position at the foot of my father's lounge chair: *Dig yourself out of that one.*

"I'm not angry, Barbara," I said. "Really. I wish you well. All the best."

"Vince. You sound like a Hallmark card."

"You and my dog," I said. "I'm outnumbered."

"Your dog?"

"I—have a dog now."

"Really? Oh my god, Royal will love this!"

"I may not be able to keep him," I said. "He belongs to the girl I'm looking for. Everything is kind of in flux."

"Oh, please bring him home," Barbara said. "Please. We need a dog."

"We?"

Another conversational hole opened, and you could have driven a truck through it.

"I want a second chance," she said.

"You've already had several."

"I know," she said. "I want another one."

"What about your—other relationship?"

"A huge mistake. I know I've hurt you. But I miss our family. I can barely manage this alone."

There were things that I missed about it too, but this was dangerous ground. "I don't know what to tell you."

"Royal wants to say hello." I heard her talking to our son in the background. She put the phone to his mouth, and he immediately began to howl. "He's tired," she said. "Sorry."

"Thank you for taking care of him," I said. "I feel bad about not being there."

"Mrs. Tomaselli called me last night. She explained what you're doing for her. Don't worry about anything here, OK? You do what you need to do."

"It's going to be a while."

"You relax, sweetie. Take care of yourself. We'll talk about this when you're home."

Home? Barbara and I had been living apart for over a year. Her home was hers, and mine was mine. I had spent a lot of time drawing the boundaries, respecting them, not overstepping, and even though I didn't have a new relationship of my own, I was reaping the benefits of my newfound privacy. Our marriage had foundered on the rocks of some very bad decisions on both our parts. A second chance sounded like doubling down on a losing bet.

"OK," I said. A one-word answer. The less said the better.

*

Shelburne Point is some of the most exclusive acreage in the state of Vermont. But it isn't dotted with pseudo-castles, and the roads aren't crowded with Teslas and Lamborghinis like you would see in Palm Beach or Naples. Vermont money isn't about the show. It's much older money, carefully camouflaged behind flannel shirts, worn-out chinos, unassuming houses, and beater cars like Trish Lussen's Saab, which was parked in the driveway of Angus Driscoll's relatively modest, gambrel-roofed house when I pulled in. The place was as perfectly kept as his daughter's farm, and what it might have lacked in architectural grandeur was made up for by the stunning views across Lake Champlain to the sawtooth profile of the Adirondack Mountains.

The driveway continued beyond where I had parked, toward several other houses: a compound, as I had gathered from the real estate records and satellite maps that I'd researched before the trip up from Barre. I knew that the gambrel was where Driscoll lived, and the nose of his Town Car protruded from an adjacent garage bay, confirming what I had learned.

Fish Falzarano emerged from the front door of the house as I approached, waving his arms back and forth in front of him like I was a runaway train. "You can't come in here, Tanzi," he said. "Private property."

"Nice to see you, Fish," I said as I got out of the car. "I heard about your military service. Very impressive."

"No thanks to you." He wore a black turtleneck that stretched over his muscles. Gary Petrullo might be too fat to whip my ass, but Fish looked like he could do it without breaking a sweat.

"Great gig you have here," I said. "You probably make three times what I did as a cop."

"It's none of your damn business, is it?"

"Plus the benefits," I said. "Medical, dental, retirement plan? I'm sure Angus sees to all that."

"Why don't you get the fuck outta here? I heard about you taking a slug, Tanzi. I don't want to fuck you up any worse than you already are." His too-small nose began to twitch like he was going to sneeze.

"And there's the girl," I said. "You pick her up in the limo late at night, you pimp her out—unless you wanted some for yourself. All part of the benefits package, right?"

"I have no idea who—"

"Yes you do, Fish."

"Hey—"

"I want to know where she is, that's all," I said, cutting him off. "Not my concern if you were screwing her."

"No way would I touch her. I never laid a hand on her. I'd be..." He stopped mid-sentence, catching himself.

"You'd be what?"

The nose was twitching uncontrollably now, but he wasn't going to say anything more.

"Where is she?" I said. "I know that you know."

Fish's face gave away his next move. He took a roundhouse swing at me, but I sidestepped him and he lurched past. He quickly recovered his balance and I was ready, but both of us froze when Angus Driscoll discharged a shotgun into the air from the porch of his house.

"There's one more shell in the chamber," Driscoll said. "On your way, Mr. Tanzi."

The shotgun was an over-under with a polished walnut stock and lots of silver filigree. A rich man's sporting weapon. Probably a

Purdey, which would cost as much as my house. I got back into the car, turned the ignition key, and drove off.

Chan looked up from the back. *That was productive.*

"Whose side are you on?"

Grace's side.

"Me too, goddamn it," I said. "It's my style, and it doesn't always work, OK? But I didn't come away empty-handed."

How so?

"Falzarano. He was afraid of saying the wrong thing. He's not the pimp."

Then who is?

"Her mother," I said. "Fish is just transportation. And Angus Driscoll is the john."

*

Maybe I should have gone to mass. Light a candle for Grace Hebert: drama major, porn model, junkie, mistress, white slave, and now fugitive. If Grace had left the country, I wouldn't blame her. Everything that I had learned about her pointed to misery.

Instead of going to church, I was on Route 15 passing by the stubbled remains of freshly harvested cornfields on the way to Johnson and thinking about my ex-wife and baby son. Being separated from Barbara was not a problem, but being apart from Royal was like going cold turkey on something that you not only needed and depended on, but that was good for you. When I was inside Royal's orbit, feeding him, changing his diaper, putting him down for a nap, or just fooling around together on the floor, I felt like a better person. My ailments and worries went away. I missed that feeling, and I couldn't wait to get back to it.

When I was with Barbara, I felt uncomfortable. I had been dating her, and she had unexpectedly gotten pregnant, and I'd figured, fine—this was how it worked, so step up and be a husband and a dad, because that's what you do. She had also helped me recover from the worst injury of my life, and I owed her. So we got married.

Then she fell in love with someone else. I could have waited until it blew over, like the sudden, torrential storms that pass through Florida in the summer. But after only a few weeks of living apart I'd had time to examine our relationship, and it didn't hold up well under the bright light of our separation. Bottom line: don't marry someone because you think you owe them. Owing isn't loving.

I was now on my way to find Karen Charbonneau. She might be at Goody's, or at the college. Or she might be somewhere completely different, and the trip would be wasted, but I have this thing about not calling ahead. I've learned that if you give someone too much notice they will come up with all kinds of plausible explanations and alibis that they've practiced in the mirror. Of the three of Goody's women, Karen seemed like the most promising. Cindy had already told me what she knew, and Lila would probably stonewall me, but I hadn't fully probed the drama department chair yet, beyond idle conversation before dinner and the few tidbits she'd tossed out when we had talked in her office.

I also sensed a vulnerability—something that went beyond being a former heroin user. If Cindy and Lila had seemed perfectly at home in Clement Goody's harem, Karen Charbonneau looked like she was being held against her will, or maybe she was going along with things out of some sort of obligation. Bad idea, like my marriage.

I decided to start at the campus, because I wasn't all that enthusiastic about going back to Goody's place. The guy creeped me out, and if Cindy had told him about my unannounced visit the previous day, he might not feel too welcoming. Karen's white Jag was in the lot next to Dibden, so I parked next to her and let Chan out for a few minutes before shutting him back in the car. There wasn't a student in sight, and I remembered that it was a Sunday afternoon and the college kids would still be in their beds, having stayed up into the single digits the night before.

Ms. Charbonneau wasn't in her office, although all the doors were open. I wandered through the hallways until I entered the main theater, which was dark except for a redheaded woman with a clipboard standing in the middle of the stage, looking upward. A single white spot illuminated her from above, giving her a ghostly look. I approached the stage, careful not to stumble in the near-darkness. "Excuse me?"

"Yes?" the woman said.

"Do you know if Karen Charbonneau is around somewhere?"

"Vince?" a voice said from far above us. "I'm up here. Fran, show him the way up, would you?"

I followed the woman backstage and down a hall that led to a stairway. "Take the ladder at the top of the stairs," she said. "You're not afraid of heights, are you?"

"No," I lied. If Karen could do it, so could I. But a few minutes later as I was inching out a steel catwalk I wished I'd been more forthcoming. Don't look down, Vince.

"Are you OK?"

"Sort of," I said. Karen was dressed in black jeans and a black T-shirt with a Magic Hat Brewery logo. Her blonde hair shimmered with light that leaked sideways from the spot that she was adjusting. "I wanted to ask you some more questions. It can wait until you're done."

"I'm done," she said. "Let's go back down. You're sweating like crazy."

"It's kind of warm up here."

"You're not going to faint on me, are you?"

"I don't think so," I said, but the jury was out on that one. I'd better not, or they'd have to call the fire department to fetch me like a kitten stuck in a tree. I carefully retraced my steps and descended the ladder. Karen followed and took my arm at the top of the stairs.

"We'll go to my place," she said. "You look like you could use a beer."

"I'd just as soon not go back to Goody's," I said.

"I have an apartment in Morrisville," she said. "I don't stay there very often unless I need some alone time."

"Do you need that now?"

"Yes," she said. She brushed some dust off of the black T. "I think I'm moving out."

"Seriously? I thought—"

"I love Clement very deeply, Vince. He's an amazing man, and he saves lives. But's he's a sex addict, and so am I. It's as bad as heroin."

"Maybe worse," I said.

*

Karen's apartment was located over a vacant furniture store near one of the few stoplights in town. Morrisville was one of the villages that the hippies invaded in the '70s, opening bars, head shops, and other establishments in a setting that had been left largely undisturbed since Calvin Coolidge—a Vermonter—was president. "Silent Cal" might not have approved of the present-day town, seeing how you didn't have to find a speakeasy to have some fun—it had a distillery, a microbrewery, and plenty of barstools from which to soak up the local hooch.

Chan and I followed Karen up a long flight of wooden stairs to her loft. The building was post and beam inside, and someone had gone to the trouble of refurbishing a huge open space that showed off the precise joinery and leftover machinery of what must have been a mill. Steel rods crisscrossed the high ceiling with gears and pulley wheels still attached. I wondered what had been manufactured here. The professor had made it her own with an eclectic mix of junk store furnishings and modern touches.

Chan found a space to lie down under a window that let in the last of the afternoon light. Karen directed me to a seat at a butcher-block table while she disappeared behind a tall purple drape that might have once been part of a theater. She came out a few minutes later dressed in a white peasant blouse and the same black jeans that she had been wearing earlier.

"About that beer," she said. "I have some Labatt, but I'm afraid that's it."

"My high school beverage of choice," I said. "So…Charbonneau is French Canadian?"

"From a couple generations ago," she said. "I grew up in St. Albans. My dad drove a milk truck."

"And you became a college professor. He must be proud."

"My father wanted us to be educated. He's gone now. And we've pretty much screwed it up."

"Why?"

"The pill thing, like I told you," she said. "It got way out of control."

She took a seat at the table and put two bottles in front of us. I took a long swig, finishing a third of mine. The cool, tart flavor brought back memories of being sixteen and getting a buzz from illegally obtained liquor with my friends of the time. "It has to be more than that," I said. "You don't just pick up a heroin habit because your sister has one."

"We're unpredictable about those things," she said. She began to fidget with a lock of her hair, rolling it up on a finger and then unrolling. "Cindy and I used to share men. She called it the Salami Swap. One of us would get a boyfriend and we'd change places in the middle of the night. I already know it was wrong, so don't be shocked."

"I'm not."

"And don't judge."

"I was a cop for twenty-five years," I said. "I did the arresting, not the judging."

Karen took a sip of her beer and set it back down. "How old are you?"

"Fifty-three."

"I'm forty," she said. "Younger than your wife."

"Ex-wife."

"Oh, right," she said. "Cindy said that she left you."

"Yes," I said. "We spoke earlier today. She told me that she misses being married."

"Really? How does that make you feel?"

"Like I need another beer," I said.

"I was married once. It lasted two months."

"That sounds like the short version of a long story."

"This is all the beer I have," she said. "There's a decent bar down the block."

"Let's go, then."

Karen Charbonneau tossed her empty bottle into a recycling bucket twenty feet away. It landed exactly in the middle with a tinkle of breaking glass.

"Three-pointer," I said.

"I like you, Vince," she said. "If we're going to be drinking, you and the dog can stay here. I'll tell you what I can, because I want to help you. But I'm not going to bed with you, just so you know. I'm done with being an addict."

"Your sister said the same thing," I said. "I must be losing my touch."

*

After two pints of Lost Nation IPA I knew a lot more about the Charbonneau sisters, and slightly more about Grace Hebert.

Karen and Cindy had spent their girlhood in a world of their own: always together and shutting out everyone else. It was safe that way. They trusted no one, and the only thing that they needed was each other's company. And then puberty arrived, as if the UPS truck had come up the driveway and dropped off a big, nonreturnable box of snakes. The man-sharing episodes were mild in comparison to some of the things Karen confessed to over our beers and enough chicken wings to count as dinner. We sat in a corner booth at Moog's Place, a down-home bar with a stage but no music, because it was a Sunday. It was my kind of joint: unpretentious, good food, and loud enough to be able to talk without the next table listening in.

The high school boyfriend swapping had evolved into a long series of ménages à trois. The twins didn't have to peruse the classifieds, much less run an ad: all it took was a visit to the nearest bar, a brief selection process, and off they would go with their mark, some of whom were married and some not, but all highly willing to participate. Lots of men fantasize about the three-way thing, but I'm not among them. I prefer to screw up my relationships one at a time.

Things had deteriorated quickly when Cindy's broken ankle started the pill habit, which became the smack habit. I asked Karen: how she had allowed herself to be drawn into that?

"You don't get it, do you?"

"No," I said, because I didn't.

"If Cindy gets a headache, I do too. That's how we are. We're a matched pair, like dueling pistols. It got really, really bad, Vince. I would be dead a long time ago if it wasn't for Clement."

I call the third beer the Pint of Truth, because it's the one when your tongue is the loosest, and is also the last one before you start making little or no sense. We were halfway through number three, and Karen had finally stopped twirling her hair in her fingers. "I want to know something," I said.

"What?"

"Why did you tell me to ask Grace's mother where she would be? You said that in your office the other day."

She looked down into her glass. "Carmela gets money. Money to stay quiet."

"From who?"

"Grace's sugar daddy. Grace told me about it, last spring, when we were doing the Brecht play and she was the prostitute. She said that she was living the part. But I can't tell you who it is. I swore to her that I wouldn't."

"I already know," I said. "Angus Driscoll."

"What?" she said. "I mean—how?"

"How did I find out? This is what I do, remember?"

"It's why I'm so worried," Karen said. "Clement doesn't know about this."

"You're worried because of what?"

"Because of what happened to Donald," she said. "My theory is that Driscoll found out that Donald and Grace were lovers, and he was jealous. Guys like him think they own people. Plus, his own daughter was being cheated on."

"I'm with you, so far," I said. "Do you have a theory on Matty?"

"The mechanic? I thought they said he killed himself."

"Maybe."

"You mean, maybe not?"

"Did you ever meet him?"

"No," she said.

"Grace never talked about him?"

"No."

"He was killed with Clement's gun," I said. "Grace had it last, as far as I can tell. It was at the crime scene. Lussen's cabin."

Karen shuddered. "And you think that someone killed him, and then made it look like a suicide?"

"Yes." I finished off my third pint. That would put me at around a point-oh-six, and if I ordered another I would be staying the night. I wasn't too comfortable with that, even though Karen Charbonneau's blonde hair and green eyes had taken on a glow that you didn't need three beers to appreciate. She was not only pretty, she was leaning her face about ten inches from mine, and our knees were brushing each other's under the table. It was the closest thing to intimacy that I'd experienced since my wife had checked out. Time to go home.

"It could have been Grace," Karen said.

"What?"

"You said it was her gun, right?"

"Yes, but—"

"A couple of weeks ago. Clement got her drunk. He likes to do that, even though he's sober himself."

"Lila told me that," I said. "The night we had dinner at his house."

"I don't know why he did it, but he got her shitfaced. And she pulled the gun on him. The big one that he lent her. It was loaded, and we were sitting around the dinner table, and she scared the hell out of all of us."

"So what happened?"

"She was aiming it at him with one eye closed like she was about to pull the trigger. And then she starts laughing, and she puts the gun away. Clement was so mad I thought he was going to thrash her, but he's a complete fool for her. He pretty much does what she says."

"Cindy said that too."

"You see what I mean about twins?"

"I have to go," I said. "I don't have any food for the dog. I'm a complete fool for him, and I pretty much do what he says."

Karen Charbonneau's smile made the room feel like someone had thrown a fresh log onto the fire. I liked her. After two marriages I hadn't been thinking about women, or relationships, or any of that crap. My bachelor life was going just fine, thank you, and Royal gave me all the hugs and cuddles that anyone could possibly want. But he was a baby, not a woman who was smart, who seemed to like me, and who had closed the ten-inch gap between our faces to five.

"I'm not going to sleep with you," she said.

"You said that already."

"She might have killed Matty, but—"

"But what?"

"Nothing," she said. "Let's go." She got up from the table and summoned the waitress. We paid the bill and walked out into the night, not talking.

"You need to finish your sentence," I said as we got to her door.

"You need to get your dog," she said. She put her arms around my neck and pulled me to her. We kissed for a long time—long enough for me to want to stay, but I had already made up my mind.

I followed her upstairs and fetched Chan. Karen and I mumbled goodbyes, and I left with the dog. We were halfway to the interstate when he sat up in the back seat and I caught his expression in the mirror.

"Don't even," I said.

You're smarter than you look, Tanzi.

"I could be in bed with her right now," I said. "But instead, here I am with man's best friend."

*

I thought about calling John Pallmeister on the way home, but that was illegal, plus I had a buzz, plus it was a Sunday night, and there was nothing about what I had learned that couldn't wait until the morning. Maybe Karen Charbonneau was right, and Angus Driscoll had killed Donald Lussen in a jealous rage. Or, he had somebody do it for him.

And worse, maybe she was right about Grace. There might have been some unknown conflict between Grace and Matty, and she could have lured the mechanic to Lussen's cabin, although I had a hard time thinking of her as a killer. I wasn't ready to pass any of this on to

Pallmeister, although I would press the lieutenant for more details on Angus Driscoll. I believed Pallmeister when he'd said that he wasn't in anyone's pocket. He was a straight arrow, like ninety-nine percent of Vermont cops. The police force of any given area reflects the population, and Vermonters are an honest, no-bullshit group. There isn't a lot of crime up here, or even sleaze, and if Angus Driscoll was rotten and I could convince my State Police friend that he was, John Pallmeister would be relentless. He would track him down and would solve at least the first of the homicides.

My phone buzzed shortly after I turned off at the Barre exit, and I broke the law and answered it.

"Sneaky little so-and-so, your runaway," Robert Patton said, "but we found her."

"Really? Fill me in."

"Burlington to JFK last night with a fake ID," he said. "Our software ran a photo cross-reference on her Vermont driver's license picture. Pretty good job on the fake. It was a West Virginia license, same photograph, but she calls herself Lucinda Kardos."

"And then she connected to London, right?"

"She'd need a passport for that," Patton said. "Are you in your car? You sound like you've had a few beers."

"I'm good," I said.

"Don't kill anybody, OK?"

"So where is she?"

"You'll like this," he said. "She connected to West Palm Beach, not London."

"Really?"

"It gets better," Patton said. "I was able to have someone at the airport. My agent followed her to her hotel. Your girl checked in under the fake ID and paid cash."

"Checked in where?"

"The Breakers," Robert Patton said. "Way too fancy for a bum like you."

"I'll wear my cleanest T-shirt," I said. "Can your people watch her until I get there?"

"Yes, but don't dick around. This is on the taxpayer's dollar," Patton said. "We're Homeland Security, not your personal babysitting service."

"If I find her, you'll have one less nut job to worry about."

"Her?"

"Not her," I said. "Me."

MONDAY

I RENTED A PRIUS AT the West Palm airport and drove to the beach. I would pull into the Breakers, toss the keys to the valet, and strut into the place like a rock star, except that I didn't have anything approaching a clean shirt: I was wearing the same one that I'd worn for the last three days, and I hadn't bothered to shave. I would be lucky to get past the lobby.

It was just after noon, and I'd had the farthest-back row to myself on the flight from New York after connecting from Burlington. Chan was at my mother's until I decided what to do with him. I was leaning toward adoption, although I've never owned a dog. Whenever Royal was at Barbara's, it was damn quiet in my house. It might be nice to have another living creature around, even if the creature had a major attitude.

A few hours of flying had given me time to think about where all of this was going. I would meet Grace Hebert, we would have a talk, and my work would be complete. She wasn't missing anymore. I would confirm that she was OK, and I would report back to her grandmother. Done. *Finito.*

Except that two people in Grace's immediate circle had recently met with violent deaths. I had to entertain the possibility that Grace wasn't just a mixed-up kid with a drug problem and a bunch of old men chasing her. Karen's description of the dinner table scene with the gun didn't sound very good. It was possible that Grace had killed Matty, for whatever reason. She was the last person in possession of the Ruger .44 magnum, as far as I knew. She could also have lured Donald Lussen to the water tower and shot him with the bow. The homicide investigations were John Pallmeister's problem, but they were mine too, because as much as I might like to report in to Mrs. T that I had found her granddaughter and then slide back into my life with Royal, it might not be that simple, and I finish what I start.

I also wanted to see Karen Charbonneau again, at least one more time, because something had started there, too. Not that it would go any further, of course. Like, beyond the long, slow kiss that had lingered with me all the way back to my mother's house…and through a few hours of toss-and-turn sleep…and the drive up to Burlington…and the entire frigging plane trip to Florida. No, that couldn't possibly be it. I just wanted to make sure that Karen was going to be all right. It was a good thing that Chan wasn't with me now, because he would have had something to say about that.

The valet took my car, because a tip was a tip after all. And nobody gave me the sniff-test as I entered the Italian Renaissance-styled hotel that had been built back in the day when Palm Beach was the winter playground of the Astors and the Vanderbilts. The Breakers is a Florida version of the grand palaces of Europe: ornate ceilings, fabulous stonework, spectacular grounds, oceanfront golf course, pools, and everything else that might make you feel that you had turned back the clock to a more glamorous era when you could see F. Scott and Zelda arriving in their Stutz Bearcat, high on champagne and trading witty remarks.

No Fitzgeralds were in attendance today. I was in a line behind four guys in golf clothes and a European family with three whirling-dervish children, waiting our turn while an elderly couple was holding everything up at the check-in desk. Robert Patton's babysitter hadn't contacted me yet, so I had decided to press ahead and see if I could finesse Lucinda Kardos' room number from a reception clerk.

Someone tapped me on the shoulder. "Vince?"

"Rose?" Rose DiNapoli stood in front of me, dressed in tennis shorts with a white polo top. She held a water bottle in one hand and a racquet in the other. "What are you doing here?"

"Watching over your friend," she said. "Patton got me the gig. I just played two sets with her, and we're going to change and meet at the pool."

"Does she know who you are?"

"Sort of," she said. Rose was a U.S. Customs agent I had met on a case around the same time that my marriage to Barbara was falling apart. She was my age, cute, and Italian American, with curly black hair. We had enjoyed each other's company—a lot—but I'd gone into my shell shortly afterward. This was the first time that I'd seen her in over a year. "She knows you're coming. She's OK with talking to you. I didn't tell her who I worked for, because I didn't want to scare her."

"How did you do all that?"

"I chatted her up over breakfast," Rose said. "We're friends now. She's a good kid. Messed up, though. You have your work cut out for you if you're trying to straighten her out."

"I know."

"You need a shower," she said. "Let's go up to my room, and then we'll find you a bathing suit. It's going to be a beautiful afternoon."

"I'm not here for fun," I said.

"Excuse me? This is the Breakers, dude. Let's enjoy it. Patton got me comped for the room, and you and I are going to order expensive drinks and go swimming with your young lady, who's quite the hottie, by the way. You can question her and do all your shit, and then you and I will return to our boring little lives, *capisce?*"

If Rose had already set things in motion, this would be a lot easier than I'd thought. Maybe I could relax a little. It sure was nice to be back in Florida, with the temperature in the eighties and the opulent surroundings. I would have a poolside beverage with Grace Hebert and debrief her, and then everyone would be happy again. Except for the two people who were dead.

"Lead on," I said. I was glad to see Rose and to be near my home, but I was worried about why things appeared to be going so smoothly. That was never a good sign.

*

Half an hour later I was dressed in a too-tight pair of swim trunks that Rose had gleaned from the lost and found. I borrowed a terrycloth hotel robe to cover up the rest of me and wore the sneakers that I'd packed for Vermont. I felt laughably conspicuous, but once we got to the pool area I realized that everybody else looked just as silly and I should just chill. This wasn't going to be a normal interview anyway. All that I had seen of Grace since I'd started looking for her was her undressed form in Clement Goody's basement, so I had no idea how I was going to play this, but I had the suspicion that any discussion between us would be on her terms, not mine.

Rose walked a few paces ahead of me with a bounce in her step. We wound along pathways and across terraces to the South Pool, which abutted the ocean and was mostly deserted except for a bartender and a few sun-seekers scattered about on chaises. The day was balmy with a light breeze coming off the ocean, and this was not feeling at all like work. But it was, and as much as I tried to go with the bathing suit, relax-by-the-pool idea, it felt wrong. I wanted to go back to Rose's suite, put on my clothes, collar Grace Hebert, and grill her in a small room. That wasn't going to happen, because I wasn't a cop, and she wasn't being held for anything, so all I could do was go along with Rose's set-up and hope that Grace would answer my questions.

I spotted Grace lying face down on a padded chaise with the top of her bikini unclasped. Her young body was so untroubled by age, sun, and cellulite that it looked photoshopped. She saw us coming, reattached the bra strap, and signaled the bartender, who came running. Twenty-one years old and she was already bossing around the help.

"Hello you two," she said as we approached. "Drinks? Any specials, Jimmy?"

"I make a killer Negroni, Miss Kardos," the man said. He had the deep tan and sun-bleached hair of a lifeguard.

"Three Negronis?" Grace said, looking at us.

"Two," I said, taking a seat at a teak table next to Grace's chaise. "Iced tea for me."

"Cuba Libre," Rose said. "And something to munch on."

The waiter disappeared. "So you're a regular at this place?" I said.

"Not really."

"How often—"

She cut me off. "I appreciate what you do for my grandmother, Mr. Tanzi. I love her a lot, you know."

"She's a lovable person."

"She adores you." She stood up from the chaise and wrapped a sheer blue cover-up around her bikini.

"She's very concerned about you," I said. "That's why I'm here."

Rose DiNapoli took off her hotel robe and draped it over one of the chairs at the table. "I'm going to get a quick swim," she said. "You two go ahead and talk."

"Have a seat," I said to Grace. She ignored me, walked over to the bar, and came back with a small bowl of macadamia nuts.

"Starving," she said. Meaning: I'll sit when I'm ready to sit, not when you tell me to. "There's nothing to worry about, Vince. I'm fine. Please tell her that."

"Maybe you should tell her that."

"It wouldn't carry the same weight."

"What if I didn't believe that you were fine?"

"Then don't," she said, looking straight at me. Her dark eyes reminded me of her grandmother, except they lacked the softness. She was ready to do battle, and the relaxed, drinks-by-the-pool thing was history.

"Karen and Cindy say you're using again."

"Don't listen to them," she said. "They're actresses."

"Were you and Matty lovers?"

"Weren't you supposed to be nice to me? Rose said you had a couple of questions. She promised me that you wouldn't be a jerk."

"I don't believe that Matty killed himself," I said. "Do you?"

Jimmy the bartender arrived with our drinks, and Grace signed the chit. Rose DiNapoli was doing a leisurely crawl in the pool near us with her head out of the water so that she could listen. I took a sip of my iced tea.

"You don't have an answer?" I said.

"Not right now."

"Please thank Angus for the drinks," I said. "He has to be feeling pretty good with Donald out of the picture."

Grace glared across the table. "You're so wrong about that. You don't know Angus."

She was right—I was pushing too hard, too fast. But the whole thing was pissing me off, because even though I was sitting right in front of her, the truth was a million miles away.

"Let's back up for a minute," I said. "Why did you sneak up on me that afternoon? On Prospect Rock?"

"That wasn't me."

"Yes it was, Grace. And I don't care about being assaulted. I just want to know why you did it. There's no need to lie."

She took a sip of her drink and looked out over the Atlantic. "You have no idea what you're dealing with here."

"Donald called you after I left his office, right? And you panicked, because you'd been getting death threats."

"How do you know that?" she said. "No, of course you do."

"There's too much that I don't know, and it bothers me. I don't know who killed Lussen or Matty."

"Neither do I."

"You're the common denominator."

"What do you mean? You think I did it?"

"No," I said, although I hadn't ruled her out, but I wasn't going to go there. "I'm worried for the same reasons that your grandmother is. You're a heroin addict, and whether or not you're using at the moment isn't the point. Addiction is addiction, and you're not dealing with it. Instead, you're fooling around with two guys who are fifty years older than you are, because they're rich and powerful. You're under their sway. You should be in college, dating men your age and learning things from smart people like Karen, but instead you're in deep shit, and two people who you cared about have died in the past week."

"Is that the end of the lecture?" she said. "Because the answer is the same. I don't know who killed either of them. So fuck off."

"Your gun was in Matty's mouth."

"That's not possible."

"Why?"

"Because Angus has it," she said. "He takes care of everything. Too bad he's not here yet, because he'd swat you like a fly."

"Don't be a punk," I said. "You can't survive forever on being pretty. I think that you're very unhappy, and you're scared too, because who wouldn't be? So stop dodging me. And if you have any respect for your grandmother, you're going to come with us and we'll get you some help. If you tell me that you're not scared and not sick of all the craziness, I'll leave you alone. But I can't believe that you're sleeping with Driscoll because it's your goal in life."

I had worked up a pretty good head of steam, and I was hoping that I hadn't gone too far. Something had to be done. For all of Grace Hebert's toughness she was still a goddamn kid, and people were taking advantage of her. I couldn't stand it any longer, and I'd sounded off. Rose DiNapoli was getting out of the pool and had no doubt heard everything because she was shaking her head as she approached as if I had completely screwed this up.

"For god's sake Vince—" she began, but Grace cut her off.

"No," Grace said to both of us. "You're right, I'm scared. But you have to leave now. I have nothing more to say."

"Grace—" Rose began, but the young woman got up from the table and walked down a flight of steps to the beach. She waded past the small waves near the shore and dived into the warm water, swimming toward the horizon.

"I just love to watch a pro at work," Rose said.

"That went better than it sounded. She's just not ready yet."

"So we're done here?"

"For now," I said. "Drink your drink."

I walked over to the bar and got a piece of paper and a pencil from Jimmy. I wrote down my cell number and left it on the table for Grace. Sooner or later she would call, because she wasn't ready now, but she was close, and she was the kind of person who had to do this on her own terms. In the meantime I had learned several things, not the least of which was that Grace's sugar daddy was coming to West Palm. I couldn't wait to see him.

*

I checked in with Robert Patton, who had enough pull with the hotel management to arrange another night's free stay, for which Rose bravely volunteered. John Pallmeister was also in the loop, as I had caught him up on everything during a half-hour cell conversation. He was intrigued by Grace's mention of the gun that had killed Matty being in Angus Driscoll's possession. It wasn't. The State Police had it, and they would for a while. Meanwhile he promised to personally check in with Clement Goody, who owned the weapon, to see if he knew anything.

Patton found Driscoll's name on a flight manifest that would put him in West Palm later in the afternoon. Rose invited me to stay at the hotel for dinner, but you could buy a week's worth of groceries for what you paid for a salad there, and Vero Beach was only an hour-and-a-half-drive north. I called Barbara, explained what was going on, and arranged to pick up Royal for the evening. I would feed him, get in some playtime, and then take him back to Barbara's, because I planned to be back at the hotel by breakfast. Forget Angus Driscoll: I could hardly wait to see my son.

*

Barbara met me at the door of her bungalow in full babe regalia: a soft pink top that outlined her shape and left no doubt as to her gender, skin-tight blue jeans, sandals with low heels, and carefully applied makeup. She gave me a dazzling smile of the kind usually reserved for somebody she wanted to charm, like the elderly male judge who had presided over our split-up.

"You must have a date," I said as she let me in. I stood far enough from her so that there was no chance that we would touch, much less embrace. It could be a dance step: the post-divorce dosey-doe.

"No, just home alone," she said. "I thought I'd treat myself to some oysters."

"You bought oysters?" Barbara had never been that fond of them as far as I knew.

"Yes, and I got way too many. You're welcome to stay for supper if you like."

Uh-oh. Something was going on here, and I didn't think that it was me being irresistible. "Is everything OK?"

"I guess."

"Where's Royal?"

"Still in his crib," she said. "We went shopping and I wore him out. You can stay. I'll make you a drink."

"I'm taking it easy on the drinking," I said. That is, I hadn't had a drop since the three pints that I'd cheerfully pounded down with Karen Charbonneau less than twenty-four hours ago.

"I'll fix you something, babe."

"No thanks," I said. "Don't worry about it. I can run some errands and come back when he's awake."

"Am I that awful, Vince?"

I looked around the living room of Barbara's small house. Some of the furnishings were things that she and I had bought during our time together. Some were new, or were borrowed from her friends. None of it looked comfortable. "I'm still working on this case," I said.

"Tonight? I thought the girl was in Palm Beach."

"I may get a call at any time. I'll just run some chores. I can't tell you how much I appreciate your doing all this."

I heard Royal's familiar cry coming from his bedroom. I opened his door, plucked him out of his crib, and held him to my chest. "Dada!" he squealed as he rubbed the sleep from his eyes, and for the first time in a week everything was good with the world.

My former wife was in the kitchen, carefully layering the oysters into a plastic container. She put it into Royal's diaper bag along with his essentials. "Enjoy," she said. "I know you love them."

"Thank you," I said, and I took my son out to the car.

*

Royal and I had played all of our favorite baby games, and I'd dropped him back at Barbara's and ran before I could be drawn into another conversation. I put away his toys, cleaned up, and took the oyster shells out to the garage so that they wouldn't stink up the kitchen. The smart thing to do now was to go to bed—my own bed, which would be very welcome after six nights on the road. In the morning I would shower, shave, dress in fresh clothes that were appropriate for the swanky hotel, meet up with Rose, and start over with Grace Hebert if I hadn't completely alienated her.

I didn't think that I had, because I'd seen more than a glimmer of fear in those dark eyes. Grace was a cool customer, but Matthew Harmony's death and Donald Lussen's murder had to have upended her world. When things like that happen you look for a rock: someone who can protect you. So, Grace had flown to Florida on Angus Driscoll's dime, and theoretically, he was going to protect her. Clement Goody could have done the same, but he and Grace were seemingly on the outs right now, and Driscoll was the rock.

The flaw in that plan was that both of them wanted to screw her. My strategy was to position myself as the better way out. I was connected to her grandmother, I would encourage her recovery and treatment, and I wasn't trying to get her in bed. I was offering a way to put this behind her and fix what had gone wrong in her life, even though I'd partially lost my temper while doing it. But Grace was from Barre, and she knew about tempers. We Italian Americans can get overexcited when we're trying to make a point, and the point that I was making was that I cared about her. I hoped that she would get the message and that my cellphone would ring before this got any worse.

I called my mother to check on her and the dog. They were getting along fine, according to her. I ran a load of clothes in the laundry, opened the mail, paid some bills, turned on the radio, turned it off again after the fifteenth car dealership ad in a row, checked my email, and I was about to start cleaning out the fridge when I realized that it was almost midnight and I was wide awake because I couldn't turn my brain off. There was just too much going on.

I sat in my recliner and tried to break it down:

My ex-wife was coming on to me, which was awkward and needed to be handled delicately if we were going to successfully co-parent our son.

Grace Hebert was shacked up with her seventy-year-old lover in a luxury hotel, and I hoped that she was considering what I'd said to her by the pool.

And last but not least, I was thinking about Karen Charbonneau's mouth covering mine, right around this time the previous night. Damn. Maybe I wouldn't be getting any sleep at all.

My phone buzzed on the glass table next to my chair.

Everything OK?

I didn't recognize the number. *Who is this?*

Karen.

I was just thinking about you.

Good thoughts?

Ha. How did you get my number?
From Cindy. She says you're in Florida.

Caught at my own game. Cindy Charbonneau had installed something on my cellphone, and I'd forgotten about it, but she hadn't. Too bad it was so late in the night, or I would call Roberto and have him remove it.

No privacy in this world, I wrote.

OMG I'm so sorry, Karen sent back.

I didn't mean it that way, I wrote. *I'm glad you got in touch.*

Really?

Yes.

I miss you, she wrote.

I didn't write anything back for a minute, and I must have waited too long, because she fired off three more texts in a row:

OMG

I just made a complete ass of myself, didn't I?

I can't believe I texted u. U must think I'm a total stalker.

Rather than keeping up the text dialogue, I dialed her, which is a known breach of texting protocol, but I was too wiped out to focus on the tiny screen and my fat fingers could no longer find the keys.

"Hello?" she said, as if she wasn't sure who had called her.

"It's Vince."

"Oh no," she said. "You're mad at me, aren't you?"

"Not at all," I said. "It's been a long day, and this is a nice way to finish it."

Karen said nothing, and I listened to the faint sound of static on the line, mixed with her breathing. Finally, she spoke. "You could have stayed here last night."

"You said you didn't want to sleep with me. No more addictive behavior."

"That was the reason you left?"

"I had to feed Chan," I said. "And…"

"And what?"

"I'm damaged goods, Karen. My wife left me because of it. I'm not really boyfriend material."

"You mean, you can't—"

"I can have a sex life, if that's what you're asking. I'm just—a slowed down version of myself. I limp, I screw up, and I'm not who I used to be. I was a pretty good husband to my first wife, for the most part, but I failed Barbara."

"Or she failed you?"

"She did some things, yes."

"Vince," Karen said. "Suppose someone met you, and they didn't know the old you, but they liked you for the way you are now."

"They'd be getting shortchanged."

"Oh my god, you really are a project."

"I found Grace," I said. "She's shacked up in a hotel in Palm Beach with Angus Driscoll. I met with her this afternoon."

"Is she coming back?"

"I don't know yet."

"So where do you go from here?"

"I'm not sure," I said. "Ideally, I would get her to Vermont and put her in rehab."

"Would you bring her back yourself?"

"Probably," I said. "I also need to deal with the dog."

"I want that to happen," Karen said.

"You do?"

"Yes," she said. "I'd like to see you again. I could use a project."

TUESDAY

AT FIRST I THOUGHT IT was Chan barking, although as I rose from my bed I remembered that he was in Vermont. Then I thought it must be the alarm that I'd set for five AM. It was neither—my doorbell was ringing.

I pulled on a pair of sweatpants and looked out the kitchen window. A white Mercedes sedan was idling in the driveway with no one inside. My doorbell continued to ring, and I opened it without bothering to look through the peephole, which is the kind of bad decision that you might make at three in the morning.

Fish Falzarano stood at the threshold, dressed in a black shirt and slacks. His eyes were set so far apart that I had to choose which one to look at. "What are you—" I began, but he stepped forward and punched me in the stomach before I could react. His fist must have grazed a lower rib, because I felt a combination of instant, breathless nausea and searing pain. I fell onto the floor tiles, gasping for breath. The moment my wind came back I drew in as much air as I could, but the room exploded into a burst of light, and I knew that I was losing consciousness.

"Where is she?" I heard him yell, although I could no longer see him.

"Who?"

He leaned down and grabbed me by the front of my T-shirt and shook it. "Don't fuck with me, Tanzi," he said. "She told Driscoll she was leaving with you."

"Know...nothing...about that," I said, trying to get air into my lungs. "I left her at the hotel."

Fish shook me again, but that was the end of our conversation, because the white light was going dark. He released his grip from my shirt. "Useless piece of shit," he said, just before I passed out.

*

I didn't call in the assault, even though I could have. Fish's prints were all over my house seeing how he'd opened every door, pulled the clothes out of the closets, and even scattered Royal's toys around while I lay on the floor of the entryway. The place had been trashed, along with the owner. I'd regained consciousness after he left, heaved whatever was in my stomach into the toilet bowl, and had gone back to bed for a couple hours of sleep, punctuated by my labored breathing. He had definitely bruised a rib. But there was no need to sic the authorities on him, because sooner or later I would pick my spot and I would blindside him like he'd done to me. It's always nice to have something to look forward to.

I called Rose at six AM to tell her that breakfast wasn't going to happen because I could barely rise from my bed. She found out from the hotel staff that Grace had taken a cab to the airport while Angus Driscoll was dining alone. Grace must have made some kind of excuse and slipped away. She also must have said that she was "leaving with me," which was encouraging but wasn't true, because I had heard nothing from her, and she had my cell number. If she had decided that I was her best option, I couldn't understand why she had taken a flight out, although even that was in question. Rose said that Patton's team hadn't found her on any of the outgoing flight manifests.

The day had only begun and already someone had beaten the crap out of me, and the woman who I'd been pursuing for a full week had disappeared once again. I thought about making breakfast, but my stomach hurt too much to consider it even though I needed the food. I needed more sleep, too. Most of all, I needed a break.

You make your own breaks, Chan would have said. I wished that he were here. I started thinking about how I might transport him to Florida if I were to adopt him. Flying in the cargo hold of a commercial jet would freak him out, and he would never let me live that down. It was a twenty-four-hour drive from Barre to Vero, and I couldn't risk a trip that long because of the whiteouts. Bus? I didn't think that they allowed animals. Private jet? Way too expensive. Those things were for the Angus Driscolls and the Clement Goodys of the world.

Private jet...

I called Rose DiNapoli. "Did you speak with the cab company directly? The one who picked up Grace?"

"No, I got it from the front desk," she said. "They said she asked the concierge for a car to the airport."

"Which airport?"

Rose said nothing. I figured that her silence meant that she understood where I was going with this. "I didn't ask," she finally said. "Damn."

"North Palm Beach," I said. "That's where most of the private flights go."

"Right."

"Let me know what you find out, OK?"

"I'm sorry, Vince. I shouldn't have assumed—"

"Forget about it," I said. "We'll find her."

*

I'd had to lie down again because I was feeling worthless after being beaten up and getting next to no sleep. My lower rib cage ached, and my ego was sorely bruised after being sucker punched by Fish Falzarano. All I could do now was to wait until Patton or Rose got back to me with Grace's potential whereabouts, and I wasn't motivated to do anything except lie back in the recliner and hope that the phone would ring. The sooner the better, because I sensed that Grace Hebert was in full crisis mode. Somehow she had telegraphed to Angus Driscoll that she was going to accept my offer to help straighten her out. And then she'd disappeared, leaving him alone at the dinner table with his forty-dollar Brussels sprouts. Grace had said enough to make Angus send Fish Falzarano all the way to Vero to rough me up, but Fish hadn't learned anything from me except that I was asleep enough to open a door to a stranger in the middle of the night.

My phone vibrated with a text from Roberto. *You're back? Saw a car in your driveway.*

Yes, I answered. *But I'm a little under the weather.*

Flu?

Somebody beat me up.

Impossible, he wrote.

I'm not Superman.

I'm done after this class. Pick me up in ten, OK?

I didn't want to contribute to Roberto's truancy, but he was a student at St. Edwards, and they didn't screw around at that school. If they allowed him to leave early, then it was probably all right. I went into my bathroom, took a five-minute shower and ran a razor across my face. I dressed in fresh clothes from my closet and brushed my teeth. All of this would make me a few minutes late for Roberto, but he would be cool with it, and I was tired of smelling like something in the refrigerator that needed to be thrown out.

Roberto stood at the curb in front of his school. I hadn't seen him for a week, and it seemed like he'd grown an inch taller. Perhaps he had. Boys his age can become men while you're not paying attention.

"Dude," he said, as he got into the Prius. "This is a rental, I hope?"

"Nah, I sold the BMW," I said. "I went all crunchy granola up in Vermont."

Roberto did a double take until he realized that I was kidding. No way would I give up the convertible that was waiting for me at the Orlando airport where I'd left it before my trip north.

"Don't scare me like that," he said, and we both laughed. Next to Royal, Roberto Arguelles was my favorite person in the universe. "Give me your cell and I'll fix it. So who beat you up?"

I filled him in at length on the events of the last several days. I talked the whole way back to my house, while he listened and simultaneously removed Cindy Charbonneau's tracking app from my phone. Roberto doesn't say a lot, but it's not that he's distracted. He's listening, parsing, analyzing, and then offering me suggestions, and sometimes, encouragement. It made a nice change from the grief that I'd been taking from Chan.

"Why don't you believe that Matty committed suicide?" he said as we pulled into my driveway.

"It didn't feel right," I said. "I met him, twice."

"Then why would someone kill him?"

"I don't know yet. It could have been Angus Driscoll. Driscoll might have killed Lussen, and then set up Matty. Somebody planted the bow in his shop, because Matty had no reason to own it. He didn't hunt."

"Where do you think the girl went to?"

"Grace? I don't know. I was hoping that she would call me and ask for my help. She needs it."

Roberto and I got out of the car and entered my house. He took a container of orange juice from the fridge and poured each of us a serving. We sat at our usual seats at the kitchen counter, and I stared at my glass while he drained his. Roberto was very quiet, but I could tell that he was giving me the once-over. "You look different," he said.

"You look taller."

"Are you sick? You're really pale."

"I might have a broken rib. Other than that, I'm just ducky." Which wasn't entirely true, because the inside of my house had suddenly taken on a bright sheen. The kitchen glowed like an overexposed photograph, and Roberto's form was backlit as if he had been charged with electricity.

"Vince? Are you OK?"

The phone rang, but I couldn't get out of my chair to answer it. In fact, I couldn't move at all. Roberto rushed to my side and attempted to prop me up, which was good, because without him I would have been on the floor.

The message machine amplified the call: *Vince? Hey, it's Rose, and you were right. There was a flight out of North Palm that went to Vermont. A private jet chartered by some group called the New Commitment Society. Does that help at all? Call me, will you?*

The room began to spin and I grabbed the edge of the counter, but I was in the lead car of a roller coaster and there was no getting off. "Clement Goody," I said to Roberto, slurring the name. My chair toppled and we both crashed down. I was about to pass out again, and in my remaining split second of consciousness I knew that this was another goddamned whiteout. It would be the last one. I was done with them.

*

"There's quite a crowd in the waiting area," the doctor said. He was tall and slender with skin the color of nutmeg. I read the tag on his lapel, which had been elongated to accommodate his surname. He peered into my eyes with a small flashlight and hummed a few notes now and then as if he was remembering every other line of a song. "Your former wife, your son, the boy who called the ambulance, his parents, and a woman who said she is your associate. I just went out and spoke with them."

"What did you tell them?"

"The same thing I'm going to tell you. You're not in any immediate danger, but you need another surgery. We took scans while you were unconscious, and I shared them with Dr. Jaffe in Vermont."

"What did she say?"

"She agrees with my diagnosis. There's a bone fragment that has moved. It's not in a good place, and it's probably the reason you lost consciousness. Has that happened to you before?"

It was time to confess, seeing how they had already decided that I would be going under the knife. "Yes. It's happened a few times, starting a couple of months ago."

"Really? I though that Dr. Jaffe just examined you."

"I didn't bring it up."

He gave me a disapproving look. "You survived a traumatic brain injury, Mr. Tanzi. You know how cats have nine lives?"

"Yes?"

"You've used up eight. Don't be disingenuous with people who want to help you. You don't have that luxury."

"I don't have time for surgery," I said. "I'm in the middle of a case."

"Does it involve leaving your house? Driving?"

"Probably."

"You can't drive. You could put off the surgery for a week or two, although you might experience more seizures. I'm going to release you on the condition that you go home and take it easy. Dr. Jaffe wants to do the procedure in Vermont if you're willing to travel."

"I am."

"Schedule it with her. You'll need a companion for the trip."

"I can arrange that," I said, although I had no idea who I would ask.

"I'll call a nurse to remove your IV and you can get dressed. I'm quite serious about the driving, sir. I can have your license pulled."

"No need," I said. "I used to be a deputy sheriff. I understand what you're saying."

"I wish you well with the surgery, Mr. Tanzi."

"Thanks, Dr. Kalanadhabhatla," I said.

He arched his eyebrows. "How did you do that? Everybody calls me Dr. K."

"I don't know," I said.

*

My entourage took me back to the house by caravan, and I shooed them all away when we got there, except for Rose DiNapoli, who wouldn't be shooed. She had called Robert Patton, and he'd "assigned" her to me, as she described it. I wondered how Patton would justify the expense of a customs agent's time, hotel bills, and everything else that he had had done to help me in my pursuit of Grace Hebert. There was nothing in it for Homeland Security, and someone had to be looking over his budgetary shoulder. I appreciated the help, and I hoped that it wouldn't land him in trouble, but I figured he'd been with the Border Patrol for years and he knew the back alleys.

Rose was looking through the barren wasteland that was my refrigerator. "There's nothing in here," she said. She left me in my recliner and came back an hour later with an armload of groceries. I helped her, but I felt like I was moving in slow motion, and I found myself staring at the labeling of whatever I was putting away. I held up a bag of crackers: *Thiamin mononitrate. Monocalcium phosphate. Ammonium bicarbonate.*

"Do you want some of those?" Rose asked me.

"What?"

"The goldfish crackers. You look like you're going to eat the package."

"I'm not hungry," I said. Rose shook her head and continued to put things away. I gave up on helping her. I was just getting in her way. I went back to my chair and picked up the paper, but I got stuck on the weather report. *Negative vorticity advection.*

"Where's your salad spinner?" Rose said from the kitchen.

"I don't have one."

She came around the corner. "Everyone has a salad spinner."

"Not me."

"Are you all right?"

"I'm fine." I thought about what Dr. K had said about being disingenuous with people who were trying to help me, and here I was doing it all over again. I wasn't fine. I felt light-headed, slightly nauseous, and I couldn't stop obsessing about small things that meant nothing. Fish Falzarano had messed me up good. But I had had enough doctoring for one day, and as much as I wanted to be honest with Rose, I couldn't. I needed to tough it out and finish this job. As soon as Grace Hebert was located and stashed in a treatment facility, I would blab about my troubles to anyone who listened, and the doctors were welcome to open my head and take out whatever they wanted.

"The jet flew to Burlington," she said. "Just the pilots and Goody on the flight record."

"How hard is it to alter that? Grace had to be onboard."

"It's not impossible. In fact, it's pretty loosey goosey in some places, particularly when the flight gets in at two AM."

"She's in Vermont," I said. "We'll get a flight in the morning. I'm going to bed."

"It's not even dark yet. I'm going to make a stir fry."

"Thanks, but I have to pass," I said. "You're going to regret this assignment. I'm a real pain when I'm not feeling well."

"Go to bed," she said. "I'm going to read up on your Reverend Goody. I want to know who we're dealing with."

*

Five hours later I was awake again, and Rose DiNapoli was asleep in the guest room. It had once been my wife Glory's room, because I snore, and later on it had been Barbara's room, because I snore. One of the things I liked about Rose was that she snored too, and the sound carried through the bedroom door as if someone was removing lug nuts with an impact wrench.

I picked up a flight itinerary that lay on the countertop in my kitchen. Rose had booked us a flight out of Orlando at seven, meaning that we'd have to leave the house by four, and it was now just before midnight. We would be in Burlington by noon provided that there were no security hassles, as I would be bringing my Glock this time. The Vermont landscape had changed, and I wasn't looking for colorful foliage—I was looking for killers, and for a mixed-up young woman who might be involved.

A wise man would have had a glass of milk and gone back to bed. But the sleep had sharpened my senses, and I was frustrated because Grace Hebert had been within my grasp and I'd let her slip. Perhaps I had misjudged the situation, but I had tried to strike the right balance of stirring her up and offering her a way out. I couldn't just grab her and haul her off to the nearest treatment center. She was twenty-one years old, and that would be a kidnapping, not a rescue, unless she fully consented.

I needed to know what had happened to Donald Lussen and Matthew Harmony if I was going to understand why Grace was running. This was the same trap that John Pallmeister had fallen into: come up with an explanation, and then make the evidence conform to it. It's other way around: sweat the details, and the conclusions will follow.

My fixation on the doctor's name, the snack food ingredients, the weather report's meteorological jargon—this was my damaged brain telling me to focus harder on the small things. Why hadn't my fingerprints been on the gun that had killed Matty? How come Grace believed that Angus Driscoll had the weapon, when the State Police had it? And where had the hunting bow come from? Somebody must have purchased it, and there would be a record. Pallmeister should be doing this kind of legwork, but he seemed to have lost momentum, and I was glad to be returning to Vermont because I would press him for some answers.

I poured myself a small glass of milk and drank it in the dark kitchen. I would go back to bed, but between Rose's snoring and my mind's attempt to untangle events like so many knotted-up shoelaces I doubted that I would get any more sleep.

WEDNESDAY

ROBERT PATTON MET US AT the Burlington airport in a rusted-out '04 Mercury Marquis that had been painted flat black and looked like the illegitimate child of a stealth bomber. It had 260,000 miles on it, the brakes hissed, the steering squealed loudly, and the seat cushion felt like a bag of marshmallows. "Take it for as long as you need," he said to us. I hadn't seen him in over a year, but he hadn't changed: short, stocky, and with a face that said: *if you argue with me, you'll lose.* Patton was a cop's cop.

"Oh, thanks a bunch," Rose said. "You obviously confiscated this from some drugged-up axe murderer."

"Rose, you exaggerate," he said.

"I'm wrong?"

"It was a hatchet, not an axe."

We drove him to the Border Patrol office that adjoined the airport and made promises about getting together, but I had leaned on his generosity enough and I let him get back to work. I opened the rear door, which groaned like it was about to fall off, and moved up front. "We're going to Clement Goody's house in Johnson," I said to Rose. "If you drive fast enough, we'll be there in time for the show."

"What show?"

"Have you ever been to a strip club?"

She turned her head sideways. "Why would I go to a strip club?"

"Have you?"

"Once, in Fort Lauderdale. Girl's night out. We were all pretty well lubricated."

"Prepare yourself," I said. "This is the play-at-home version."

*

Somewhere between the airport and Johnson the muffler of the Marquis decided that it was time to literally hit the road. I heard a

113

bumping noise under the chassis, as if we had run over a log. Afterward, there was a continuous, muffled roar that made it impossible to talk.

Rose was driving up Hog Back Road. The foliage had become a rust-colored carpet that circled the bare maples along the driveway into the West Eden Bible Camp. The afternoon had suddenly turned cold, and I remembered how fickle autumn was in this state: you could be basking outside one day and making a snowman the next.

The perimeter gate was wide open. I hoped it meant that someone was home, as I was eager to confront Clement Goody. And if he fed me some line about how Grace needed to be rescued by his Love Society, I would feed him a knuckle soufflé. Rose pulled in front of the house and turned off the muffler-less car, which had announced our arrival at least a mile ago. Cindy appeared from the main house, and Clement Goody approached from the barn wearing coveralls and a John Deere cap. "Howdy," he said, grinning as we got out of the car.

"I'm looking for Grace," I said. "I know that you flew her back here."

"Whoa, Vince, slow down, my friend," Goody said. He held his hands up in front of him. He wore the smile that I had learned to distrust, because it wasn't really a friendly gesture, it was a defense mechanism.

"I can't slow down. I'm in a hurry. Go get her, and we'll be on our way."

"Aren't you going to introduce me?" he said, gesturing toward Rose.

"Agent DiNapoli, U.S. Immigration and Customs Enforcement," she said.

"Interesting," Goody said. Cindy Charbonneau was now at his side, staying silent. She stood next to her master like she would take a bullet for him.

"Just get her," I said.

"Help me understand this, Vince—and Ms. DiNapoli," Clement Goody said. "You're here because you would like to pick up Grace and take her somewhere? And, for some reason, U.S. Customs is involved? Now, Grace is of the age of majority, and she hasn't broken any laws that I'm aware of, much less done something that would involve Customs. So, I'm just curious—what would be your legal authority?"

"Bring her out and I'll establish the authority," I said.

"You know me, Vince," he said. "I'm a southerner. We don't rush things. Let's go inside and we'll have a drink."

"You don't drink."

Clement Goody ignored me and addressed Rose. He gave her a wide grin. "Young lady, I have to confess something to you. I have a tremendous weakness for curly hair."

Rose turned to me. I fully expected her to roll her eyes and tell Goody what a jerk he was. Instead, she smiled.

"We're not in that much of a hurry," she said.

*

"I prefer bourbon when the weather gets cool," our host said. We were seated around the glass coffee table in the foyer where I had passed out the week before. Clement peeled the wax off the top of a large bottle of Maker's Mark and poured each of us a generous shot of the brown liquor, including one for himself.

"Karen told me you were sober," I said.

"Ah, Karen," Goody said. "She was correct. I've been abstaining for several years now. But I have to admit, I've been under some stress lately, with Grace leaving us, and then Karen."

"Thanks to you," Cindy said, glaring at me. "Pretty soon my sister will be strung out again."

"Or she'll be living a normal life," I said.

Cindy said nothing, and Clement continued. "Your work is done, Vince. Grace is safe and sound. Away from temptation, and from that man."

"Angus Driscoll?"

"He's part of her problem," Goody said. "You already found that out, didn't you?"

"And so you flew to Florida and got her?"

"Yes." He took a long pull off of his bourbon glass. People who have successfully abstained for years don't usually jump back in unless something pushed them. Grace had ditched Goody, and flown to Palm Beach for a shack-up with Driscoll. Karen Charbonneau had checked out of the West Eden Bible & Sex Camp. Goody's harem was down to Cindy and Lila, and I wondered if that had been the catalyst. In fact, Lila wasn't even around.

"Where's Lila?" I asked him.

"She had to go away," he said. "She's on a spiritual retreat."

"Is everything OK, Clement? Your women are deserting you."

"You worry too much, Vince. And you ask a lot of questions."

"Speaking of questions, do you hunt?"

"No."

"Do you know how to use a compound bow? Ever owned one?"

"No," he said. "Go ahead. Keep asking. You'll find that I'm entirely innocent of anything except for caring about Grace's welfare."

"You know Driscoll? You've met him?"

"We don't talk about those things," Goody said.

"What does that mean?"

"We call him Angus," Cindy said. "We don't use last names."

Ahh. The Program. Goody, Driscoll, and the Charbonneau sisters knew each other, all right. All of them were dealing with addiction issues, including Angus Driscoll, and they had become acquainted through twelve-step meetings. I knew a whole lot of people who had turned their lives around with the help of A.A., and I had nothing but respect for it. Also, I was aware that sometimes the members would develop a bond that went beyond the meetings.

"Where does Donald Lussen come into this?" I asked. "And Matthew Harmony?"

"Matthew was Grace's most fervent admirer," Clement Goody said. "Stone jealous. I believe that the police have that exactly right."

"You think he killed Lussen? And himself?"

"He might have killed me too. Fortunately, the Lord took him first."

"I'd like to get Grace's take on that," I said. "Where is she?"

"Do you read the Bible, Vince?" He pronounced it *bah-bull*.

"I studied it some."

"Then you know about the book of Revelation. Have you any idea how close humanity is to the apocalypse? Do you realize that there are more than sixteen thousand nuclear weapons out there, and that any one of them can rain down fire and brimstone on us at the touch of a button?"

"It's not that simple," I said.

"Oh, yes it is," Clement Goody said. He had his preacher voice on again, and he stood up from his chair with the bourbon glass in one hand while he gestured with the other. "It's so simple that it was laid out in scripture, two thousand years before our time. Our lord Jesus will make his triumphant return, and those of us who have devoted our lives to him will be gathered by the angels under a glass dome. And the destruction will begin, and the sinners will perish from a fiery death without any hope of salvation or resurrection. We will then be transported to Heaven, to sit at the feet of our Lord. And that's where Grace Hebert will be, because she has found Jesus, thanks to my program of commitment and love, just like Cindy right here. We're going to be saved, and you can be, too."

Rose DiNapoli began to laugh, and the preacher stopped mid-rant. She turned to Clement Goody. "So, let's think about this from the girl's perspective. You're a twenty-one-year-old drama major. And you get yourself messed up on heroin. And then two guys your grandfather's age want to fuck you, because you're young and beautiful—"

"Now hold on—"

Rose shushed him. "One of them gives you a bunch of money, and he even buys off your mother. And the other one tells you that he can cure your addiction and save your soul as long as you suck his dick whenever he feels like it. You can handle this because you grew up tough. But it starts to unravel, and you realize that you're somebody's whore."

"Ms. DiNapoli, you're speculating, and—"

"I'm a woman and you're not, so zip it," Rose said. "I don't know if you've killed anyone, Goody, but that's not why we're here. We're here to pick up the girl, and if you don't tell us where she is, we're going to rain down some shit on you. Actual shit, not your biblical fire and brimstone. You got that?"

"She's not here," Goody said.

"She flew back to Vermont with you," I said.

"I had to get her away from him," he said. "She's safe and sound, and frankly, y'all aren't welcome in my house. Go on home."

Rose looked at me, and I gestured with my head toward the door.

*

We didn't stop laughing until we reached the end of Clement Goody's driveway. "You're going to rain down some actual shit on him?" I said to Rose. "I could never pull off a line like that."

"Ah have a *tremindous* weakness for y'all ladies with curly hair," she said, and we dissolved into giggles all over again. None of this was getting us any closer to Grace Hebert, but we needed to blow off some steam after a long day.

"I was worried that he'd charmed you."

"Not a chance," she said. "I just wasn't ready to leave. You were giving up too early."

"He wasn't about to tell us anything."

"On the contrary," she said. "He told us that he'd started drinking again, and that's a big deal. People don't stay sober for years and then backslide without a reason. Something has to be very wrong in his life, and I don't think it's because all his girlfriends are ditching him."

"I thought the same thing. What is it?"

"I don't know yet," Rose said. She had to yell over the noise of the car's exhaust to be heard. "We also found out that Goody knows Driscoll from A.A., and that may play into this."

"Do you think that Goody really believes all that stuff? I don't remember a glass dome in the Bible. I'm wondering if he has any religion at all."

"He's dangerous," she said. "And yes, I think he's sincere, and that worries me even more because he's scared. His faith is shaken, and he's in some kind of crisis. Where are we going, by the way?"

"To my mother's house."

"Aw, Vince, you're taking me to meet your mother?" She flashed a smile from the driver's seat. "That's so sweet."

"Don't get any ideas," I said. "I'm taking you to meet my dog."

*

The urgency that I felt about finding Grace was based on my concerns about her well-being, but there was also the issue of my waistline. If this case was going to take much longer I would to have to buy a new wardrobe, which I couldn't afford, seeing how I wasn't getting paid. My mother served us *giambott*, a vegetable stew that wasn't all that fattening by itself, except that you couldn't possibly do it justice without sopping up the remains of the sauce with garlic bread. She had prepared not one but two loaves, and with the help of Mrs. Tomaselli we polished them off like prisoners who were being served their final meal. I hadn't stopped eating since Rose and I had arrived at my mother's house: platters of sliced sorpressata, olives, marinated artichoke hearts, a wedge of aged asiago, and crostini from the oven drenched in olive oil and spices. And that was just the antipasti, not the meal.

Chan watched us eat from the dining room floor. He was curled up at Rose's feet, not mine. He had ignored me when we entered the house, as if my two-day trip to Florida had meant abandonment. I passed him a piece of the bread under the table, which he grudgingly accepted. "Good boy," I said.

Don't even.

My mother and Mrs. T debriefed us over the meal and a bottle of wine that Rose had bought on the way through Barre. I was abstaining, because it was going to be a work night. I'd already had a phone conversation with John Pallmeister and had prodded him about the origin of the bow. He said that he'd get me the serial number, but he was pretty sure that it had already been checked out and was deemed too old to trace. I would turn over whatever information he had to Roberto and would give him a crack at it. Roberto could go to strange, revelatory, and probably illegal places on the computer that the police only dreamed of.

I had also called Patton, who caught me up on Angus Driscoll. The financier had booked a first-class seat home, cutting short his Florida vacation. I put Driscoll on the calendar for a visit in the morning: his brokerage office was in downtown Burlington, half an hour away. Rose could chauffeur me in the Stealth Bomber, and we would see if we could get past the secretaries and rile him up a little. Was he married? I didn't know, but I would research that tonight.

"Vince," Mrs. Tomaselli said, putting down her fork. "You said that this priest told you that Matty was in love with Grace?"

"He's Baptist, not Catholic," I said. "They don't call them priests. And yes, he insinuated that Matty and Grace were lovers. That's what the police believe, too. I'm not so sure."

"Why do the police think that?"

"Their theory is that Grace was in a relationship with the professor up at the college. Matty got jealous, he killed the guy, and then he committed suicide."

"When you say in a relationship, you mean sex?"

"Yes."

"Oh dear, dear, dear," Mrs. T said, shaking her head. "This is all my fault and no one else's."

"You're being ridiculous, Donna," my mother said. "Every woman makes these choices on her own."

"I used to brag to Grace about my boyfriends," Mrs. Tomaselli said. "That was nothing but foolish, sinful pride on my part. It was ancient history, of course, but it must have made her think that it was acceptable. Her own grandmother was a flirt, not to mention her mother. Oh dear god, I'm such a useless old wretch." She removed the napkin from her lap and dabbed at her eyes.

"Rubbish," my mom said. "You had nothing to do with it. You've always been there for Grace. Have some more of this nice wine and pipe down."

Both of them had a point. People think of their elders as role models. Sometimes that's good, because it can open a whole world of life experience to a shy teenager. And sometimes it backfires. I wasn't always a perfect role model with Roberto, or even with Royal, but it seemed to balance out over time. Parenting is more about being there than being any good at it.

I excused myself from the table because my phone was buzzing in my pocket, and I had sneaked a look: Karen. I took the call in the bathroom. "Hello?"

"Where are you?"

"My mother's house," I said. "We got into Burlington this afternoon, and we went up to see if Grace was at Goody's, but no one was too helpful."

"We?"

"I'm with a U.S. Customs agent. She's helping me out."

"Customs? Why are they involved?"

"Rose is an old friend, and I needed a driver."

"Are you all right?"

"I had a little setback. I'm not supposed to drive."

"And so, this Rose. Your old friend. She's not young and good-looking, right?"

"Hold on—"

"Forget it," Karen said. "I'll pick you up in an hour. We're going to Sweet Melissa's, in Montpelier. They have the best beer."

"Karen, I'd really like to see you, but—"

"This isn't about us, Vince," she said. "This is about Cindy. I'm about to betray my twin sister, and I'm going to need a drink."

*

Karen was on her second beer and I was still nursing my first one when the band started up. Sweet Melissa's was one of those hole-in-the-wall joints where the music, the liquor, and the small, noisy crowd made it seem like you had just been let off of the bus at honkytonk heaven. A guitar player in a cowboy hat was growling out a Lefty Frizzell tune called "That's the Way Love Goes" from the dimly lit stage. He was accompanied by drums, bass, and a pedal steel guitar, and the music was as smooth as Clement Goody's bourbon.

"You were going to tell me about Cindy," I said. Karen was dressed in jeans and a light-blue sweatshirt with the hood pulled up. She wore makeup, and her eyes were smeared around the edges.

"Cindy and I were like one person," she said. "Our mother dressed us the same, and our parents always got off when we'd do the same things. They thought it was cute. So we learned how to be carbon copies of each other, because we wanted their approval."

"Including going to bed with the same man."

"They never knew about that," Karen said. "But it came from the same place."

"You said you were going to confess something."

"I don't know what to call it. I'm afraid for Cindy. This has gone too far."

"How?"

"What happened to you, Vince? How come you aren't driving? And who's the woman? You told me that she wasn't pretty, but she is. I don't think she liked me."

Karen and Rose had been in each other's company for a total of thirty seconds in the doorway of my mother's house. Neither of them had said a word, but that hadn't stopped them from sizing up each other. "You're dodging my question," I said.

She began to draw circles on the polished wooden table with her fingertip. "My sister and I aren't the same person anymore. It's been going on for some time. I have a career, and she's floundering. She got into drugs, and I allowed myself to get sucked into it with her. The worst part was that she fell for Clement. All the way."

"She's in love with him?"

"It's more of an obsession. I have some of it, too. Clement knows how to exploit people's weaknesses. He's a very charismatic person. Don't ask me to explain love, Vince. The older I get, the more I realize that nobody has a clue."

"Amen," I said.

"My sister and I grew up west of here. That's the part of Vermont that used to be all dairy farms, but a lot of the land has gone back to woods. Everybody hunts there. Our dad took us hunting when we were kids, but I cried the whole time, and he finally gave up and left me home. But he always took Cindy."

"She learned how to hunt?"

"Yes."

"Rifle? Or bow?"

"Both," Karen said. The band finished the song, and we clapped politely while the other people in the bar whooped and whistled. The guitar player lifted the brim of his cowboy hat, nodded to the audience, and smiled. His face was deeply lined, as if he had lived the lyrics of the songs he sang.

"Do you think that your sister killed Donald Lussen?"

"She still holds the county record for the biggest buck shot by a teenager. She and my dad had a tree stand in the woods, way up a hill beyond our house. They went there afternoons, in the fall. I played on the field hockey team and got black and blue marks on my legs while they shot deer and filled up our freezer."

"Is Cindy capable of killing someone? A person, not a deer?"

Karen stopped drawing circles and looked up at me. The musicians began a slow waltz that matched her expression. "If Clement told her to, she might."

"Damn," I said.

Karen said nothing, but the tears were welling up in her eyes.

"You're doing the right thing," I said.

"Betraying my sister? That's doing the right thing?"

"We should go," I said. "You can stay with me. We'll figure this out in the morning."

"I don't want to think about the morning," she said. "And no, I'm not going to stay at your mother's house with that customs lady."

"She's just a friend."

"It's too late to drive home," she said. "You and I are getting a room."

"Karen, that's crazy."

"You're turning me down?"

More than a year had passed since I'd slept with anyone but myself. Two failed marriages and a bullet in the head had left me thinking that I should be labeled with one of those propeller-shaped orange signs that said: *radioactive*. I wasn't fit for a relationship. I couldn't drive a car, I could barely manage a beer, and I didn't want to think about whether or not I would be of any use in a motel bed. Plus, I had a full day ahead of me tomorrow. No way.

"Vince?" she said. "You don't want this?"

The pedal steel player began a solo in a minor key. The slow, mournful music brought to mind the many things that I had done wrong in my life, and the inevitability of doing them wrong all over again. But Karen Charbonneau was looking at me like none of that mattered.

"Do you know how to waltz?" I asked her.

"No."

I took her hand, led her to the dance floor, and put my arm around her waist. We shuffled back and forth until she pulled me closer and rested her head against my shoulder. After a while we got into a rhythm, far back in a darkened corner where we wouldn't collide with the other dancers. It wasn't really waltzing, but we didn't care.

THURSDAY

KAREN DROPPED ME OFF AT the bottom of my mother's driveway just as the sky was starting to lighten in the east. I didn't think that anyone would witness my Walk of Shame between her Jaguar and the house. I was wrong.

Mrs. Tomaselli opened the door for me as I fumbled for my key. She was dressed in a black terrycloth bathrobe that she kept at my mother's for the nights when she slept on the couch. Her hair was down. I hadn't ever seen it like that. It was beautiful.

"You have very nice hair, Mrs. T," I said.

"Aren't you full of compliments, Mr. Just Got Lucky," she said. She leaned over and whispered in my ear, "I'm pleased that you had a good time, Vinny. But you have some fences to mend."

"What fences?" I whispered back.

"Your girlfriend," she said. "She hardly slept at all."

"She's not my girlfriend."

"You'd better straighten her out then. She's sweet on you."

I made my way into the kitchen where Rose DiNapoli was removing a sheet of biscuits from the oven. My mother was at the stove, stirring a pot.

"Don't tell me," I said. "Biscuits and gravy, right Mom?"

"I didn't make enough for four people," my mother said. "You didn't tell us when you'd be back."

"You're kidding?"

She wasn't. She was scowling, and Rose wouldn't even look at me. They had closed ranks. I might as well slink off to McDonalds and get an Egg McSawdust or whatever they sold there, because I wasn't going to be offered any sustenance in my mother's house.

"No problem," I said. "I'll just starve to death." I smiled my most winning grin, but it was lost on them. Chan was in the corner of the kitchen with one eye open.

I sure hope that was worth it.

124

"It was," I said, but nobody seemed to hear. I had prepared myself for some explaining, but the truth was that the last few hours I'd spent with Karen had been a blissful escape. All of the crap that I'd been dealing with had vanished the moment she turned off the bedside light and pulled the sweatshirt over her head. She had made me feel like someone could still find me attractive despite all of my afflictions. She had surprised me with her tenderness, and I had surprised us both with my stamina.

"I'll just hop in the shower," I said to the room. "I'll get something on the way to Burlington. Rose and I are going to drop in on Angus Driscoll."

"You must have been too preoccupied to answer your phone," Rose said. It was the first time that she had acknowledged me.

"I left it here. It's in the bedroom."

"Then you don't know?"

"Know what?"

"Angus Driscoll is in the ICU at Fletcher Allen Hospital. Somebody lobbed a pipe bomb into his car window. It killed his driver, and Driscoll is on life support. Pallmeister has been trying to reach you, and so have I. But you were too busy for silly little things like that."

*

The Middlesex State Police barracks is a squat, no-frills building with low ceilings that would be more suited to elementary schoolers than big, hulking cops filling out reports and bustling around the halls with coffee cups. John Pallmeister's office was at the far corner. It had one small window and all the charm of a holding cell. Rose and I took the two wooden visitor's chairs while Pallmeister sat ramrod-straight behind his veneer desk. "Clement Goody has a box of pipe bombs in his cellar," I said to him.

"You waited to tell me this?"

"You weren't interested," I said. "You had it all figured out. And now that Driscoll's in the hospital, you're suddenly interested again."

"Meaning?"

"You said you weren't in Driscoll's pocket—"

"And I'm not," the lieutenant said. "You can just leave that right there."

Rose must have felt my blood pressure rising, and she tried to intervene. "Vince, what are you trying to accomplish here?"

"I'd like to see the State Police get their heads out of their asses," I said. "That's what I'd like to accomplish."

Pallmeister glared at me from behind the desk. "We can get a warrant, if you're telling me that he has explosives in the house. Maybe we'll find your runaway in the process."

"She's not a runaway," I said. "She was kidnapped by Clement Goody. He's holding her somewhere."

"This is a guess? Or do you know something else that you're not telling me?"

"It's an educated guess," I said. "You have three murders now, and the girl is connected to each of them. You need to focus on helping me find her. We find her, and you solve all three homicides."

"Where do you think she is?"

"No idea, unfortunately. Every time I get close, she's gone."

Rose DiNapoli was finishing the coffee that she had served herself while we'd waited to see the lieutenant. She had been quiet for the last few minutes, but I could see that something was on her mind.

"What's wrong?" I said.

"It could be her," she said.

"Who? You mean Grace?"

"You're the one who brought it up," Rose said. "She's connected to all these guys. Matty had a thing for her, and he's dead. She was screwing Lussen, and he's dead. Fish Falzarano chauffeured her back and forth to her sugar daddy, and he's dead. And Driscoll might not survive, either, so that's four. The girl's a black widow."

"No way."

"Why not? She's a junkie, her mother is trailer trash, and frankly, everything that you've told me has reinforced the case against her. I only spoke with her a few times while we were at the hotel, but I can tell you that she's shrewd. She has you conned."

"Impossible," I said. "Her grandmother is a close friend of mine. I know the family. Grace isn't a murderer."

"That would be the easy assumption, wouldn't it?" John Pallmeister said. He had risen from his chair and was putting on his jacket.

"You agree with her?"

"Vince, you're the one who took me to task for accepting the murder-suicide theory," the lieutenant said. He had donned his Smokey the Bear hat and was adjusting the leather strap to fit around the back of his head. "Rose has a point. You told me earlier that the girl was the one who attacked you on the mountain."

"But she didn't kill me," I said.

"Not yet," Pallmeister said. "Listen, you've accomplished what you came here for. I'll put more resources on finding Grace Hebert. Just don't be disappointed if you can't save her."

"She needs rehab," I said.

John Pallmeister opened the door to his office, indicating that the meeting was over. "If she's behind any of this, she won't need rehab," he said. "She'll need a very good lawyer."

*

I would just as soon forget about what happened on the ride up Interstate 89 to Burlington, because it reinforces my worst failings as a man, and even as a friend. Rose and I had a fight. I hadn't meant for it to happen—in fact, I was in a pretty good mood since I had finally secured John Pallmeister's full cooperation, not to mention that Karen Charbonneau had buzzed me with a saucy text that I'd snuck a look at and had made me smile.

Rose was convinced of Grace Hebert's guilt, and she had tried to make her case as we drove north. I defended Grace, even though I still barely knew her. It might have been a rational, give-and-take argument, but there were complications. Rose was sweet on me, as Mrs. T had put it, and I had shown up early in the morning with a post-coital grin on my face. So what had begun as a discussion among peers had degenerated into pass-the-grenade.

"You're pussy-blind, Tanzi. Grace Hebert can do no wrong because she's young and hot. You're no different from the rest of them."

"That's completely unfair," I'd responded, but she was on a roll. We were on the Bolton Flats, and she had the Marquis up to about eighty with her hands gripping the wheel so tightly that her knuckles glowed pink in the slanted morning sun.

"I didn't get five fucking minutes of sleep last night. I thought you were passed out somewhere in a ditch. But noooo, you were getting your bean waxed by a potential witness."

"And that's none of your business, is it?" I had to shout, partly because the noise from the car was so loud, but mostly because I was pissed.

"I fly all the way up here from Florida to help you out, and what do you do? You take off the minute some bimbo college professor gets all clingy."

"Who's getting clingy?" I said, which was a mistake.

Rose held up her hand like a traffic cop. "Excuse me? What did you just say? You're calling me clingy? Like I give two shits about you?"

I tried to answer, but she was talking as fast as she was driving.

"You could never be happy with a normal woman, could you? You're one of those guys. Addicted to the drama queens. Men need to save somebody, like in a play. I have to admit it, Vince; your theater professor hottie might be perfect for you. You two can stage your little love scenes, and you'll be happy because you can't handle a real relationship."

"Rose, you have no idea what you're talking about."

"Don't I?" The needle on the speedometer had crawled up toward ninety, and we were flying past the rest of the morning traffic like it was stopped.

"No, you don't. Not at all. I was married to one woman for twenty years, and I loved her. Barbara and I didn't work out, but that doesn't mean that I'm some kind of playboy. And yes, I like Karen. And I like you too. You're a really nice person."

"Oh, so I'm Miss Congeniality. That's every woman's worst nightmare, in case you wondered."

I tried to answer, but it was the end of the conversation as far as she was concerned. We rode in silence the rest of the way to Burlington. I reached behind the seat to calm myself down by stroking the fur of Chan's neck. For once his deep brown eyes showed sympathy rather than disdain.

"I'm right on this," I whispered to him.

Maybe so, he said. *But you still lost.*

*

The crowd in the waiting room of the Fletcher Allen hospital intensive care unit was a who's-who of Vermont politics. The governor stood near the entryway, surrounded by assistants, handlers, and the press. One U.S. senator had already come and gone. State legislators and their minions abounded. Lobbyists, business leaders, and various other influence-peddlers crowded out the nursing staff, and even though Angus Driscoll was still clinging to life somewhere beyond the doors, it felt like a wake.

I had left Rose in the car to sulk with the dog while I found the waiting room and waited. I didn't approach anybody, and I didn't ask any questions. I quietly took a seat and tried to be as inconspicuous as the six-month-old magazines that were stacked on the table next to me. All I wanted to do for now was to observe. Pallmeister and his group would be working the obvious angles. They would be all over Clement Goody's place, looking for bombs—the real kind, not the emotional kind like Rose and I had been tossing back and forth. My job was to look for the nuances: the body language, facial expressions, and the possibly unguarded comments from people who were in Driscoll's circle and might accidentally drop me a big hint, because I needed one if I was going to wrap this up and get back to my life.

I thumbed through a tattered golf magazine while I listened to the chatter around me. The waiting room smelled of old carpet, stale coffee, and worry. I was one of the worriers, and I had every reason to be one. In the eight days since I'd come up to Vermont to get my head looked at, three people had died, another one was in bad shape down the hall from me, and I wasn't exactly all roses and sunshine myself after Fish had hit me hard enough to send me back to surgery. Pretty soon I would be in this very same hospital making my own recovery, although it was unlikely that the press would cover it, or that a senator would be by my bedside. I needed to get in touch with Dr. Jaffe and schedule an appointment, but that was low on my list because I currently felt better than any time since I'd been shot. Maybe Clement Goody was right, and sex was the cure for everything. If the scientific community ever decided to research that, I would volunteer, although I'd probably end up in the control group.

The double doors to the patient area opened, and a doctor came out with Trish Lussen at his side. I'd seen them both shortly after I'd arrived, when the surgeon had briefed the press about the extent of Driscoll's injuries. The bomb had landed more or less in Fish Falzarano's lap. The fragments had traveled low, passing through the front seat and into Angus Driscoll's legs and lower torso. The doctors believed that they could save his legs, but his intestines were a mess, and there was already trouble with sepsis.

"Is he conscious?" I heard someone ask.

"Yes," the doctor said. He seemed young for someone who would be assigned to a high-profile guy like Driscoll. He was my height, with a goatee and a shaved head that was deeply tanned like he'd been somewhere warm. "Mr. Driscoll is sedated, but he refuses to go under. He asked me to thank you all for coming, and to go home."

"No way," a young guy in a suit said, but others in the room began to filter toward the exit. Trish Lussen saw me and made her way through well-wishers who shook her hand or hugged her. By the time she got to me she looked spent, but there was the same resolve in her expression that I'd seen when I had been on the doorstep of her farmhouse.

"He wants to speak with you," she said. "I made the mistake of telling him that you were here."

"What about?"

"His girlfriend, I presume," she said. "He thinks that I don't know about her, but men are blind in that regard. Even the smartest ones. My father is in a hospital bed and my husband is dead because of Grace Hebert."

"Do you think that she killed your husband?"

"One way or the other," she said. I noticed that her teeth were crooked at the bottom, although nothing else about her was out of place. She must have had less sleep than I had, but she looked perfectly composed. "You're the investigator, Mr. Tanzi. You tell me."

"The police thought that it was Matthew Harmony. Your mechanic. And they also think that he killed himself, out of remorse."

"Come with me," she said. She took my elbow. "Let's get this over with."

*

Angus Driscoll's huge body draped over the sides of the hospital bed like a too-big slab of prime rib on a dinner plate. It was a natural human response to be intimidated by people of his physical stature, but that had never applied to me. Evil can come in any size, and I was starting to think that Clement Goody was more of a threat than his much larger rival, who took up a lot of real estate but didn't appear to be a threat to anyone at present.

Driscoll's eyes were open when Trish and I entered the room, but it was clear that he was struggling for consciousness, and even survival. He raised a weak hand and motioned for me to draw closer. I leaned over him to hear what he was trying to say.

"Want to hire you."

"Excuse me?"

"To protect Trish," he said. It was no more than a whisper, and his daughter was across the room. I wondered if she could hear him. "Fish is dead. Can't do it myself."

"Protect her from who?"

"Whoever did this," Driscoll said. "I'll pay triple your rate. You stay with Trish, and if you can find Grace and protect her too, there will be a bonus."

"Who tossed the bomb in your car? Did you see them?"

"I was reading the newspaper," he whispered. "Fish must have known the person, or he wouldn't have stopped."

Driscoll began to cough violently. Two nurses rushed into the room and pushed us aside. Trish Lussen took my elbow again and led me out. "Let's hope you didn't just finish him off," she said. "And in case you're wondering, I heard what he said. I don't need your protection, Mr. Tanzi. You can leave now."

I seldom take on two clients at the same time, but Angus Driscoll had thrown me a curve ball. He was worried about Grace, and I was thinking that this might be the break that I had been looking for.

"You heard him," I said. "I'm accepting his offer."

"Don't be ridiculous," she said. "Nobody is going to babysit me."

"I have a car outside," I said. "The muffler is shot. It sounds like a Sherman tank. There's a pissed-off female customs agent in the front seat and a hundred-pound dog with a bad attitude in the back. You'll fit in nicely."

*

I dropped Rose DiNapoli and Trish Lussen off at the estate on Shelburne Point. The local cops had already posted a patrol car at the end of the driveway, and I had a word with them. Trish had bitched the whole way over from the hospital while Chan growled at her, but eventually we made a deal: she would stay in the house for a minimum of twenty-four hours while I did my job. Rose would stay with her for a couple of days, with the added security of the police car at the end of the drive. Chan and I took the car, despite Rose's strong protest, but I made the case that the best way to protect Trish was to assist John Pallmeister, find the killer or killers, and locate Grace. I had inside knowledge of the players, and I needed to be out there circulating and stirring things up. I promised Rose that if I had the slightest hint of another whiteout I would call her for help, but I was still feeling at the top of my game, thanks to Karen Charbonneau's unique brand of physical therapy the night before.

I knew exactly where I was headed: the West Eden Bible Camp. Pallmeister had texted me an hour earlier, saying that they had a warrant and were on the way. By the time I arrived they would probably be done, and even if they couldn't apprehend Clement Goody and sweat him, they'd be able to give the forensics team a sample of the bomb and match it to the one that had killed Fish. If Goody was still there, he'd be arrested for possession of the explosives, which would easily earn him a year or more of jail time. But he was too smart for that, and I wondered where he might be right now. A guy with his money and resources could go anywhere.

I also wondered if Cindy Charbonneau was with him. Cindy had worked her way up my suspect list because of Karen's revelation that her sister was an expert with a bow and arrow. Karen had also told me that Cindy would do Clement's bidding. Did that extend to tossing a bomb into somebody's car? Possibly. The evidence was mounting up, but I couldn't figure out the motive. Goody was a rich guy. A power broker, like Driscoll, and those types weren't usually killers, at least not overtly. They settled their scores in other ways. Unless they had lost control, because they were infatuated with a beautiful young woman.

My phone buzzed with a text. I pulled the Marquis into the driveway of a farm a few miles short of Johnson and called Roberto. I had put him on a research task the day before, and my cell displayed the answer: *Found the weapon. It was sold on Craigslist.*

He picked up on the first ring. "Vince?"

"You found it how?"

"The ad was deleted, but we retrieved it," he said. "It was kinda complicated, so I got some friends to help."

Aha. Roberto had a cadre of hacker buddies with whose assistance he could find out what Vladimir Putin had eaten for breakfast. "So the bow was sold on Craigslist?"

"Yeah, about two weeks ago."

"Same description that I gave you? With the quiver and the carbon arrows?"

"It's the same make and model bow," he said. "There wasn't anything about the arrows. Where are you?"

"On the way out to Clement Goody's."

"I called the seller," he said. "He said he'd already sold it, which I knew, of course. To a woman. I could trace his street address."

A woman had bought Donald Lussen's murder weapon on Craigslist? "No need," I said. "You answered my question, although I don't like the answer."

"Was it the girl that you're looking for? Grace?"

"No," I said. "One of Goody's friends is an expert archer. He must have put her up to it."

"Why?"

"I wish I knew," I said.

We hung up, and Chan climbed into the front seat as I left the farm driveway. In a few minutes we'd be at Goody's house, the place would be swarming with cops, and Goody and Cindy Charbonneau might already be in custody. I would pass the information about the Craigslist buy to Pallmeister, and he would build his case. They would be arrested. Interrogations would happen, lawyers would be hired. Clement and Cindy might cop a plea and get fifteen or twenty years, or they might get life. It didn't matter to me, because all that I cared about was that Grace Hebert would be found, rehabilitated, and given another chance. I wanted that to happen, for her grandmother's sake if for no other reason.

"I think we're close to wrapping this up," I said to the dog. He didn't look so sure.

*

John Pallmeister wasn't in Clement Goody's driveway when I arrived. Neither was anyone else, except for a sleepy-looking deputy in a Lamoille Sheriff's cruiser who was listening to the radio chatter with his window rolled down as it was an unusually warm October day.

He told me that the State Police crew had shown up along with three local deputies. They'd gone through the entire house. There were no pipe bombs to be found. The room that I'd directed them to was empty—not even a bullet remained. The place had been left open, but no one was home. Food was in the refrigerator. The plants were freshly watered. But no guns, let alone explosives, and the deputy told me that Pallmeister had left in a foul mood, which was an uncharacteristic display of emotion for the cool-headed lieutenant.

Goody had somehow cleaned up and cleared out. Pallmeister would be questioning what I had told him. After all, I was a P.I., not a cop, and I'd screwed up plenty in the past, plus I'd taken a few hits and might be as reliable as a punch-drunk boxer. I thought about calling him and telling him about Roberto's discovery on the bow, but I was at a loss.

I sat in the car for a while to consider my options. I could go back to Shelburne and consult with Rose. I could hang around at Pallmeister's barracks and hope for some scraps. Or I could fly back to Vero Beach, where I was way overdue with my young son, and say to hell with it. Sorry, Mrs. T, I couldn't locate your granddaughter, and she's a lost cause anyway, so let's all move on.

Rose might be right about Grace. She could be a black widow, and I realized that I hadn't bothered to ask Roberto if he'd gotten a description of the woman from the seller of the bow. Grace and Cindy didn't look at all like each other. A simple inquiry about the buyer's hair color would solve that one, but I was too discouraged to call Roberto and have him pursue it. I would just hand the information over to Pallmeister, and they could go interview the guy. I felt like a loser. A hack who was past his prime. I had no business here. Pallmeister and Patton were trying to help me out, but I was in over my damaged head. Florida was looking better and better.

"What am I missing?" I asked the dog, who was curled up in the back seat. "And don't you do anything besides sleep?"

I get more done sleeping that you ever will awake.

"Meaning what?"

Meaning use your brain for once. What's left of it.

"I'm missing something?" The animal didn't respond, nor did I expect him to. I was simply using our imagined conversations to work things out, and what was clear in the work-out process was that I was missing something. The hair color of the woman who bought the bow? Was that important? Possibly, but that didn't seem to be it—obviously Cindy Charbonneau had bought the weapon, given her archery background.

Bow and arrow, Ruger .44 magnum, pipe bomb—there were three murders now, with three different weapons and entirely different sets of circumstances. The level of violence was escalating with each killing. All three deaths were connected to Grace Hebert. And Clement Goody was connected to all three of the weapons, via his female companions, or his armaments cache, which had conveniently vanished right before the cops arrived. I'd stood in the room and seen it only a few days ago. There was a lot of nasty, lethal stuff in there—way too much to sweep under a bed at the last minute. Goody had moved it, very deliberately, and it must have taken him some time.

He was a prepper, according to Eric the Electrician, and this was his ultimate hideout for the End Times, fully stocked with canned food, hot women, and bullets galore. The recent circumstances had disrupted his preparations for the apocalypse and the weapons had been moved temporarily, but this was ground zero for when the Huns started running up the driveway.

Or was it?

I began to suspect what it was that I'd been missing.

One of the great things about Vermont is that you don't need a phone book, or Google, or any high-tech snooping devices to find someone: you just stop in at the local store. I drove the Marquis to Johnson Farm and Garden, less than a mile from the bottom of Clement Goody's road, and waited to speak with the proprietor, who was in the middle of demonstrating a chain saw to a customer who looked like he might be there for a while. I was in a hurry to get the information, but the quickest way with Vermonters is to wait your turn. The customer finally made up his mind and counted out bills for the saw. I approached the owner.

"I'm looking for a guy named Eric," I said. "He did some electrical work for Clement Goody, up the road."

"You with the police? They were there today," the man said. He wore coveralls and had a broad moustache that covered his dark-stained teeth. "You don't look like a policeman."

"Private investigator."

"They got some shenanigans goin' on up there, by jimbo. Nobody's gonna miss that guy when they take him away."

"Except Eric," I said. "He told me there was some money to be made."

"Oh yeah, Eric, he cashed in," the man said. "Mr. Goody never spent a dollar here. Don't care for the man, personally. I got two daughters, and that fella would screw a heifer if she mooed at him."

"I'd like to know how to get in touch with Eric," I said. "I don't know his last name."

"Gagnier," the man said. "He's in my contacts. Hang on." He took a cellphone from his pocket and dialed. He handed the phone to me.

"Eric?"

"Yes?"

"This is Vince Tanzi. You and I met at the bottom of Clement Goody's driveway, when you were installing an electric fence."

"I remember you."

"I'm a private investigator. I need some help. You said that he had a lot of weapons in his house."

"So?"

"I saw them. Guns, ammo, even a box of pipe bombs."

"Don't know about no bombs." He sounded sleepy, like I'd woken him.

"He had a box of them, but they're gone now. The cops just searched the place."

"He's in trouble?"

"Yes."

There was a long silence. "My wife don't like this," he finally said. "We heard that the State Police was there. There ain't no easy money, is there, Mr. Tanzi? Money for nothin', like the song says?"

"No," I said. "How much did he pay you?"

"Twice my usual."

"That's a lot."

"My wife told me it was all gonna end bad," he said. "I wish I could give the money back."

"Where is it?" I asked him. "His hideout?"

"Top of the hill," he responded without hesitating. Once somebody decides to get something off their chest you don't have to push very hard—you stand back and get out of the way. "It took me a good part of last summer. I borrowed an excavator, and I poured most of the concrete before some other guys took over. He paid me a bundle so's I wouldn't tell nobody."

"You didn't do anything wrong. But some people have died, and I need your help."

"It's cut into the side of the hill. Used to be an old root cellar but it's a lot bigger now. The door's on a special lock and it weighs a ton, so I put in a pneumatic assist. You need a remote fob thing I had made up."

"Can you get me one?"

"Where are you?"

"Johnson Farm and Garden."

"Ten minutes," he said. "I'm gonna feel better once this is over, right?"

"Yes, you will. You're going to be a hero."

"Don't know about that. My wife thinks I'm a fool."

"I've had two wives," I said. "That's part of their job description."

*

I was on my third mug of coffee at the Lovin' Cup when I called Rose DiNapoli. It wouldn't be dark for another hour, and I didn't dare approach Goody's hidey-hole in the weak afternoon light. The coffee shop was closed, but the manager had allowed me to linger while she cleaned up and paid bills. I told Rose about my discovery.

"You'll need back up, of course. I'll get someone to watch Trish."

"I'm doing this solo," I said. "A few days ago the State Police told me I was getting in the way."

"Vince, you don't have to prove anything."

"I'll have my Glock with me," I said.

"Impressive," Rose said. "Meanwhile they have a box of pipe bombs."

"I'll take a flashlight, too," I said. "And some Band-Aids."

"You're being stubborn, but you already know that," she said. "Here's the deal. You call me before you get there, and then no later than an hour afterward. If you don't phone me, I call in an air strike. Pallmeister, Patton, everybody. Got it?"

"You're breaking my *gul*," I said.

"Yes I am, and don't you forget it," Rose said. She was busting my ass all right, and in a strange way it felt good. It had been a while since anyone had worried about me like that.

*

I left Chan in the car and walked up from the bible camp buildings at the very bottom of the hill. A half-moon lit the way, which was fine, but it was also a liability, as Cindy Charbonneau had no doubt installed security cameras, and the extra light would make me more visible. I stayed well away from the driveway and snipped the electric fence with bolt cutters that I'd picked up at the Farm and Garden store. Cindy might see that the fence had been disabled, but she wouldn't necessarily know where. And if she did, and they sent someone to intercept me, I had my gun and the cover of semidarkness.

It was a long way up a sloping pasture to the house, and then several hundred yards further to the root cellar near the crest of the hill. Beyond it was a barn that was too small to hold much in the way of animals or hay. Perhaps it was a springhouse, which was a common structure on the older farms. By the time I approached the entrance to the root cellar I was breathing hard enough to inflate a queen-size air mattress. If Chan were here he would be giving me grief for all my huffing and puffing, but I had left him behind because I had no idea what I'd encounter, and I didn't want him to get hurt.

I had reached the hideout fifteen minutes after my initial call to Rose to tell her that I was under way, leaving me with forty-five minutes to complete my task before I'd promised to check in. The exterior of the root cellar was faced with irregular stone and looked like it had been there for a century, although I knew that Eric had done extensive work to the interior. The door was a gray rectangle of Barre granite—I recognized it because it was the same material that my father had fashioned into memorials and monuments during his forty years of working in the Barre sheds.

I flicked on my penlight and read an inscription that was carved into the face of the granite: *Behold, I stand at the door, and knock: if any man hear my voice, and opens the door, I will come in to him, and will sup with him, and he with me.*

I recognized the passage as scripture, and it had Clement Goody written all over it: Y'all come in, have a drink or two, dine with me and my women, and hell yeah, we'll end up in the sack. I decided not to knock. I didn't need to, because I had Eric's key fob, and he had told me how to use it. I stood back from the slab and pushed the button.

What happened next is hard to explain, because I don't remember all of it.

I did see the slab swing open, hinged on the side. I remember the hiss of the lifters that Eric had installed. I remember the light coming out, and leaning in to see what was below, and then making my way down a narrow set of stairs. And that's pretty much everything, because after that it was a blank—until Rose DiNapoli, Robert Patton, half a dozen SWAT guys from Patton's team and two Lamoille County deputies woke me, lying on my back on a circular bed in Clement Goody's hilltop hideout. The room around me was a near-duplicate of the one upstairs in his house with all the sex toys and video equipment. A motor under the bed hummed softly while I rotated in a slow, 360-degree arc. Rose found the control panel on the wall and turned it off. "Getting a little dizzy there, fella?" she said.

"What the hell?"

Robert Patton helped me sit up. "Didn't know you were into the kinky stuff, Vince."

"I don't know what happened," I said. "I came down the stairs, and that's all I remember."

"We had a look around while you were resting," Patton said. "No pipe bombs. Pretty slick little bunker, but not even a firecracker."

"I must have passed out," I said as I sat up. The blood rushed to my head and I almost fell back onto the mattress, but I was regaining my consciousness, slowly. It must have been another whiteout, and someone had lifted me onto the bed. Or, several people had, because at six feet and two hundred pounds I'm not all that portable. "I've been doing that lately."

"Related to your injury?"

"Maybe," I said. "They want to operate on me again."

"Let's go," he said. "Unless you're waiting for your date, and we're interrupting something."

"I'm his date," Rose said. She turned to me. "I'll drive you home. And just so you know, you have one very pissed off dog waiting in the car."

*

It was a long ride back to Barre with Rose at the wheel, Chan in the back seat, and me in the doghouse. Fortunately for me the Marquis' exhaust noise made conversation impossible, which was fine, because I needed to be alone with my thoughts to process what had happened.

I had suffered a whiteout, and this time there had been no warning at all.

I'd ended up in Clement Goody's super-secret boudoir, and somebody played a game of spin-the-detective until Rose had mercifully turned off the rotating bed. If Goody's arms cache had been in the bunker, it was gone now. So much for my big bust.

My mother was asleep when we got to her house. I let Rose take the guest room and curled up on the living room couch to nurse my bruises from keeling over on Clement Goody's floor. Someone must have been there, as I hadn't dragged myself onto the huge bed.

I heard Rose's snoring through the thin walls of the house. She'd put in a long day, first babysitting Trish Lussen and then rescuing me. She deserved the sleep. *Sleep that doth knit the raveled sleave of care*, as Macbeth had described it. I, on the other hand, didn't deserve sleep. I'd thought that I was so close, but had come up empty-handed. I was still missing a common thread that would tie everything together, and it was something beyond where Goody's weapons were hidden.

Human beings can generally stay out of trouble except for two things: money and sex. And if money was the root of all evil, sex was the rest of the tree. I had been operating on the assumption that Grace Hebert's problems had to do with sex, seeing how every male I had met was trying to get into her culottes if they hadn't already. Sure, money was involved, notably between Angus Driscoll and Carmela Tomaselli, who was pimping her own daughter. Money could also have been a factor between Donald and Trish Lussen. But I hadn't taken a purely financial motive into account, because Goody and Driscoll seemed to be pulling all the strings, and they were both rolling in dough.

The cops weren't even close to solving Donald Lussen's murder, and they'd given up too easily on Matthew Harmony's so-called suicide. Add in Fish Falzarano's execution by pipe bomb and too many people were dying for the sake of a college drama major. What was it that Rose had called me? Pussy-blind? She had meant that I was oblivious to Grace's negative qualities because she was beautiful. But that wasn't my real blind spot: everything that I'd discovered so far had pointed to love, sex, and jealousy, and I'd accepted that as the motive behind the murders.

Perhaps that was wrong.

It was almost midnight and Roberto would have school in the morning, so I would have to do this myself. I dressed in my bathrobe and sat at my mother's kitchen table with the only light coming from the glow of my laptop. I began to search, first for Clement Goody, and then for Angus Driscoll. My queries brought up thousands of hits— mostly accolades for their various accomplishments and puff pieces by journalists. Each of the men was a classic American success story in that they were stinking rich, and a fat checkbook meant automatic respectability in the good ol' USA.

But the Internet is a deep and fertile valley, and a river of sludge runs through it. I would spend the next few hours wallowing in that muck to see if I could find what I was looking for. This was normally Roberto's domain, but he had taught me a few tricks, and I had some of my own. I worked while Rose and Chan snored, and I hoped that I would find something before someone else died, like Grace Hebert, or even me.

FRIDAY

WHERE ARE YOU?

My phone buzzed with the text, and I realized I'd dozed off in front of my now-dimmed laptop. No matter—I'd found what I was looking for, as the checkout girl at Wal-Mart likes to hear me say. Oh yes, I'd found the goods all right, and it put a different spin on everything. Meanwhile, I was reading a text from Karen Charbonneau at four o'clock in the morning.

Nodding off at my mother's house, I wrote back.

I need to see you. Urgent.

Where?

Morrisville, she wrote. *How soon can you come?*

Fast as I can drive. What's wrong?

Tell you when you get here.

I slipped out of the house without waking anyone, including the dog. I took my mother's venerable Subaru, as the Marquis' bad exhaust would roust the whole neighborhood. The roads were dark and clear except for fallen leaves from the almost-bare trees. I felt a rush of adrenaline running through me, so much so that I didn't bother to stop for coffee at the all-night gas station on the road that led to the Interstate. Karen must be in some kind of awful trouble, and I was deeply worried.

And once I straightened out whatever the problem was, I had some questions. I'd pulled a very smelly fish out of the River of Sludge, and Karen had to know about some of it, because she was close to Goody. His entire empire was a sham, and the New Commitment and Love Society was in financial ruin. And that was just for starters.

My search on the web had yielded foreclosure proceedings on the NCLS by an outfit called Sunbelt Capital Opportunity Fund against virtually all of Goody's real estate holdings, including the bible camp. He was facing bankruptcy and was fighting to save his properties, but the money had dried up. The church membership currently numbered in the hundreds, not thousands, according to various message boards, and the weekly pledges had dwindled to a trickle. In addition to the real estate negotiations there had been a number of lawsuits and out-of-court settlements for sexual harassment, which didn't surprise me in the least. Some of the chatter on the so-called Christian message boards was outright scathing and looked like it belonged on a teenage gamer board, not one that was supposedly populated by God-fearing adults. The worst of the invective came from the pastors of competing mega-churches, who had fallen on the harassment and bankruptcy rumors with a giddy, decidedly un-Christian display of contempt. They must have subscribed to an alternate version of the Golden Rule: *Do unto others before they do unto you.*

So, Goody's back was against the wall, which explained his return to the bourbon bottle. And it might also explain why three people he knew had died in the past ten days. Three going on four if Angus Driscoll didn't pull through.

I wondered how much John Pallmeister knew about this, and decided that he knew nothing. He'd fallen for the rich-equals-respectable paradigm, just as I was now going for the broke-equals-desperate theory. They were both assumptions, and were likely flawed, but I've seen a lot of bad things happen when the money evaporated, especially when people had become accustomed to a certain lifestyle. Clement Goody wasn't the type to let the repo man haul away his toys without a fight.

The question in my mind as I neared Karen's apartment in a somnolent Morrisville was: what was Goody's plan? He had to be scrambling for a solution. And how were the three murders related, if they were?

I found a parking place next to the building and rang the bell at the bottom of Karen Charbonneau's stairs. I heard footsteps coming down. Just as the door opened the outside light shut off, and I blinked in the sudden darkness. She was standing at the foot of the stairs, shrouded in a black cape that covered her head and wearing sunglasses. As soon as she let me in she turned and began to climb the stairs without saying a word.

I followed and tried to take her arm but she shrugged it off. "Karen? What's going on here?"

"I don't want the light," she said.

"This is a vampire movie?"

"Not funny," she said as we reached the top. "Get over there. On the bed."

"Aren't you going to tell me what happened? You said something was wrong."

The shrouded figure turned toward me. A single candle on top of a bookcase across the room provided a weak backlight to her shape.

"It's fine now," she said. "Take your clothes off. You're going to make love to me."

"What? Karen? This is—"

"Just do what I say and I'll let you go."

"Let me go?"

"You want me, right? You love me?"

"Karen, what happened? You need to calm down and tell me about it. I came here to help you. You said it was an emergency."

She lowered her sunglasses to look at me. "I want sex, Vince. That's the emergency."

"No way. Not until—"

"We'll do this the hard way then," she interrupted. "Get on the bed."

Something was way, way wrong. I didn't know her that well, but I hadn't had the slightest inkling that she could go off the rails like this. The time was just before dawn, which is when peoples' emotional clock is at its weakest—it was when we got the most suicide calls back when I was a cop—but Karen Charbonneau didn't look vulnerable. She looked crazy, even though I could barely make out her face in the darkened apartment.

But I did see the gun. It was a Kimber Solo Carry, a center fire automatic that had just enough silver finish on the barrel to make it gleam in the candlelight. She held it a few feet from me, far enough away so that I couldn't snatch it. "Clothes off," she said. "You're about to have the greatest lay of your life."

"Karen, that's wrong," I said. "Put the gun down. You know that I have a two-year-old kid waiting at home for me, right?"

"Don't guilt trip me, Tanzi."

"Put it down," I said. "I need your help. I found out that Goody is broke, which you must already know."

"No way," she said. I saw the gun lower by about an inch.

"He's in foreclosure," I said. "Everything is crumbling. That's why he's drinking, and desperate, and it's probably why people are getting killed."

The Kimber dropped to her side. "Why are you saying that? It's a lie. Clement is fine."

"Why are you acting crazy? And it's time for you to tell me everything. I also found out about your sister. She bought the bow that killed Lussen. You were right to worry."

"That's another lie."

"No it isn't."

"Oh for god's sake," she said. "This is a fucking waste of time. You're not even that sexy." She walked across the room and down the stairs. I heard the door slam as she left.

I found a wall switch and turned on the overhead light. The bright wash blinded me for a few seconds until my eyes adjusted and I noticed that I wasn't alone.

Karen Charbonneau was seated in a straight-backed wooden chair across the room from me. Her hands and feet were bound with clothesline and her mouth was sealed shut with masking tape. She couldn't say a word, and her eyes were glazed over with shock. I hurried across the room and pulled off the tape, trying to be careful not to hurt her.

"That was my sister," she said.

"I realize that now," I said. "How did she tie you up like that?"

Karen rubbed her wrists where the ropes had been, while I untied her ankles. "I was asleep," she said. She wouldn't look directly at me, as if she was ashamed. When I finally did catch her glance she looked exhausted and out of it, like she was somewhere far away from here.

"I have some questions," I said.

"You're wrong. Clement's not desperate. He's just going through a tough time."

"Are you sympathizing with him? He might be behind these murders. I'm thinking it's about money, and not about Grace."

"I can't think," she said. She was freed now, and she began to walk around the room. "You want coffee? I need a coffee."

"I want some answers," I said.

*

Karen served me a cup of French roast that burned my lips because I was too anxious to let it cool. She said that Cindy had let herself into the apartment in the middle of the night with a spare key. Cindy knew all about Karen's and my entanglements. Karen was supposed to share her men, and Cindy was off-the-charts jealous. So

Cindy had tied up her sister, called me with Karen's phone, and then turned out the lights. She was going to bed me with her sister watching, even though I wasn't her "type." I had news for her: she wasn't mine, either.

Cindy Charbonneau was now solidly at the top of my list. The woman was an expert archer, and she had pulled this latest stunt on her own twin. I would call Pallmeister to have him bring her in. He could get the details on the bow sale and have the seller ID her, and they could build a case against her for Donald Lussen's murder. If he worked her hard enough he might also find that she'd been involved Matty Harmony's death, and had tossed a bomb in Fish Falzarano's lap. All he had to do was do his job.

And all I had to do was find Grace and get her out of here. The rest was for the cops. Goody had hidden her away, but Karen said she didn't know where. Grace could be anywhere.

Karen could barely keep her eyes open, and I decided that I'd gotten what I could from her. There was no reason to stay in the apartment any longer. She needed to sleep, and I needed to get on the road, because I had work to do. I was going to start by following up with one of my best sources so far: Eric Gagnier, who had built Clement Goody's bunker. He'd held back that secret, but had spilled it willingly when I pressed him. I had a feeling that he knew more about Goody than I'd been told, probably because I hadn't known what questions to ask. I did now.

*

Eric's van was outside Sudsy's Wash-N-Dry, a defunct laundromat in the middle of Johnson village. His wife had told me that he was uninstalling the equipment that was headed for auction. I found him inside, bent over the back of a commercial dryer with his tools. The only light in the building came from a battery-powered work light that sat on the dust-covered floor next to him. He looked up as I neared.

"Me again," I said.

"You found the place?"

"Yes," I said. "Nothing there."

He put his tools down on the top of the machine. "What was it you were lookin' for, if ya don't mind my asking?"

"A young woman. Her name's Grace Hebert. She's being held against her will."

"The dark-haired girl with the dog? I seen her coming and going while I was up there."

"When did you see her?"

"Let's go outside," Eric said. "Get a smoke and some daylight."

I followed him out into the parking lot, where he took a pack of cigarettes from his pocket and lit one. "Tell me about the girl," I said.

"She started coming a lot last spring. Sometimes she had her own car, sometimes she was with that professor. The one who got killed."

"Lussen?"

"Yep. And a couple of times in the limo. Near the end of the summer when I was working on the fence."

"She arrived in a limo?"

"Town Car, you know. Big ugly guy driving it. Don't think it was a boyfriend, 'cause she sat in the back, and besides, the guy looked like a freak. Like he was lookin' at you two ways at the same time."

Fish Falzarano? He had driven Grace to Goody's place?

"Did you ever talk to the driver? Get his name?"

"No, but I seen him up at the barn, too. Couple a times. Once by himself, and once with the young dude with the tattoos. He was helping him move in the welding equipment."

"Hold on," I said. "What barn? And what do you mean about welding equipment?"

"A job Goody had me do up in Lowell. Next door to the asbestos mine. He owns one of the machine sheds, and the tattooed kid was using it to work on shipping containers. They fix up rusted-out ones and sell 'em. They had me put in three-phase power for the welder."

"Did you get a name for the guy with the tattoos?"

"Nope. He was a local though—drove a Saab with Vermont plates. They left me alone, and I didn't bother them none."

"The Saab was bright yellow, right?"

"Yep."

So, Matthew Harmony and Fish Falzarano had been seen together, way up in the boondocks near a closed-down asbestos mine. And Matty was doing a job for Clement Goody, involving shipping containers and his welding skills. This was the Clement Goody who was out of money, according to my web search. Why would he be involved in something as mundane as that?

Back when I was learning to knit I would occasionally screw up a whole row, curse loudly, and fix it. Some days I spent more time cussing than I did knitting. Solving a case was no different. If you are a person who needs to be right all the time, don't become a P.I., because you will be miserable. You have to take it stitch by stitch, you do a lot of fixes along the way, and eventually it comes together and your sweater begins to look like a sweater. I had made a number of mistakes over the past two weeks, but I could finally feel things coming together with this case, and I sensed that what I had just learned from Eric Gagnier was at the center of it.

I would call John Pallmeister and would bring him up to date. I'd check in with Rose and would make up some kind of explanation for my early AM departure without getting into even more trouble. And then I would drive north to Belvidere Mountain to find Clement Goody's machine shed where the now-deceased Matthew Harmony had been in the business of restoring old shipping containers. I would poke around a bit to see if I could add a stitch or two to my investigative sweater, because the idea of fixing up containers didn't sound like a business venture that was going to save Goody's fortune. It sounded like bullshit.

*

The trip to the mine should have taken half an hour, but it took me twice as long. I spent the first ten minutes on the phone with Rose, who pried the details of the previous night's events out of me and was incensed that I wouldn't wait for her. I promised that I'd be back as soon as possible, and asked her to relay everything to Pallmeister. I'd tried him first, but he wasn't in, and I was about to go out of cell range. Somebody needed to start on the police work and lock up Cindy Charbonneau, and probably Clement Goody too.

The next half hour was a blur. I had felt another whiteout coming on and pulled over into a driveway. I spent twenty minutes slumped back in my seat until I came to. The seizures were happening closer together, which couldn't be good. I got out of the car, stretched for a while, and continued north.

The trees that lined Route 100 were now completely bare, as autumn would soon yield to the long Vermont winter. My GPS pointed me down a road to the west, and a few miles after that the asbestos mine came into view: a two-mile-long defacement of the pristine landscape, as if someone had taken a box cutter to a priceless oil painting. Immense piles of gray tailings flanked either side of the central road, empty structures loomed over overgrown parking lots, and rusted mining gear was strewn around the fenced-off grounds like abandoned toys. The place was an environmental graveyard. If you had worked here and could still breathe, you were one of the fortunate ones.

I drove the length of the perimeter road looking for the building that Eric Gagnier had described. He said it was newer than the rest, and I figured that there would be signs of recent activity. I located it at the far end, surrounded by stacked-up shipping containers and partially obscured by another small mountain of tailings. The structure had a painted metal roof, new-looking siding, and fresh car tracks leading up to it. No vehicles were parked in front, except for a kind of crane-on-wheels thing beside a pond that had turned gray from the runoff. I drove around the back of the building and found a small car under a blue tarp. I parked the Subaru next to it, got out, and looked beneath the covering. It was Grace Hebert's Ford Aspire. I was suddenly glad that I'd made the trip.

I checked the doors for an easy entry point, but they were all locked. Not a problem: I didn't have my full kit with me, but I had the wire in my wallet, and I brought it out. The back door had a sliding bolt with a padlock that was too old to put up a struggle. I was in within seconds.

The interior of the shed was an open expanse of concrete littered with welding equipment and tools. A kitchenette was tucked into one of the corners, next to a small dining table, a chair and a single bed. Somebody lived here.

In fact, the somebody was still in bed, and she sat up when she heard me enter. It was Grace, dressed in jeans and a sweatshirt with her hair uncombed and her eyes full of sleep. "What are you doing here? Don't tell me you're working for them?"

"I'm working for your grandmother," I said. "Let's go. I'll take you to her house."

"Not happening," she said. She held up her left hand. On it was a leather manacle attached to a slim steel cable that led to a girder above our heads. "I'm on a leash. I'm Clement's sex toy, and he's gone completely insane, if you haven't figured that out already."

Her face was pale and she was shivering. I sat down next to her on the bed and held out my hand toward the manacle. "Let me get you out of that." The young woman eyed me, unsure. I took the wire from my wallet and showed it to her. "This shouldn't take long," I said. "Goody told me he was protecting you."

"Clement has been manipulating me from the start. He tracked me down when I was living in London, and he got me clean. He underwrote my performances at the college. And then I started seeing

Donald, and he went crazy. I found out that it was Clement who wrote the letters with the threats. He told me that he would protect me, but what he really wants is to own me."

"And you were also seeing Matty? And Angus Driscoll?"

"Matty was like a brother. And Angus is like a father. It's not just sex."

I would leave that one to the psychiatrists. "How did you end up here?"

"I was in his bunker until yesterday. They said the bunker wasn't secure anymore."

"How did Goody get you to fly back from Florida? I don't get it, Grace. You say he's crazy, but you go along with whatever he says."

She used her free arm to roll up the sleeve of the arm I was working with. Her veins were dotted with needle marks, some of them fresh. "I stayed clean until a month ago. Clement gave me some, because he realized he can't control me unless I'm stoned. Matty went crazy when you told him I was using again. Clement has the best junk in the world."

"He gives you heroin?"

"You have no idea how good it is. Nothing like the garbage you buy on the street. He gets it from Albania, and they bring it down from Canada in these containers. It's welded into the walls, and Matty cuts it out. Clement likes to pretend he's not in the dope business, but he's huge. He says someone else would be doing it if he wasn't, and he can use the money to save souls."

Goody was a heroin smuggler? Lord have mercy. That was twisted criminal hypocrisy at its finest. The Reverend Clement Goody, great saver of souls, was happy to spread around the most addictive, poisonous scourge known to humankind if it meant bailing himself out of a financial hole. I have been chasing after bad guys for most of my adult life, and the one thing that they all have in common is the ability to rationalize *anything*. Sell heroin, and use some of the proceeds to save pretty girls from heroin? It was classic perp-think.

I wiggled my pick in the right direction and Grace's manacle clicked open. She surprised me by putting her arms around me and giving me an embrace. It was the nicest moment I'd experienced with her since I had met her.

But it didn't last long.

"Thank you," she said. "And I'm sorry, but I have to do this alone."

She sprinted out the door and slid the bolt into place before I could react. I kicked at it, but it was securely shut, as were the other doors. I would have to call Rose and have her rescue me yet again.

Several minutes later, while I was trying to get a signal, I heard the bolt slide and the door opened. Karen Charbonneau stood at the threshold, dressed in blue jeans, a tight black sweater, and hiking boots. She wore the same distant look in her eyes that I had seen earlier in the morning. "How did you find this place?"

"Where's Grace?" I said. "She took off a few minutes ago and locked me in."

"What did she say?"

"She told me about the containers. She said that Goody was keeping her here. This is his heroin depot, and Matty was doing work for him."

"Don't listen to her," Karen said. "You look really bad."

"I had another seizure," I said. "I have to get Grace to her grandmother's. My car is around the side of the building."

"Leave it," she said. "You shouldn't be driving. You can ride with me. I need to show you something."

She took me by the elbow and led me to her Jaguar. My head was still spinning from the last whiteout, and too many people were telling me too many different versions of events. "Where did she go?" I asked Karen.

Karen ushered me into the passenger seat and got in behind the wheel. "Don't worry about Grace. She's an actress, remember? We'll deal with her, but you and I have to make a stop first."

"Where?"

"Clement wants me to show you something," she said. "It will explain everything."

*

Karen Charbonneau and I had a one-sided conversation as we drove out of the mine road and back onto the highway. I told her what I'd learned, but she didn't respond to anything I said. She looked like she hadn't slept since I'd left her apartment, and her silence was unnerving.

Rose DiNapoli flew past us in the Marquis going at top speed toward the mine. I yelled at Karen to go back, but she paid me no heed. Instead, she turned up the road that I'd been on the previous week: the primitive gravel drive that led to Donald Lussen's writing cabin where I had discovered the corpse of Matthew Harmony.

The Jag struggled to take the bumps. I wondered if we'd make it to the top, but Karen skillfully avoided the roughest spots, and we approached the clearing where the cabin stood. Instead of stopping, she continued onto a narrow road beyond the cabin that was little more than a trail. It looked like a leftover from the last time that the hillside had been logged, and Karen maneuvered the Jaguar as if it was a Jeep. I was impressed, but most of all I was wondering what it was that she wanted to show me. The cops would have searched the whole area after Matty's death, and I doubted that they would miss anything significant, even though they'd ruled it a suicide. We continued for half a mile until we were at the upper boundary of the gash on the face of Belvidere Mountain where the topmost excavation had been done.

Karen stopped the car on a level area fifty yards from the edge, and turned off the ignition.

"Get out and have a look," she said.

"What do you mean?"

"It's a beautiful view," Karen said. "Once you see it you'll understand."

I got the same read from her expression that I'd had when she had opened the door to the workshop. "Why don't you just tell me?"

"Vince—this is what you've been waiting for. You can only see it from up here."

I couldn't guess what I might learn from gazing down into a valley of asbestos slag, but I'd been down too many false trails in the last two weeks, and I wanted to solve this. And after I solved it, I would get my brain operated on, I'd go back to Florida, and everything would be right again.

So I went.

The vista from the top of the mine was as appalling as it was beautiful. In the distance were layers of fog-draped mountains extending to the Canadian border. Directly below me was a series of mine terraces, as if a gigantic rice paddy had been gouged into the surface of Mars. Perfection and destruction. And none of it enlightened me in the slightest, except to illustrate how people can destroy a spectacular landscape when they want something within it. I turned back to the car.

Karen Charbonneau had gotten out of the driver's seat and stood by the open trunk of the Jaguar. She removed a hunting bow, strung it with an arrow, and pointed it at me.

151

I jerked away as her shot released. The arrow flew low and hit me in the side of my ass. It punctured the muscle and protruded out of the back of my pants. I fell to the ground at the top edge of the mine screaming in pain as Karen approached with the bow, stringing a second arrow as she strode across the clearing. She raised the bow and aimed it at my face.

"You killed Donald," I said through the scorching pain. The slightest movement telegraphed waves of agony through my body.

"Clement sent Cindy for Donald," she said. "He assigned you to me."

"You're a junkie again, aren't you?"

"Clement saved me—"

"No, Karen. He's a killer, and you're his pawn. And Cindy didn't overpower you last night. You two staged everything."

"I'm a drama teacher, Vince." She drew back the string for the kill shot. Karen Charbonneau would put the second arrow into my head, just as her twin had done at the water tower with Lussen.

"Why?"

"Because you found out too much," she said. Her arms began to tremble with the tension of the drawn bowstring. "We were seeing what you could uncover. Clement wrote the play, and my sister and I acted it out."

"But you and I—"

"It wasn't all acting," she said. "I have to do this. You're a danger to us."

"You would kill me because he told you to?"

"You don't understand. You have no idea about his work."

She inched nearer—near enough for me to kick out hard with my good leg and knock her off balance for a split second. The arrow shot into the ground, and she screamed and dived for me.

I grabbed her by the hair and used her momentum to throw her past me and over the rim. She tumbled down the escarpment and landed on a terraced road fifty feet below with a hoarse shriek. The bow went with her and stopped near her feet.

There would be no way for her to climb back up—it was far too steep. But she tried, digging her boots into the gray slag, and she began to make progress. If I didn't do something immediately, she would be back. I picked up lumps of earth and threw them at her, but it didn't stop her. She found her balance on a small ledge and strung another arrow. I turned and hobbled back to the car.

The vehicle was locked. I was bleeding, and Karen would be back on top of the ridge within seconds. I didn't think that I could run very far, if at all; the wound in my buttocks wouldn't kill me, but it would certainly immobilize me.

There have been times in my life when my brain stops and my body takes over, as if I'm watching a video of myself doing something that I would never believe that I was capable of. I reached back and pushed the arrow the rest of the way through the flesh so that the flights came out of the bloody hole where the point had protruded. I didn't pass out, or even scream. There was no soundtrack to this film, just the silent shock of adrenaline taking control.

I stumbled across the clearing and into the woods.

*

When a deer is wounded in the hindquarters it goes uphill. My father taught me this on the singular occasion that he took Junie and me along to hunting camp. We asked too many questions and were far too rambunctious to be invited back. Besides, having young kids around interfered with his drinking, and the booze was my father's primary motivation to disappear into the forest for a weekend, not the hunting.

I was trying to disappear too, as quickly as I could, although every step was pure agony. I couldn't go downhill because the scar of the asbestos mine stretched for a mile in both directions. There was nowhere to go but up, just as a deer would.

The forest had been logged and dead branches and slash lay in my way, making the going even harder although it provided extra cover. My immediate objective was to get out of sight and pray that Karen Charbonneau wasn't any good at tracking, because I'd left a trail of blood in my wake even though I had wrapped my fleece jacket around my posterior in an effort to staunch the bleeding. Losing this much blood was dangerous. But the far more pressing danger was the woman with the bow. She must have scrambled to the top, because I heard her scream:

Vince Tanzi!

Karen was close. I heard her breathing hard, gasping after the difficult climb up the slagheap, but I couldn't see her. I crouched down as low as I could behind a thicket and waited.

Tanzi! You'll die out here!

That's right, bitch, I'll die sooner or later, but I'll do it on my own terms. I could barely contain my rage, I was so incensed at having been conned. I had gone along willingly to my own execution. But she had missed, and I had run. Now, I had to stay quiet and pray that she wouldn't see me.

I heard her roaming around the woods, calling out my name, which let me know her position. That was fine with me—I needed every advantage that I could muster. When her voice sounded like it was farther away, I decided to start moving again and go deeper into the woods. Uphill, like a deer with an arrow in its flank. The pain was still intense, but it had somehow become less important. My thirst was greater than my pain, and I knew that wasn't a good sign. I was bleeding and dehydrated, and I was very possibly not going to make it through this.

I was stunned by Karen Charbonneau's betrayal. I had been expertly played, and that hurt, because I should have seen it coming, but it also didn't matter. What mattered was my little boy who I desperately wanted to see. I missed my son Royal, and my almost-son Roberto, and Florida, and my normal, mundane existence. Why had I even come up here? Chasing Grace Hebert through Vermont and elsewhere had been the worst mistake of my life, I had put my family obligations on hold to do it, and now all the people who depended on me would suffer. I was a useless, washed-up P.I. with a faulty brain and a wound that was seeping blood, no matter how hard I cinched the fleece jacket. Oh yeah, I had one hell of a pity party going on out here in the deep woods.

I took my phone from my pocket and tried to get a signal, but couldn't. I could barely focus on the screen because my head had begun to wobble as if it had become unattached to my neck. Goddamn phones. Hate them anyway. I don't need a phone, I need a canteen. I put it back in my pocket and kept walking.

Uphill, uphill, uphill. I had no idea how far I'd gone. A hundred yards? Miles and miles? The sun was weak now, and was struggling to filter through the trees. I badly needed water, but I couldn't find a source. Karen Charbonneau's voice had faded away, but I no longer cared. I just had to keep going.

Uphill. Find water.

The pain gradually disappeared. What pain? It was so calming to walk through these beautiful woods. Yes. I would show them to Royal one day. Just look at all of the gorgeous leaves on the ground, my son, like an oriental carpet in hues of orange and faded bronze. Isn't this beautiful? This is where your father grew up.

Wait...I'm somewhere different now. We went there once, do you remember? There was lots of water, out there in the mountains. You could hear the streams trickling through the forest. Cold, clear water. Our knees buckled, and we dropped face down onto the soft earth next to the brook. We could reach out, cup our hands, and drink all of the fresh, cool liquid that we wanted. All of this lovely water.

Except that everything was white. Impossibly, catastrophically white. Too white to take even the smallest sip. I would drown in my thirst.

Karen Charbonneau was right. It was a beautiful view, and it explained everything.

*

When you die, they say that a glorious shaft of light descends from the heavens to take you away. This is according to people who have died, briefly, but then mysteriously came back to share their experience with the rest of us on nationally syndicated talk shows, or through a lucrative book deal. So they must be telling the truth, right?

I saw a light too, but it was no divine shaft. It was the harsh, fluorescent kind that you see in the back of an ambulance: the kind that makes the injured and sick look even worse than they feel. I was floating in and out of consciousness, taking in bits and pieces of the surroundings as the vehicle caromed and bumped down a darkened road.

Rose was belted into a jump seat next to my gurney. A dog was licking my hand. An IV bag swayed with the bumps, suspended on a pole above my head. My ass was on fire.

I was alive.

"Where am I?"

"You're in an ambulance, Vince." Rose said in a hushed voice. The lighting created a halo effect around her curly black hair. She looked like an angel. Maybe I *was* dead.

"I detected that," I said. "I'm a detective, you know."

"You're a brain-damaged P.I. with an arrow hole in his butt," she said, louder this time. "And you'd be dead if it wasn't for this dog."

"Chan?" I raised my head off the gurney to look at the animal that was still licking my hand.

"He found you," Rose said. "I got to the building at the mine, and he jumped right out of the car window and took off. I watched him climb the hill, way up, barking like crazy. I thought he was after an animal or something. Then we started looking for you, and somebody heard him in the woods. When we got to you, you were facedown next to a stream with the dog by your side, howling."

"Howling?"

"Saddest thing I ever heard. The other guys thought it was a wolf."

I looked at the dog. "You saved my life?"

No big deal, he said. His furry chest was puffed out. I could swear that he was smiling.

"Who are you, Lassie?"

Don't go all sarcastic on me.

"You wouldn't have lived if the arrow had been a broadhead," Rose said. "It was a target arrow. A hunting tip would have killed you a lot quicker."

"She was going to finish me off, but I pulled her over the edge."

"Cindy? She left the scene. We have the whole state looking for her."

"Not Cindy," I said. "It was Karen. We passed you in her Jag going the other way."

Rose's eyes widened. "Oh, really? So I guess your hot date didn't work out so well?"

There was no way to answer that without making it worse. Fortunately for me, whatever was in the IV bag began to kick in, and I drifted off to a warm, sunny place where there were no jealous customs agents, no gloating dogs, and no P.I.s with perforated backsides.

SATURDAY

I HAVE SEEN MY SHARE of hospital rooms, and they are all the same. When you want to sleep, they wake you for reasons known only to them. When you're wide awake and your body is screaming for more painkillers, the entire staff has suddenly disappeared because they are "in rounds" or "on break." Hospitals are a business, you're the customer, and in the medical world the customer is always wrong. You know nothing, they know everything, and from the moment that you surrender your street clothes you are at their mercy. After all, how much credibility can you have when you're shuffling to and from the bathroom in an outfit that exposes your lily-white derrière with the slightest breeze?

Chan was asleep at the foot of the hospital bed, tethered by a leash that was fastened to a side chair. Rose had managed to get him past the front desk by declaring him a service dog and flashing her badge. She was also asleep in the visitor chair, snoring lightly with her mouth open. It was ten in the morning, and I figured that they had both been up all night worrying about me.

Me, I was fine. Sure, my wound hurt, but the pain only served as motivation. I was angry as hell, and I could hardly wait to get out of this stupid hospital and right a few wrongs. I'd been shot with an arrow and betrayed by a woman who I had thought was on my side. I'd even believed that there was an attraction, and had allowed myself to share a bed with her, which I have become much more careful about in recent years after some disasters. Karen Charbonneau wasn't a black widow, she was a praying mantis: have sex and then bite the guy's head off. Not most peoples' vision of the ideal male-female relationship, although it does eliminate the whole thing about sitting by the phone wondering if he'll call.

I worked while my visitors slept. I left a message for Barbara to let her know that I would be in Vermont longer than I'd thought. The doctors wanted to get my vital stats back to normal and then operate on my brain. My ex picked up halfway through the message and put Royal on the phone for a few seconds to coo and ramble in toddler non sequiturs. He didn't really understand that it was Daddy on the line, but it still cheered me up.

After I finished with Barbara I had a conference call with John Pallmeister and Robert Patton. The State Police hadn't seen a trace of the Charbonneau twins, or Grace Hebert, or Clement Goody. No one had come back to the bible camp, the bunker, Karen's apartment, or the machine shed by the asbestos mine. Karen's Jag was gone, as were Cindy's van and the Hummer. They had all vanished.

Robert Patton filled me in on the heroin-smuggling operation. Three trucks had entered the country in the last month bound for the machine shop. Each had been noted in the customs records at the Derby Line station as "unladen," carrying only an empty, rusted-out container that was going to Belvidere, Vermont, to be restored. Three containers had been found at the shop with marks that indicated the removal of a false panel. A forensic accounting team from ICE headquarters in Burlington had gone through Matthew Harmony's financial life and had found three deposits into his bank account of $9,000 in cash—just under the reporting limit. Pretty good pay for some quick work with a torch.

Pallmeister had reopened the murder investigation, and had learned from the coroner's report that Matty's blood alcohol content at the time of his death was point-two-eight, which would have made him far too drunk to kill himself. You can barely hold a gun with that amount of booze in you, let alone stick it in your mouth and pull the trigger. No one had put that together before, but they did now. Someone had gotten Matthew Harmony shitfaced and had blown him away. My chips would have been on the dissembling and deadly Ms. Karen Charbonneau, except that it could have been anyone, because I now knew that there was big money involved—more than enough to get someone killed, especially if they were about to jeopardize a multimillion-dollar drug ring.

Robert Patton estimated that over a hundred kilos of heroin could have been hidden in each of the containers. He admitted that the scheme was ingenious, as even an experienced border agent wouldn't have looked too hard at an empty truck, nor would they have bothered with the X-ray equipment or a detection dog. At fifty thousand dollars per kilo, three container loads would equal fifteen million bucks worth of the drug at wholesale prices. Once it was on the street, the dealers would step on it—mix it with all types of ungodly chemicals—and would mark it up many times beyond that. Where in the unholy hell had Clement Goody come up with the money to finance this? He was broke, or at least he had been until recently.

Goody must have had a backer. Someone who could front him several million dollars.

And I had a notion about who it was.

I was in and out of sleep for most of the day. A steady stream of visitors came into the room, including my brother and sister, both of whom lived near Burlington. My mother made the trip up from Barre with Mrs. Tomaselli, but I shooed them off before they could set up permanent camp. They had watched over me in this same hospital during the weeks after I had taken a bullet to the head two years ago, and I told them that there was no need for a sequel: this was a flesh wound, and I would be fine. Mrs. T smothered me with a garlic-flavored kiss, and my mom left me a plastic container full of her homemade amaretto cookies, which would surely cure me a lot faster than whatever was in my IV drip.

During the time I was awake, Rose and I chatted and theorized about who was guilty of what. I didn't let on to my theory about the front money. It wasn't that I wanted to hold back or because I was testing her. It was because I had worked hard on this goddamn thing for the past two weeks, and I wanted to own the answer when it arrived. You get possessive when you spill your own blood over something.

I got my chance at around eight in the evening when Rose had taken off for Trish Lussen's with the dog. The new shift of nurses had arrived and settled in, the doctors were gone, and the patients were bedded down for the night. The wing that I was on was quiet except for the bleeping of machines and the occasional noise of a television from someone's room.

I sat up in the bed and felt everything that was in my IV bag rush to my head. Whatever was in there was good stuff, because I felt hardly any pain. I took hold of the wheeled pole that held the bag, and used it to help me navigate out of my room and into the hall. I was dressed in my hospital johnny—just a 200-pound ex-cop with his ass in a sling, going out for a little stroll.

A young nurse with spiky dark hair looked up from her computer. "Everything OK, sir?"

"I felt like moving," I said.

She smiled. "That means you're getting better."

"Hope so," I said, smiling back. "Is Angus Driscoll still here?"

"You know him?"

"We go back a long way," I said. Like, two weeks. "I'd love to say hello if he's still awake."

"He's on the secured floor," the nurse said. "I can call up there. You're a policeman, right?"

"Sort of."

"They have a bodyguard outside his room. Someone came in last night and shut off all his support devices. He might have died, but a nurse heard it, and the person took off. The police were here."

Driscoll was on somebody's hit list? My theory was looking better and better. "Which way?"

"End of the hall, take the elevator to McClure Six. You look a little unsteady. Are you sure you're up to this?"

"Oh yes," I said. "It will be great to see him."

*

I wheeled myself into Angus Driscoll's room after giving a perfunctory smile to the guard sitting outside. The guy didn't seem interested in anything except for the wrestling magazine he was reading. I must not have appeared to be a risk, seeing how my flimsy hospital outfit looked about as threatening as a tutu.

Driscoll was in his bed watching the TV with the sound off. He was hooked up to a rack of machines and his complexion was as pale as his bedclothes, although he looked better than the last time I'd visited him. His eyebrows rose when he saw me. "What happened to you?"

"The Charbonneau sisters," I said. "They happened to Donald Lussen, too."

"What do you mean?"

"I heard someone tried to kill you last night," I said. "Was it one of them?"

"I'm alive," he said. He pushed a button to make the back of the bed rise up. "And I don't know anyone named Charbonneau."

"I have some questions," I said. I would have taken the visitor's chair but my ass hurt too much to sit, so I stood next to the bed. "About the import business you had with Goody. Which is history, by the way. I doubt you'll get your investment back."

The gray eyes narrowed. "You can leave right now, Tanzi. Or I can have the guard escort you out."

"These holy roller dope dealers are pretty touchy," I said. "I only scratched the surface of what was going on, but they decided to kill me just in case. They've already taken two shots at you, and eventually they'll get you. And your daughter Trish."

"Trish has nothing to do with any of this."

"That doesn't matter," I said. "Goody is in too deep, he's scared, and he's irrational. Fear makes people do stupid things. Don't tell me that you're like that."

"I'm not."

"You're a pragmatist," I said. "You make deals happen."

"You're looking for a deal?"

"I'm looking for a young woman who is caught up in a very bad situation."

Angus Driscoll sighed. The sound was like a tire deflating. "Go ahead," he finally said. "Ask."

"Where are they? Where's Grace?"

"Clement has a hideout up the hill—"

"She's not there," I interrupted. "And they're not at the house, or Donald's cabin, or at the machine shed."

"Then I don't know. He comes from somewhere in Florida. He owns a lot of real estate. He has houses all over the world. He needed money, and I thought that I was bailing him out with a short-term loan."

"How many kilos were in each container load?"

"What? You've lost me, Tanzi."

"Heroin," I said. "Don't play dumb."

"It was a short-term loan on his properties," Driscoll said. "His creditors were after him. Everything was signed and documented. We set up a company in the islands, I loaned him five million, and I got seven million back. He still owes me three million."

"A hundred percent markup on a real estate loan?"

"He was in a bind."

"How does he get rid of the stuff?"

"Look, this is going nowhere," he said. "I'm a businessman. I move capital around for a profit. This has nothing to do with drugs."

"They killed your son-in-law," I said. "Your driver was helping them, and he's dead, too. They went after me, and you and Trish might be next. So let's stop the posturing, OK Angus? Do you really want your daughter to die?"

Driscoll looked away, as if he was talking to someone else. "This goes no further than this room," he said. "I'm paying you to protect my daughter, remember?"

"She's being looked after."

"It was Fish who found out where the money was going. I had no idea. Goody knows a guy at the college who has a New York connection. They drive up here and collect it once it's out of the container. They send middle-aged men in SUVs with their families, like they're in Vermont for a vacation. People the police would never look at. They drive the speed limit, and they don't get pulled over."

"Why did they kill Donald? And why you, if you were the bank?"

"Donald started this. He knew a person in Europe who he'd met in grad school. Someone from an old family, not a street thug. The narcotics traffickers there are cultured people. Donald dreamed up the idea, and Goody took it and ran with it because he has more balls than Donald, and because he was broke. Donald had visions of being richer than his wife. You should never marry a woman with more money than you."

"So why did Cindy put two arrows in him?"

"I don't know, but my guess is that he got cold feet and told one of Goody's women that he was going to bail. Donald was a talker and a wimp. Trish could have done far better."

"Did you argue over the money that Goody owed you? Why the pipe bomb?"

"Pipe bomb?"

"The one they threw into your car."

"I thought it was a hand grenade. That's what the doctors told me."

"It was a homemade pipe bomb, like they make in the war zones in the Middle East. A length of pipe filled with gunpowder and a short fuse. As deadly as a grenade."

"That kid made those for Goody," Driscoll said. "Clement showed them to me one night at his house. He had a lot of weapons. I should have known he was crazy."

"What kid?"

"Trish's mechanic. The one with the tattoos."

"Matty made the bombs? Is that why they murdered him?"

Driscoll shook his head. "I've told you enough," he said.

"We're just getting started."

Angus Driscoll pushed a button to lay his bed back down. "We're done," he said. "When you find them, do everyone a favor and kill them."

*

By the time I made it back to my room I was hurting, confused, and depressed. Hurting because the medication was wearing off and I had to beg a night nurse for another hit of the happy juice. Confused, because as much as I'd learned from Angus Driscoll, I knew perfectly well that I was being fed a few tidbits of truth mixed in with a load of crap. He was going to throw Goody under the bus and claim that he'd made an innocent loan. He couldn't tell me where anyone was, nor could he finger anybody for any of the murders, although I suspected he knew exactly who had killed whom.

I was depressed because I was still smarting from Karen Charbonneau's treachery, and especially from not seeing it coming. Goody had a cultlike hold on the women who surrounded him, à la Koresh, Manson, Jones, and all of the others throughout history. The unexpected part was how rational she had seemed during our conversations. I used to believe that people who were under someone's sway like that were unthinking robots who mumbled in monotones as they carried out their master's dastardly instructions. Karen's demeanor was a lot subtler, far more convincing, and was a reminder: there is no such thing as absolute good or evil when it comes to people. We all carry elements of both, and only rarely can a person ignore the other side long enough to become a paragon, or a pariah.

I had learned from Driscoll that Matty had made the bombs for Clement Goody, which didn't surprise me, because everyone in this case was connected to everyone else like Velcro. I'd also learned how Donald Lussen had fit in to the whole scheme, and that Driscoll hadn't liked or respected his son-in-law. I'd found out that the smack ultimately went to New York, and Angus had also told me how much he had invested and what the vig was: five million of profit on five million of front money, which was typical of the drug business and was enough of a lure to pull in even the hyper-respectable types like him.

And then there was the coda: *kill them*. I didn't believe that Angus had said that because he was concerned for my personal safety. More likely because it would be convenient for him if they were all dead because he wouldn't have to explain his connection to a huge heroin operation. *It was a loan to a trusted friend. Good lord, I had no idea.*

*

I couldn't sleep because my wound hurt, and because the nearer I got to solving this case, the more complicated it became. I tried to make myself drift off by thinking about Royal, imagining us on the warm sand of South Beach where I would take him to play. My little boy was old enough to go into the water now, and there were days when my muscles would ache from holding his arms and swinging him back and forth in the shallows. We collected shells, chased after shore birds, watched the pelicans fly in formation over the condos, and ate our snacks along with some accidentally embedded sand. This was my go-to visualization for sleeping, but it wasn't working. So I was wide awake when the phone buzzed on the bedside table with a text.

You OK? It was Rose.

Fair to middling.

I'm bored to death babysitting Trish. She's such a spoiled brat.

Her father was the banker for the heroin deals. Donald came up with the whole idea.

Wow. You're good.

I'm not feeling that way at the moment.

Why not?

Frustrated.

Can I ask you something?

OK…

Why are you alone? No woman in your life?

A really good detective never gets married.

Excuse me?

Raymond Chandler said that.

But you've been married twice.

Kind of proves his point, doesn't it?

I didn't hear back from her, so I returned to my imaginary beach with my baby boy and tried to sleep. It might have worked, except that half an hour later the door opened and someone came in. "Wake up," Rose DiNapoli said. "It's time for your sleeping pill."

"What are you doing here?" I attempted to sit up. "What about Trish?"

"Trish is a big girl," Rose said as she began to take off her clothes. "Move over. Two of us can fit in that thing."

I didn't protest. Instead, I scooted over as far as I could. The room was dark except for the readouts on the machines. Rose slipped into the bed dressed in her underwear and put an arm around my chest. It felt better than anything I'd felt all day. Maybe all year.

"I can't do anything, you know," I said. "I'm useless."

"That's not why I'm here. Go to sleep."

"Impossible," I said, and it was, but it hardly mattered.

SUNDAY

"DID YOU KNOW THAT the average groundhog excavates seven hundred pounds of dirt just digging out one den? And they usually have four or five dens?"

"Fascinating," I said. I was sitting up in the bed drinking coffee that Rose had brought in. She was in the visitor chair with her laptop open. Her curly black hair was unkempt, but she still looked great. "We call them woodchucks up here."

"And, according to this, the average groundhog den has three or four boltholes so that they can escape if they have to."

"Gee whiz," I said. "Just think what the above-average groundhog might have? Why are you telling me this?"

Rose closed the laptop. "Do you remember when I found you spread eagled on the bed in Goody's root cellar?"

"I'd blocked that out until now."

"That bed was huge. Eight feet across. You remember the stairway? Narrow, with stone steps?"

"Vaguely."

"OK then, Sherlock. How did they get the bed in there? No way would it fit down those stairs. Goody's a groundhog. People are the same as animals. They need to have an escape route."

"I thought the cops went through the place."

"It was dark outside, and they were too busy laughing at you. But listen—maybe we only saw part of it. Where's the air intake? They'd have to have a ventilation system, and I didn't see anything. Did you get plans from the guy who built it?"

"They might not exist," I said. "He was being paid to keep it a secret, and he didn't do the whole job. I could call him."

"Don't bother. I want to check it out myself. I think Mr. Goody is hunkered down with your girlfriends."

"I'm going with you."

"No way," she said. "You don't have the strength yet."

166

"And you don't have the key," I said. I fished through the bag of clothes that was next to my bed, found the fob I'd gotten from Eric Gagnier, and held it up. "See? You're not doing this alone. I already tried that, and look where I ended up."

Rose sighed. "No offense, Vince, but you'd be in the way."

"This is what happens when you share my bed," I said. "I get all clingy."

*

I had managed to talk my way out of the hospital, but Rose was right: I was in rough shape, and every one of the bumps on the way to Johnson felt like a ski jump from hell. I called Pallmeister for back up, and he explained that the Lamoille sheriff had assigned deputies to watch the place. He said to check in with them when we arrived, and to keep our guns handy.

Two county cruisers were parked side by side at the bottom of the bible camp driveway. The cops were talking with each other through their open windows. I explained our business, and they said to go ahead and look all we wanted, but no one had come or gone for days. They'd been through the whole place, and as far as they could tell their stakeout was a waste of resources.

Clement Goody's root cellar looked different in the crisp morning light. I could see where the land had been disturbed, smoothed over, and reseeded. A stretch of newer grass extended toward the springhouse thirty yards away, and I followed it while Rose went down the cellar stairs.

We had announced our arrival via the roar of the Marquis' muffler, but no one had come out to greet us. Nor had anyone been at the stone door when I'd opened it with the fob. I wasn't up to doing stairs, as the painkillers were wearing off and every move hurt, so I wandered around outside looking for boltholes, as Rose called them. If there was one, I didn't see anything obvious. Maybe Rose was wrong, and the gigantic bed had been stuffed down the stairway somehow. I'd called Eric during the trip up to Johnson, but his wife told me that he had scored a moose permit this year and would be at his hunting camp for a week. Bagging a moose, as an old Vermonter once said, was about as sporting as shooting a parked car. The real challenge would be hauling a thousand pounds of Bullwinkle out of the woods without having a heart attack.

The springhouse was exactly that: a small wooden structure about a dozen feet across with big wooden doors that swung open at one side. The spring itself was in a corner and consisted of an old bathtub with a pipe extending into it. It looked like it had been dry for years. There were tire marks on the wooden floor from a large vehicle, possibly a tractor. Goody could be using the place for storage, but it was empty now, and there was no sign of a super-secret bolthole. Rose had guessed wrong, and it was time to collect her and get back to my hospital bed. I was woozy from the hospital stay, and the pain was coming on strong.

On my way out of the springhouse I looked up. Tucked into the rafters was a tiny device: a security camera so small that you could mistake it for an insect. It was no doubt transmitting my image to Cindy Charbonneau somewhere. I resisted the temptation to raise my middle finger at the lens.

I returned to the root cellar and called for Rose, but there was no answer from below. She must be exploring the area outside, and I'd missed her. I decided to lie my sorry, aching butt down on the back seat of the Marquis and wait.

Fifteen minutes is my ultimate threshold of worry. After five minutes I begin to fidget, after ten I start imagining random, dire scenarios, and after fifteen I know that something is wrong. Rose was nowhere to be seen. She wouldn't let this much time elapse without checking in with me. Something was screwed up. I took my Glock from under the seat and fastened the holster to my waistband.

I got out of the car and inched down the stairs of the root cellar, partly because I was trying to be stealthy, but mostly because every movement hurt like sin. The lights were on, but no one was home. I checked out the space where I'd passed out three nights ago: about twenty feet square with a galley kitchen at one side, a small bath with a shower, a stainless steel table with two chairs, a TV, and the circular bed. The wall behind it was covered by floor-to-ceiling closets holding articles of clothing and canned food. No guns, no bombs, no bricks of heroin. There was nothing to see here.

The only sign of a ventilation system was a louvered slot to the side of the closets. I took a chair from the table and climbed up for a closer look. Between the slats was the glint of a tiny lens: another camera. I was being watched again, and the hair at the back of my neck began to rise. This was messed up. Rose shouldn't have wandered away like that, even though the place was deserted. I would go outside, honk the car horn, and give her a minute or two to come back. If she didn't, I would drive down to the bible camp and get the deputies.

I heard the stone door hiss to a close above me at the same time that the overhead light went out. I reached for the key fob with one hand and my gun with the other. No response from the door, no matter how many times I pushed the button. I unsnapped the holster at my waistband, drew out my gun and switched off the safety, but there was nothing to point at because the darkness was so complete that I couldn't even see my outstretched arm. No light coming through the vents, no cracks under the door, not even an LED on the television set, because the power had been cut. My eyes couldn't adjust. It was as if I'd been buried alive. I felt along the wall to the stairs, thinking that I should wait by the door and try to surprise anybody who entered. Someone had been watching me, all right. They had sealed the place and left me in total darkness.

More than once I saw the familiar glow at the edge of my vision— a whiteout in the making. What if they just left me here? Would I run out of air? You think crazy thoughts when you're in the pitch black and you're teetering on the edge of unconsciousness. Focus, Vince. Think about the people who need you. Think about Rose DiNapoli's warm skin next to yours in the hospital bed. Think about kicking somebody's ass when you find out who did this. Think about...nothing.

The darkness was slowly giving way to white.

Lie down, man. There's a nice big bed. Just like the last time. Take a load off.

No...

"Mr. Tanzi?" The door opened with a sudden explosion of sunlight and I was blinded, but I didn't kick anyone's ass, because I recognized the voice: Duffy Kovich, the big campus security officer. He took me by the elbow. "Here, give me that gun, OK? Let me help you up these stairs. You don't look well. In fact, you look terrible."

"I was locked in," I said, as he led me out into the daylight. "Where's my partner? She was here with me."

"No idea," he said. "Come on, come with me. I'm taking you to the health center."

"I need to call the State Police," I said. "She's a customs agent. Something happened."

"Let's get you into the car, OK? Then we'll make the call. Come on, Mr. Tanzi."

My eyes were starting to adjust, and I caught his expression as he slipped my Glock into the pocket of his jacket. He didn't look sympathetic. He looked like he was about to cuff me and haul me downtown.

"Look, Duffy, I—"

"Just do what I say, please," he said, cutting me off. We were standing next to his car; a mud-brown Lincoln that had Vermont plates but wore a Queens dealership logo on the back.

Queens, as in New York.

I was still blinking, but I wasn't blind to what was happening here, and I realized that I had just handed over my weapon to an adversary, not a friend: Clement Goody had a contact who knew heroin dealers in New York, according to Angus Driscoll. Someone who worked at the college.

"I want my gun back," I said.

"Not now," he said.

"Were you really NYPD, Duffy?" I asked. "Is that where you made the heroin connection?"

"No idea what you're talking about." I saw his hand edge toward his pocket.

"We're not going to the health center, are we? And you were never a cop. More like muscle for somebody."

He took out the gun and pointed it at me. "I was NYPD for nineteen years, and they took away my fucking pension," he said. "One screw up and they toss me out on the street. You know what I make here? Sixteen dollars an hour. How am I supposed to live on that?"

"So you put Clement Goody together with some big-city dealers. And people start getting killed, and you stand by and watch."

"What would you do for a hundred grand, Tanzi? I know about you. You got kicked off the force, too. You're no innocent."

"So now what? You take me somewhere and kill me?"

"I don't kill people unless I have to," he said. He was trying to look tough, but I felt him weakening. Maybe I could talk my way out of this.

"But you're all right with letting someone else do it? I saw you when Donald Lussen died. You're too old for this, Duffy. You'll never be able to live with yourself."

"Lussen was an OK guy."

"So am I."

"He was going to take us down," he said. "Same as you."

"You're already going down. The cops know everything. Put away the gun and let's talk this over. I can help you."

"No way."

"How are you going to get past the deputies?"

"I sent them out for lunch," he said. He smiled. "They were glad to go. You and I are supposed to be watching the place while they're gone."

"Where's Rose?"

"She's collateral," he said. "Goody's leaving the country because you fucked everything up, and she's his insurance policy. Now get in the goddamned trunk." He popped the back of the Lincoln open with his key and pushed me inside. So much for my persuasive skills.

Duffy Kovich had said that he wasn't a killer, but if I had to ride in the trunk of his car for any length of time the pain would do me in. He slammed the lid shut, and my world went back to darkness.

The car engine started, and we bumped down the grassy hill, every jolt taking a toll on my body. I tried to calculate where we were going by the terrain, the curves, the speed, and the stops. Thirty seconds down the hill to Goody's house…a minute and a half farther down the long driveway to Hog Back Road…a quick dash to the stop sign where it met Route 15…a couple of minutes at highway speed into the village…slow down…sharp turn left…and then, accelerate again…

This had to be Route 100, going north. That was the road that led to Donald Lussen's cabin. Duffy wasn't going to kill me; he was the delivery man, like I'd guessed. Someone else would do it, and I knew exactly who it was. Karen Charbonneau would complete the job that she had botched two days ago. Open the trunk, pull me out, and put a bullet in my chest, or maybe an arrow.

When I was a kid playing hide-and-seek, some nimrod would invariably hide in the trunk of a car and get locked in, and the rest of us would have to go find a grown-up, which meant a scolding and the end of the game. It wasn't just the kids on my street who did this, it was children everywhere, and after enough of them had died from heat stroke or suffocation, the carmakers began installing glow-in-the-dark emergency release handles. The Lincoln was old, but it wasn't that old: it must have one. I slowly twisted around, every movement making me want to cry out in pain. The handle should be dangling somewhere near the latch. My eyes were fully adjusted to the darkness now, and I couldn't miss it.

But it wasn't there.

The car made a turn, and the road became bumpy again. This had to be the Old Mine Road that led to Lussen's cabin. We turned again, and I knew that we were in his driveway, slowing down for the rough patches. We would be at the cabin within seconds.

I felt the surface underneath me and pulled up a carpet-covered panel that exposed the spare tire. A jack was fastened to the top of the spare, along with a lug wrench. I freed the wrench and inserted the tapered end into where I figured the trunk latch would be, and then pried as hard as I could. It wouldn't give, no matter how much force I applied or what angle I came at it from. I began to beat on the trunk lid with the wrench. It wasn't going to accomplish anything, but that hardly mattered. I needed to whack on something because people were trying to kill me, and I wasn't going to lie here and take it. I would make one hell of a noise on the way out.

The vehicle pulled to a halt and I heard Duffy's door open. I continued to bang the wrench against the sheet metal, and at the same time I curled up on my knees with my back against the trunk lid, praying that he would be dumb enough to open it.

He was.

The latch clicked, and I burst the lid open. Duffy took a startled step backward, and I swung the tire iron and connected with his crotch. He fell to the ground in pain, gasping for breath, but still clutching the gun.

For the second time in two days I ran into the woods.

*

I don't do marathons, or half-marathons, or quarter-marathons, or one-sixteenth marathons, or even the fifty-yard dash. It's all that I can manage to roll out of bed and scramble down the hall to Royal's bedroom when he panics in the middle of the night and begins to howl. I call that the five-yard dash, and I believe that I hold the record, at least for my age group.

But injured or not, I had bounded like a whitetail into the pucker brush in a crazed attempt to get out of range of Duffy Kovich's gun. Make that *my* gun. He had finessed it from my grasp while I'd been dazzled by the light and weakened by pain and an oncoming seizure. How could I have let that happen? A few years ago he wouldn't have stood a chance.

I could beat myself up about that, but the fact was that I had been operating well beyond my abilities since I'd come to Vermont. Sure, I was sick with the whiteouts, but that was only the latest symptom of a larger problem: I was getting older. I was no longer able to shape events to my liking and call all the shots. Taking a bullet to the brain had sapped my confidence along with my strength, and I was a different person now, even if I hadn't yet accepted it. I was pushing my luck—and everyone else's—with this fantasy of being able to continue my career as a hard-boiled private investigator. I was soft-boiled at best.

The farther into the woods I went, the angrier I became: partly at my bad decisions, but mostly because I couldn't stand hearing myself whine. So what if I wasn't as sharp and robust as I once was? I still knew more about this business than most people ever will, and I had something else on my side: determination. When I want something, I plod toward my objective, and I sometimes make a few missteps, but I usually get there. I'm a dog with a bone, and when I've been screwed over by someone, I'm almost more Chan than I am Vince.

I was a good quarter-mile away from the car when I stopped for a status check. Status: my wound hurt like sin, I was dehydrated, and I might face-plant at any moment, just as I had two days ago when Karen Charbonneau had tried to kill me.

But I was still alive. And nobody was going to chase me through the forest like a game animal, because I was going on the offensive, and Clement Goody's play was about to close down.

My first task was to fashion a weapon. I broke off a branch from a poplar tree and peeled the bark from one end. I found a stone outcropping that provided a chip of slate to use as a sharpening tool. After fifteen minutes of work I had the beginnings of a primitive spear.

By now Duffy would have recovered and would be looking for me. I assumed that others were also in the area, as Duffy had intended to deliver me to my executioners. They had Goody's arsenal to draw from, and I had a sharpened stick. Not very good odds, and I was going to have to watch every step if I was going to move them in my favor.

I came up with a very basic plan: find a source of water and a hiding place, and wait. Get some rest, and let the weak October sun warm me until it was dark and I could move more freely. I figured that I was somewhere between the clearing where Karen Charbonneau had shot an arrow into me, and Lussen's cabin below. I'd found a stream that time, but it was elusive now. I spent almost an hour on the move, taking pains to make no noise or sudden motions that would give me away. The Charbonneaus had learned to hunt from their father, and it's not hard for a trained eye to detect movement in the woods. That was how you distinguished yourself from the amateurs and came home with a dead buck in the back of the pickup. I didn't want to be their prize.

If I were patient enough, they would be mine.

I found a tiny brook and a hole nearby under a ledge overhang that might have once been home to a bear but was unoccupied now. I lay on my stomach and drank my fill, and then collected leaves and twigs to make a blind in front of the hole. The space was big enough to crouch in, but not to lie down. That was good: if I let myself sleep, I might not wake up, as the whiteouts had been lingering at the fringes of my consciousness ever since I'd sprung from the trunk of Duffy Kovich's car.

I busied myself by continuing to sharpen my stick with the rock fragment. Caveman 101. By the time the light began to fade I had peeled off all of the bark—out of boredom more than necessity—and had whittled a point at the end that could do some damage. Anyone who got in my way was fair game, because I'd had enough of their lies. Duffy Kovich had pretended to be a distressed campus security cop when Don Lussen was murdered, although he probably knew all about it. Clement Goody had invited me to dinner and a striptease, when his real motivation was to string me along, find out what I knew, and then take me out as he had done with Lussen: identify the threat and eliminate it. Carmela Tomaselli and Angus Driscoll had tossed me scraps of information while holding back the important parts. And Karen—she would be up for Best Actress. *It wasn't all acting*, she'd said, as if she had cared for me, at least a little. It might have been more convincing if she hadn't been pointing an arrow at my face.

I have to disagree with Raymond Chandler: detectives can be married, and maybe they should be, because it makes them more human. Love will constantly remind you that you are imperfect, which is good, because perfection is a dangerous illusion. Falling for Karen was a mistake, but love is all about mistakes, and not accepting the possibility of love in my life would kill me just as certainly as her arrows would.

None of my philosophizing was helping the searing ache in my hindquarters. I got up and moved around every half hour or so to keep my body from freezing up and to distract myself from the pain. I heard movement near my hideout on a few occasions, but nothing that resembled a person passing by. Maybe they would give up, and I could walk out of here.

That wasn't likely. I knew enough to put them all in jail for a long time, and Clement Goody wasn't the aw-shucks-you-got-me type. He would see this through until I was dead. Even then the cops might be able to build a case against him, but if I was gone and he and the girls were far away, it would be complicated. Goody needed to kill me and run. He had Rose DiNapoli as a bargaining chip, which infuriated me. Rose was the one person who had dropped everything to help me out, and who I trusted completely. I was way more concerned about her safety than I was about nailing Clement Goody, and it only added to my motivation.

By six o'clock it was dark enough to start moving. I slowly made my way downhill, pausing every few steps to listen. By seven I was back at the primitive road where I'd bolted from Duffy's car, and it was now completely dark. I walked down the road toward the cabin, staying near the edge of the woods in case I heard someone approaching and had to dive back in. No sounds, no cars, no people. A screech owl, the rustle of an animal, the night breeze gusting through the few remaining leaves, but no human sound.

Perhaps they had left after all.

I got to the clearing where the cabin stood just as the moon rose. Matthew Harmony's yellow Saab was still parked at the edge. The building was in sight, but no light came from it. I circled around it from the edge of the trees, twice. My eyes had adjusted to the darkness, aided by the moon, and I finally gained the confidence to approach one of the windows and look inside.

Just then the headlights of an approaching vehicle cast a glow on the road from below, and I bolted for the perimeter of the woods. I froze behind a bush as a van pulled next to the cabin and the motor stopped. The front doors opened, and two people were illuminated by the interior light. Goody and a woman. It could be either Cindy or Karen—I wasn't sure, but it didn't matter, because they were equally dangerous.

They opened the side door of the van and grabbed a passenger by the arms, shoving the person along the path to the door. I watched the three of them enter Lussen's cabin, and within a minute the flickering glow of a kerosene lamp lit the windows.

I could hear voices from inside. One was loud and agitated—it sounded like Rose's voice, and my pulse jumped with the knowledge that she was alive and was only a few feet from where I hid. I wanted to dash to the cabin and get her out of there, but I waited.

The talking stopped, and Goody and the woman came out of the front door. I ducked back behind my cover but kept my head high enough to see what was going on. Neither of them talked to the other. They went back to the van and opened the rear door, and this time I could see them clearly: Cindy Charbonneau and her master were dressed in hunting camouflage. Each of them took an assault rifle from the van, along with gear that they fastened to their heads: night vision goggles. Damn. If they happened to look in my direction I would be lit up like a jacked deer. I ducked back behind the bush and crouched to the ground.

Cindy began to walk up the road while Clement stayed behind. He paced around the area as if he didn't know what to do next. I caught a glimpse of him, backlit by the cabin window, and got a better look at the weapon; a short-barreled Uzi with a magazine loaded into it, ready to shred me into pieces if he spotted me. That wasn't a hunting weapon; it was a means of extermination.

Goody paced for a few minutes and then walked up the road that Cindy had taken. I could do three things: stay here and do nothing, slip back into the woods and look for a more secure hiding place, or enter the cabin and get Rose the hell out of there.

I chose the third option.

I was halfway across the clearing when a whiteout hit. It was sudden, and it was a bad one—I fell to my knees and knew that darkness would follow the whiteness within seconds. I would pass out, face down in the grass, and Clement Goody would find me and would kill me. I now realized that this was a set-up: they had placed the bait—Rose—where I would see her and I wouldn't be able to resist coming to her rescue. Goody and Cindy would be standing a few yards away, waiting for me to fall into the trap.

I was conscious enough to hear him approach, and I felt him prod me with the muzzle of the assault rifle. I was prostate on top of my sharpened stick, wondering if he would shoot me in the back.

"Wake up, damn you," he said. "I want you awake before you die. You need to know how much damage you've caused us."

I groaned, but I couldn't lift my head. Goody smashed the butt of the weapon against my side. "Tell me why you did this," he said.

"Did what?" I managed to say.

"Ruined...everything," he stammered. "I fed you, I offered you my women. I could have saved you. I save people." He kicked me for emphasis. "God damn you, Tanzi."

"You save them, or you kill them?" I said. "Which is it, Goody?"

"I've never killed a living thing," he said. He was crying now. "This was my mission. Jesus wanted me to spread his love. You were sent to ruin that, but the Lord will prevail."

The gun barrel was inches from my face. I slowly rotated my body toward his gun and reached underneath me. "Cindy?" I said, looking beyond him.

There was no Cindy nearby, but Goody turned his head. I grabbed my homemade spear and shoved it at his chest as hard as I could. It entered the flesh above his belly and he fell back onto the ground, getting off a burst of gunfire into the dark night before dropping his weapon. I heard a sucking noise, as if the air from his lungs was escaping from the wound that I had caused. But it wasn't air, it was freely-flowing blood, and I knew that the weapon had reached his heart. He would be dead within seconds.

The preacher made a beckoning motion. He wanted to tell me something, and I leaned over his body.

"I forgive you," he said, part whisper and part death rattle.

Forgive me? I watched as his head fell back and the life slipped away. Clement Goody's final words were to absolve me for the sin of killing him, shortly after he had tried to kill me. I would leave that one to the angels.

I snatched the Uzi and ran toward the cabin. Rose was inside, tied to a chair next to the kerosene lamp and gagged with a leather strap. I untied her bounds as quickly as I could and released the gag. She took a deep breath and clutched me by the arm. "They're waiting out there! It's a trap!"

"Goody is dead."

"Where's Cindy?"

A burst of shots rang out, making one of the cabin windows disintegrate in a shower of glass. I pushed Rose to the floor and cradled the Uzi in my arms, pointing it toward the open door. A second burst took out the lamp and spread flaming kerosene across the table. Cindy Charbonneau had returned. If she didn't shoot us first, we would burn to death.

I grabbed a cushion from a couch and beat it against the flames. I had nearly contained it when I heard a scream from outside, followed by a single shot.

Everything was now quiet except for Rose's and my breathing. I crawled toward the door, keeping low in the darkened cabin. No sound, no movement. A minute passed, or maybe more, because the world was going white, and I was losing track of time. Rose got to her feet and walked over to where I lay.

"Stay down!" I tried to yell, but it was more of a mumble.

"It's over, Vince," she said. She knelt next to me and put her hand on my shoulder.

I looked out the open door. Cindy Charbonneau's body lay slumped backward over Clement Goody's moonlit form, with the barrel of her gun next to her mouth.

WEDNESDAY

I SLEPT FOR FORTY-eight hours after the operation, thanks to the thiopental drip. They had weaned me from it earlier in the morning, and it was now evening and I was starting to get my mojo back. I was hooked up to various machines that monitored my heart, my breathing, my brain activity, and a couple others that I didn't recognize but might have brewed cappuccino or calculated my horoscope. My mother and Mrs. Tomaselli had come and gone, as had my brother Junie, my sister Carla, John Pallmeister, Robert Patton, a dozen different nurses, orderlies, and med students, and Dr. Noelle Jaffe, who'd beamed when she told me that everything went perfectly. Half of my head was bandaged up tight, and I knew that when they removed the dressing I would spend the next few weeks looking like some kind of electro-punk DJ until the hair grew back. I might not want to get my picture taken, but I was grateful to be alive.

Various people had filled me in on what had happened, including Rose, who was once again asleep and snoring in my visitor's chair. My mother told me that Rose hadn't left the room since I'd been wheeled in from post-op, except to walk the dog. It was Pallmeister who explained that Rose had run two miles down the road from Lussen's cabin to get help, and that I was in and out of consciousness with the mother-of-all whiteouts when the EMTs got there. He told me that Goody and Cindy were in the morgue, Karen was nowhere to be found, and that both the State Police and Robert Patton had teams of people trying to reconstruct everything. They'd confirmed that Cindy Charbonneau had killed Don Lussen, based on phone location records. She had lured him to the water tower, no doubt on Goody's instructions. They also backtracked to find the person who had sold her the bow, and he had identified her from a photograph, just as Roberto and I had suspected. He actually sold her two bows that day, including the one that Karen had shot me with. Diana the Huntress and her twin sister.

179

Duffy Kovich had been taken into custody with no resistance: a tire iron to the balls will do that to you. The campus cop wouldn't have to worry about his pension anymore, because he'd be spending most of his retirement in jail, even with a plea deal. Kovich had told the State Police investigators that it was Fish Falzarano who had killed Matthew Harmony, and that Duffy had planted the bow in the mechanic's shop. Matty was going to run off with Grace, and had threatened to expose everything if anyone tried to stop them. Fish was Angus Driscoll's enforcer when needed, just as Duffy was Clement Goody's, and the two tough guys had gotten to know each other. Fish told Duffy over a beer that Matty was stone drunk when he arrived at the cabin, probably because Grace had never shown up. It had been simple to put the gun in his mouth. Fish used the Ruger Super Redhawk that Grace had left with Driscoll, which had confused me before but made sense now, even in my postoperative fog. So it wasn't just Goody who would kill to protect his smuggling operation; he and Driscoll had worked together, although Angus had covered his tracks more effectively.

No one knew who had lobbed the pipe bomb into Fish Falzarano's car window. Pallmeister speculated that it wouldn't have been Goody or his entourage, because although Goody and Driscoll were rivals for Grace's affections, they also were partners in a multimillion-dollar criminal enterprise. Whoever had done the job had been pretty determined considering that you would have only a few seconds of fuse time to act before the bomb blew up in your face.

Grace Hebert was gone. She and Karen were the loose ends. After more than two weeks of trying, I still couldn't deliver on my promise to Mrs. Tomaselli to find her granddaughter and get her into rehab, and she was still at risk.

Angus Driscoll had been released from the hospital and had hired nurses to care for him in his home where Trish Lussen was also staying. Private guards were stationed around the property, and the State Police had backed off, as no one could tie Driscoll to anything indictable. I could testify about our bedside conversation, but the financier been vague, and a defense attorney would tear me apart if I took the witness stand. Angus had given me just enough information to point me toward Goody and take him out, which was exactly what he wanted, seeing how things had gotten out of control. I had unintentionally done his bidding.

I told this to the lieutenant, and he nodded in assent. He and I were finally working toward the same end, because what John

Pallmeister needed was to find Grace, just as I did. In fact, he might have needed it more. Five violent deaths in two weeks was a big deal in the small state of Vermont, and Grace Hebert was the person who could tie them all together in a neat bundle. The doctor had told me that I would be out by Saturday at the latest, and I could go home to Florida, but that wasn't in my plans. I was going to finish what I'd started: find the girl, and help John Pallmeister nail Angus Driscoll.

I felt Chan's tongue licking my hand at the bedside. I was beginning to like the mutt.

Mutt?

"Oh, pardon me, I meant purebred."

Grace is a long way away. Continents.

"That's crazy," I said aloud.

"What's crazy?" Rose said, waking up.

"I was talking to the dog, not you."

"Oh, here we go," she said. "You were bad enough before, and now you're looney tunes. That surgeon scrambled your brains like a frittata."

"The dog thinks that Grace is somewhere far away," I said. "Or— what I mean is—he's a reflection of my subconscious, and—"

"And I'm going to get a nurse in here to lower your dosage before you strip off that hospital gown and start doing the chicken dance."

I smiled. "Don't encourage me, or I might."

"Go to sleep, Tanzi," she said. "They'll find her."

I was going to answer, but the medication was taking over, and the raveled sleave of care began to knit itself up again, along with my twice-punctured body.

SATURDAY

Spending the better part of a week in a hospital bed gives you plenty of time to think, and even with my partially mended brain I had put a few things together. The cops were working feverishly on locating the two missing women and had come up with nothing, but I had some ideas, and they weren't just random observations from my dog-savant.

I acted on one of them by calling Eric Gagnier, who had returned from his hunting camp having bagged nothing aside from a three-alarm hangover. We had a discussion about his work for the recently-departed Clement Goody, and I learned a few things that I hadn't known before. I also lined up a few resources, including a building contractor near Johnson, Vermont, who owned an excavator, a jackhammer, and a ground-penetrating radar device. Because heck, you never know when you might need one.

According to the morning shift nurse they were going to free me sometime before lunch, which was a crushing disappointment seeing how grilled cheese sandwiches were on the menu again and by my count this would have been number sixty-seven. I know how to make a grilled cheese sandwich, and the hospital's version was like a layer of Velveeta spread between two pieces of wet sheetrock. The longer you stay in a hospital, the better the chance that they will kill you, which is what motivates people to get cured and get the hell out of there.

Rose picked me up in the Marquis with the dog. Robert Patton had found some slush money in the Border Patrol budget to fix the muffler, and the silence was blissful. Rose initially thought that we were headed to my mother's house, but I directed her onto Route 15 toward Johnson. We had some demolition to do.

Robert Patton was waiting for us when we arrived at Clement Goody's bible camp. John Pallmeister would be joining us later. The place still looked pristine, although it would probably fall into decay while the preacher's estate was sorted out, and would eventually be sold to someone who didn't mind that the previous owner was a deceased heroin importer who had spread drugs in the name of salvation: Goody's financial salvation, not the eternal kind. Patton opened the door of the car for me and I lumbered out. I had a cane, but I hardly needed it. My left leg had relapsed to the time when my limp was known as the Vinny Shuffle, but I felt completely well otherwise. I was on the cusp of solving a mystery, and that is the most restorative tonic known to man.

"What's this about?" Patton said as we walked toward Clement Goody's hilltop bunker. My friend the Border Patrol chief had his Saturday clothes on: a sweatshirt, beat-up jeans, and work boots. He'd neglected to shave, and he looked like he'd come from working on his woodpile. He pointed to the contractor I had hired who was backing an excavator down the ramp of a semi trailer. "This guy has been walking around for the past hour with a GPR unit. You got dead people buried in there?"

"Quick question," I said. "What would you do if you had a hundred kilos of heroin in your basement? Sell it? We're talking five million dollars, wholesale."

Patton rubbed at the stubble on his chin. "I'd buy a big fucking yacht," he said. "Loud music all night, chicks in bikinis, open bar, waiters running around with bacon-wrapped scallops, you know. Same as you, right?"

"You would?"

"I have this flaw, Vince. I need to be able to look myself in the mirror in the morning. That kind of puts a damper the whole bikini yacht thing."

"Too bad."

"Yeah, I know."

"Let's dig it up anyway," I said. "We could always give it away to someone less fortunate than ourselves."

Rose had gotten out of the driver's seat and stood next to us. "Are you guys going to stand here and bullshit each other all morning?" She pointed to the approaching excavator. "You're in the way."

The three of us moved to the side while the big machine did its work. Half an hour later it had exposed an expanse of concrete that was even larger than the adjacent section where I had been held captive in the dark. Eric Gagnier didn't have the plans, but he had given me the gist. What was underneath was anyone's guess, because Eric didn't know: another company had finished the project after he'd poured most of the cement, and they were long since paid off and gone.

But I'd done the math after Angus Driscoll had told me from his hospital bed that Goody still owed him three million dollars. Each load of heroin had sold for five million. That was a guess, but it sounded about right. Driscoll had fronted five, and he was expecting to double his investment. Goody had paid off Driscoll seven of the ten million that he owed him, and my thought was that the rest of the money hadn't been paid because the third lot of dope was still unsold. No wonder the preacher had been hitting the bottle after years of sobriety. He had entered a treacherous world of greed, paranoia, and big-city scumbags who would kill people over a lot less than seven figures.

Rose and I took refuge in the car while the construction guys jackhammered through the concrete because it was impossible to talk outside. The noise stopped, and two of them lifted a ladder from their truck and lowered it down the hole they'd made. Rose and I got out of the car and joined Robert Patton, who was looking down into the darkened space.

"You up for this?" he asked me.

I shook my head, and Patton nimbly descended the ladder. Five minutes later he climbed back up and switched off the flashlight he'd been carrying. "Looks like friggin' *Architectural Digest* down there," he said to us. "It's a whole house. Everything is top of the line, hidden under eight inches of cement."

"Did you see any drugs?" I asked him.

"There's a wall of cabinets, but they're locked. They back up to the part where you got shut in. That was a blind, and we never would have found the rest of the place." He held up a rumpled plastic bag filled with white powder. "But I did find this, lying on a table."

"Sampling their own goods?"

"I also found a coffee pot, and it was still warm."

"Someone's down there?" Rose said.

"Not that I saw."

Thirty yards away from us, the doors of Clement Goody's spring-house opened up and the wooden floor began to rise. It tilted back at a forty-five degree angle, supported by lifters that were hidden under the sills.

Goody's bolthole had been right under my nose.

Karen Charbonneau's white Jaguar roared out from underneath building and tore past us. "Get the car!" I yelled to Rose.

Patton put up a hand to calm me. "No rush, Vince," he said. "Pallmeister called me from the village. He's almost here."

Robert Patton radioed the State Police lieutenant from his Border Patrol cruiser. Soon afterward we were at the bottom of Clement Goody's driveway, where Patton stopped to clear a row of tire spikes from our path. John Pallmeister had used them on the Jaguar, and the speeding car had skidded helplessly on four flat tires, fishtailing across the main road and into a field. Karen was outside of her vehicle, barefoot and dressed in a faded blue T-shirt and her underwear. She leaned face down over the hood while Pallmeister cuffed her. The lieutenant took her arm and walked her across the corn stubble to where we stood.

She rocked her head from side to side, eyes down, as if she wanted to say she was sorry, but she couldn't face me, or mouth the words. The rhythmic head bobbing continued, and I realized that there was no apology coming. I'd seen it a hundred times when I was a cop: the Junkie Nod.

Karen Charbonneau was in heroin nirvana.

TUESDAY

I WAS ABOUT TO DO something that I seldom do: give up.

Rose had already gone back to Florida. We promised to see each other again, and this time I would follow through. I cared about her, and when we'd said goodbye in my mother's driveway, she'd kissed me so hard I thought she was going to suck the fillings right out of my teeth. I like that in a woman.

Mrs. Tomaselli and my mother assured me that Grace Hebert was a lost cause. No one could fix the young woman's problems except for Grace herself—assuming that she was still alive. I had done everything possible, used all of my skills, and had watched the body count rise. I should leave Vermont before more people got killed. John Pallmeister would appreciate that, seeing how I'd left him with weeks' worth of paperwork on five violent deaths over the course of my investigation.

I booked an evening flight out of Burlington and bought a travel crate for Chan, who would accompany me home. Robert Patton offered to send a car, and I took him up on it, as my mother didn't like to drive at night. Patton's team had fully excavated Clement Goody's hilltop bunker and had found the third load—ninety-five kilos of pure, uncut heroin locked inside steel cabinets. The hideaway was a warren of interconnected chambers and passageways with a control center that tracked every movement on the property. Karen Charbonneau had no doubt watched us arrive and drill into her refuge, and had then panicked and bolted, dressed in her underwear.

I almost felt sorry for her and for her dead sister—they had been sucked into the vortex of Goody's deadly charisma. Of course this was not what the nuns had drilled into me in school: people are responsible for their own behavior, period. I have always accepted that as true, but there is another truth that is equally valid: we're all suckers if the con is good enough. Anyone can be led astray, screwed over, and even sent out to do horrible things if the corrupter is skillful, and Goody was among the best I'd ever seen. He was rich, handsome, obsessed, and he was convinced that God was on his side, but as a lapsed Catholic and a practicing cynic I have figured something out: God doesn't take sides. God is smarter than that.

I had several hours until Patton's driver would come, so I spent the first few walking the dog around my neighborhood in Barre. We passed by the church where I'd sat in my starched Sunday clothes and fought off sleep during mass. We walked along the street where Fish Falzarano had grown up, a few houses down the block from where I'd visited Marie Rocchio's little second-floor slice of heaven and had traded insults with Gary Petrullo. We strolled through the town center that had recently been gussied up with granite curbstones and new streetlights and looked better than it ever had, even in its heyday. We wandered past the cemetery where I'd slipped away with my underage friends to drink beer and smoke Kools. This was my home turf, both familiar and not, because the years have frayed the memories like a scrapbook with pages missing.

The dog and I ended up at the door of Carmela Tomaselli's house. We didn't arrive here by accident: I had intended this to be our last stop before going back to Florida. Carmela answered the door, dressed in a black turtleneck sweater and lime-green stretch pants with a cigarette dangling from her lips. I tied Chan's leash to a railing and stepped inside through the smoke.

"I thought you left," she said.

"Soon," I said. "I couldn't find your daughter."

"She's still alive, right? Everyone else you found is dead."

"I honestly don't know. I wish I did."

Carmela led me into her kitchen and took a stool at the counter. I stood while she extinguished her cigarette. "So what do you want, Vinny?"

"Fish killed Matty," I said. "You knew that before I did. Who told you?"

"I ain't answering any questions. I already did that with the police."

"My guess is that Fish told you, because he wanted to scare you."

"Falzarano was pond scum," she said. "Do you remember him back in school? The guy was a zero. I can't believe he didn't get himself killed in the army."

"Did Matty teach you how to use the pipe bombs?"

Carmela Tomaselli gave me a blank look, and I continued. "Fish told you that he killed your lover, and then he threatened to do the same to you if you said anything about Angus Driscoll's heroin business."

"Driscoll was—"

"Was paying you to pimp your own daughter, and you finally felt guilty enough to do something about it?"

"You're recording this, aren't you? You're still a fucking cop, right?"

"I'm not recording anything."

"You're going to turn me in?"

"I haven't decided yet," I said.

"I lost my job, you know," Carmela said. "They did a random drug test, and I flunked. I can't even pay the rent now."

"I'm sorry."

"But you're still going to call the cops on me."

"I didn't care much for Fish," I said, "but you killed a man, and you almost killed Driscoll. You even tried to finish him off in the hospital."

"So you already decided. You came here to tell me I'm fucked, right Vin?" She turned her face away before the tears began. I gave her a few moments to settle down. "Matty loved those stupid things. He made them in his shop. He took me up to the asbestos mine one afternoon and we blew up a few of them. My ears rang for days afterward. Matty was like a tough little kid, and they murdered him. You should have seen their faces when Fish opened the car window for me and I lit the fuse. It was like they already knew they were going to die. Fish tried to throw it back out, but it blew up in his lap, and I was halfway to my car with pieces of window glass sticking out of my back like a porcupine. I couldn't hear nothing after that, either."

"Driscoll saw you?"

Carmela turned to face me. Her cheeks were tinted with rivulets of mascara. "Yes, he saw me. I hate the bastard. And I hate myself for what I did to my daughter. I'll take what's coming."

Angus Driscoll had told me that he'd had no idea who threw the bomb into his car, and that was a lie. A calculation. If he had told the police that it was Carmela, ugly things might surface. Safer to bide his time, find another enforcer like Fish, and quietly take her out. He might have already hired someone.

"I'm going to help you, Carmela," I said. "And yes, I'm going to call the police, but I have friends there. You might be able to make a deal if you help them convict Driscoll. But you'll still do jail time."

She shrugged. "I'm already doing time, Vinny. Only the location will change."

FRIDAY

NOVEMBER IS AS NICE AS it gets in Vero Beach. The snowbirds haven't arrived yet, at least not in force, the worst of the hurricane season is behind us, the weather is still warm, and the kids are in school. I'd been doing double daddy-duty with Royal for the three weeks since I had returned home in order to compensate Barbara for her coverage, which had only added to my pleasure. My adopted dog, my little son, and I had settled into a routine of mealtime, playtime, naptime, and fun outings, and I wondered if I would ever work another case. The last one had turned out to be such a failure that I had lost confidence in my abilities. I hadn't accepted a job since I'd been back.

On the plus side, I felt better than I had since being shot two years before, and I was reveling in my newfound abilities. My balance was good, my leg shuffle was gone, and the whiteouts were history. Noelle Jaffe had worked her surgical juju. I was healed.

I had stayed in touch with Robert Patton and John Pallmeister, and had kept an eye on the news from Vermont. Karen Charbonneau was cooling her heels in the women's jail in Swanton. Carmela had been charged with Falzarano's murder and was lodged in the Chittenden County Regional Correctional Facility. Angus Driscoll had been indicted for financing the heroin operation after Patton's team had done the forensic accounting and Pallmeister had taken statements from Carmela and me. They didn't have enough to charge him with conspiracy on the Matthew Harmony murder, but that was not a problem. I'd spoken with the Chittenden County D.A. who had told me—off the record—that Carmela would be looking at no more than ten to fifteen, but Driscoll was toast. The heroin epidemic in Vermont has been front-page news for the last few years, and people were outraged. Driscoll had coughed up two million bucks to post bail and was hiding in his compound on Shelburne Point, but he might have been safer in a jail cell. If the general populace didn't tar and feather him first, the D.A. would put him away for life. Either way would be fine with me.

Royal was asleep in his toddler bed and I was in my recliner with Chan at my feet when Rose called. We spoke every day. She had come up twice from Fort Lauderdale to check my bandages, as she put it, although the dressing was gone and my hair was growing back—more quickly than my confidence. The unfinished business of finding Grace Hebert, combined with the stinging betrayal of Karen Charbonneau, had brought me down a few notches. I took the phone and the dog outside to the patio so that I wouldn't wake Royal. The sunshine felt welcome, like Rose's voice.

"Do you have plans for this evening?" she asked.

"Not unless you call ordering pizza and watching Sesame Street a plan."

"Dinner and a show."

"Exactly. What did you have in mind?"

"A babysitter," she said. "Time for a night off, Vince. I'm taking you out to the Mermaid for a beer."

The Kilted Mermaid in downtown Vero is my current favorite watering hole. They have a selection of beers that would require multiple visits to enjoy without getting busted on the way home. A man needs a goal, and this was mine.

"Deal," I said. "Roberto will watch him. He wants the money for college."

"Great," she said. "I have something important to tell you."

"What?"

"It can wait."

"Let me guess. You're pregnant."

"Oh damn, you spoiled it." She laughed. I liked the sound of Rose's laugh, which alternated between a low hee-haw and a girly titter.

"It's not mine," I said. "Obviously."

"Obviously," she said. "I'll pick you up at eight."

*

We arrived at the restaurant just as the sky began to turn black. It's dark at this time of night in November, but this wasn't normal evening darkness; it was a storm approaching, and I could hear the rumble of thunder close by. Rose and I jogged hand-in-hand toward the entrance, dashing inside just as the first sheets of rain lashed against the front windows.

A lanky young dude with a man-bun seated us and took our drink order. I chose a Cigar City Tocobaga, and Rose ordered a Duvel. We glanced at the menu, but I was more curious than hungry. "So what's the big news?"

"Let's wait until the rain passes," she said. "We'll take our beers outside. It's quieter there."

"You're going to make me beg, aren't you?"

"It's good news, Vince."

"Good news would be nice."

The storm continued for half an hour, and I ordered another pint while Rose switched to water. We ate a couple of light items from the menu while we talked. I caught her up on all of the adorable things that Royal had done and said, while she told me about her new job with Immigration and Customs Enforcement: she had been promoted to second-in-command for ICE's activities in northeastern Florida from Melbourne to the Georgia line. Rose would be on the road a lot, but her pay grade was going up and she would be the top-ranking female agent in the state.

I hoisted my glass. "You're right, that's huge news. Congratulations."

"That's not the news," she said. "Let's go outside."

We found a table on the rain-soaked patio under an awning that hadn't deflected all of the water. Man Bun came out with a towel and wiped off two seats. Rose removed a tablet computer from her bag and fiddled with it.

"It's three in the morning in Amsterdam," she said. "That's when she told me to call. She's a night owl."

"Who?"

"A friend," Rose said. "Check it out. She's on."

She turned the tablet toward me. The face of a young woman appeared and then froze. It was Grace Hebert, who had shorn her hair down to the scalp like my postoperative haircut, only the effect was far more stylish. "Vince?" she said. "It's you, right? The picture isn't very good."

"Hello, Grace," I said.

"I've been talking with Rose," she said. "Every day for the last week. I asked her to say nothing, so please don't be mad at her."

"I'm not," I said.

"This is going to take some explaining," she said. Her image was moving on the screen in fits and starts, but the sound was perfect. "Lila Morton sent me some money. She's in Mexico. She freaked out when she found out how Donald died. She was in the dark about that, like I was."

"Why are you in Amsterdam?"

"I'm at a treatment center," she said. "I checked myself in. The Dutch know about heroin. They don't make it into a huge deal like in the States. They just help you get beyond it."

"That is really good news."

"I have another month, and I should be out by Christmas. And then I want to go home to Vermont, and I'll deal with the police, and I'm going to live with my grandmother and start over. I've already cleared it with her. She said to say hello, and to tell you you're..."

"I'm what?"

"Oh my god, I can't say this. It's too weird."

"Say what? You don't know me that well, but I'm hard to shock."

There was a silence, and then she spoke. "Grandma said to tell you that you're hot."

I heard her laugh, and watched her smiling image on the tablet that Rose was holding up. It was a beautiful sight.

"Tell her to take a number," Rose said.

"They won't release me from the program until I have an *opdrachtgever*," Grace said. "Meaning, someone to watch over me. Someone super-trustworthy. Not a big deal, just a person to touch base with now and then and keep me honest. It wouldn't be a lot of time on your part. I'm clean now, and I'm staying that way. People have died because of me, and I'm not going to let that happen again."

"You're asking me to sponsor you? Like A.A.?"

"Yes," she said. "I'll pay for your trip here. They interview you to make sure that you're the right person. I know I'm asking a lot."

"I have a question," I said. "Why did you choose me?"

"You almost got killed trying to help me," she said. "All the men I've ever known have wanted to take me to bed, but you're not like that."

Perhaps when Noelle Jaffe had entered my brain to clear out the remaining fragments from my bullet wound she had rearranged something. For most of my life I have been at a loss when it came to what women said versus what they really meant. It was not within the male cognitive realm to understand such things. But I did now. Grace Hebert needed to trust someone, because she'd never had that. She wanted to shed her demons, put the past behind her, and face the kind of future that a twenty-one-year-old woman should be facing. She needed someone to watch over her.

"I'll be there," I said.

"Thank you," Grace said. "This means so much to me. I'll be in touch."

The screen went dark, and Rose put the tablet in her bag. "Surprised?"

"Yes," I said. "I thought that she might be dead because I screwed up so bad. I was thinking about quitting the business. I—"

"*Basta*," Rose interrupted. "Let's go back to your place. It's remotely possible that you could get lucky tonight."

I took the last sip of my beer. "It's remotely possible that I'd like that a lot."

Chan wasn't in the restaurant with us, but I could guess what he might say:

Oh, please, people. Get a room.

Acknowledgements

Heartfelt thanks to editors Joni Cole, Deb Heimann and Elizabeth Owens, and to early readers Bob and Heidi Recupero, Bee Bigelow, Kate Annamal-O'Connell, Roy Cutler, and especially to Dr. Betsy Jaffe for all things medical.

About the Author

C.I. Dennis lives in Vermont and New Hampshire with his family and a whole lot of dogs.

Also by C.I. Dennis:

Tanzi's Heat
Tanzi's Ice
Tanzi's Game

As Zig Davidson:

Unglued

Cover artwork and concept by Alexander Dennis
Additional cover design and production by Morgan Kinney Designs
Author photo by Peter Lange
Formatting by ebooklaunch.com

www.cidennis.com

10/17 BK 4

48245569R00120

Made in the USA
Middletown, DE
13 September 2017